3/02

02
03

ILL JUN 02

GAYLORD MG

/02

THE HOUSE ON BELLE ISLE

The House on Belle Isle

and other stories by

CARRIE BROWN

A Shannon Ravenel Book

ALGONQUIN BOOKS
OF CHAPEL HILL
2002

 JR
A SHANNON RAVENEL BOOK

Published by
Algonquin Books of Chapel Hill
Post Office Box 2225
Chapel Hill, North Carolina 27515-2225

a division of
Workman Publishing
708 Broadway
New York, New York 10003

Grateful acknowledgment is made to magazines and other publications
where several of the stories were originally published, some in a slightly
different form: the Museum of Contemporary Photography's exhibit
"Some Southern Stories" and the *Oxford American* for "Father Judge
Run" and the *Georgia Review* for "Wings."

Library of Congress Cataloging-in-Publication Data
Brown, Carrie, 1959–
      The house on Belle Isle and other stories / by Carrie Brown.
          p. cm.
      Contents: Friend to women — Minature man — The correspondent
— Wings — Father Judge Run — Postman — The house on Belle Isle.
      ISBN 1-56512-300-X
      I.   Title.
PS3552.R68529 H68 2002
813'.54—dc21   2001055234

10 9 8 7 6 5 4 3 2 1
First Edition

*For John
and with great thanks
to George Garrett and
Shannon Ravenel*

Contents

Friend to Women

Duncan drove and Claire sat in the passenger
seat beside him, the letter with directions to the
house they were renting for the next year open on her lap.
They had slowed down for Claire to look for landmarks,
which she was trying to do while also listening to Duncan.
The couple to whom they had rented their own house in
Providence, a perfectly sane-seeming art history professor
and his wife and their two children, were young and friendly,
a matched set of sinewy runners who rolled their eyes in
feigned despair at Providence's steep hills, though Claire
knew perfectly well that they thought themselves equal to
any ascent. She herself felt more than usually earthbound in
their presence by her own elliptical shape, at five foot two
and a straining D cup.

Still, the young Lehmans seemed incapable, to Claire's

way of thinking, of any but the most innocent injury—stains on the floor from overwatering the agave in the sunroom, perhaps, or even a broken window here and there. Weren't the children boys? She had a recollection of having been shown a photograph of them, both rather touchingly toothy, with shaggy, dark hair.

But Duncan could imagine a million opportunities for something to go wrong, starting with the ancient fuse box and equally ancient furnace, and he went on to list for Claire, as though she were a stranger, the swimming pool, the storm windows, the chimney, the slate roof. A frayed wire inside a wall might burst into flames, he suggested. An insidious leak might begin in the basement. Why, the entire foundation of the house could be infiltrated by an unseen and fatal decay.

Claire took her eyes away for a moment from the un-remarkable passage of small, dusty trees going past her outside the window. She had suddenly remembered the disturbing scorched smell she'd detected when she'd used the dryer early that morning before they'd left. The dryer was old and lived on the inside back porch amid a welter of coats and boots and browning philodendrons and cracked flower-pots, because it was too noisy to be borne anywhere else and because it left a little powdery hill of rust on the floor every time the door was opened. Claire gazed ahead, wondering how to remind herself later of this potential problem, when she might just call the young and able Lehmans and mention it to them.

Outside the window, the trees flashed past, their gray-green line broken occasionally by a small building, its window shades pulled down, close beside the shoulder. Sun streamed in the car window and fell on her lap with an almost palpable weight. Before her, the white line of the road ahead drifted and wavered, and her eyes had almost closed when an enormous beetle hit the windshield in front of her face with a loud *pock*. Claire jumped. The beetle, dark metallic green and the size of a hickory nut, slid slowly, inevitably, across the glass, approached the edge of the windshield, trembled violently, and then blew suddenly off the car and away behind them into the tall yellow grass by the side of the road. Claire blinked.

What had Duncan been saying? She tried for a conciliatory tone. "We'll only be two hours away," she said, hoping she sounded comforting rather than argumentative, although as she heard the sound of her own voice, she realized that her reply was coming too late in the conversation now; Duncan would accuse her of having fallen asleep. Better just to continue, though. "You can go right home if anything happens," she went on, as if she'd been thinking it over. "Try not to worry."

But Duncan frowned at the road ahead as though something untoward—an elephant, a steamship, an avalanche, something preposterous—had just moved heavily onto the white line. He often frowned in the face of uncertainty, as if the force of his disapproval might weaken an enemy's resolve, should an enemy appear.

"What's the name of the street?" he asked.

Claire had told it to him already, twice just on the drive this morning. "Forest," she said again, but happily, because she didn't feel irritated with him this morning, despite his grumbling. "It'll be on the right. After the church." She reached over and patted his knee. "I'm excited," she said. "Aren't you?"

Duncan hunched over the wheel. "What sort of church?"

"Oh! That's it!" Claire cried, as they drove past it and she caught sight of the small street sign just beyond it, a few yards from the black Gothic railing of a tiny cemetery. Duncan braked and bumped onto the sandy shoulder.

"It came up so quickly!" Claire craned around and looked behind them. "Go on and back up. No one's coming."

But Duncan would do no such thing. After a series of excruciating maneuvers on the grass, he managed to turn the car around and they drove back in the other direction. Duncan turned the car onto the lane.

The house was situated at the end of the street. After two small, gray shingled houses facing each other at the beginning near the main road, their mailbox posts ringed with white stones, there were no other dwellings, and trees closed in against the car as it pushed on. Loblolly pines and beach plums and blackberry brambles crowded the edges of the sandy lane, but chunks of white light filled the shadowy interiors of the shrubs and made Claire feel they were near the transparent edge of something. She rolled down the window. The ocean was still hidden from view, but the roar of the nearby waves was immense. She had forgotten how the scale of the sound, so enormous, so overpowering, excited her. She had forgotten her great satisfaction, even gratitude, at the ocean's size.

Inside her chest, her heart took a sudden minor leap, as if it had been touched with an electric prod, and began beating hard. Claire reached involuntarily for the door handle as the familiar hot flush rose in her cheeks and her throat tightened. Diagnosed with a heart murmur many years before, when she was pregnant with their third child, she felt obscurely that the condition had somehow worsened over the years, though she had been told heart murmurs were harmless. But it seemed to her, at fifty-one, that she had to wait through such incidents almost daily now, and it was a great effort to appear normal while they were going on, as she completed transactions at the bank, for instance, and chatted with the teller, or sat with friends over lunch, or worked in her office, unrolling sets of blueprints at the big table under the round window. She pictured her heart like the sacks villains were tied up inside on children's cartoon shows, the ones where you could see the struggle taking place inside, fists and feet flying.

If she was alone during one of these moments of arrhythmia, she would freeze, standing utterly still and listening, for it seemed to her then that she might hear the news of her own death coming toward her, while the thickened sound of her pulse rose in her ears and stars began to blister the edges of her field of vision. She hoped at least that something certain might make itself understood out of her heart's failure—a horseman blowing out from behind a black curtain on thudding hooves, or the immense and salty-smelling wings of angels wafting air around her burning cheeks. She hoped, at least, to be surprised by the denouement of her own death.

But it had never gone that far. After a moment or two, her heart would settle back into a steady pattern, her ears ringing, and she could go on, shaken, but smiling brightly.

As she had sat in the cardiologist's office after her first echocardiogram twenty-five years ago, clutching her purse over the bulge in her lap that was her daughter Greta, six months along, the doctor had told her that many women, especially thin women, had similar murmurs. Mitral valve prolapse, he called it, which made Claire think of tunnels fallen in on themselves, of escape routes suddenly closed. He'd recommended she take antibiotics against infection during dental work or any other surgery. "Otherwise," he had said, patting her chart, "I suggest you forget all about it."

Claire had asked why the murmur had made itself felt then, after so many years. The doctor had shrugged, and afterward, when she tried to remember the conversation in order to repeat it to Duncan, she could not recall exactly what he'd said, or whether he'd answered her question at all. "It's nothing to worry about, Mrs. Morrisey," he had said as he led her to the door, his fingers cool and absolute beneath her elbow. "You've a perfectly good heart. A fine heart."

Still, ever since then, Claire had to struggle to apply cool logic to the terror the incidents created in her. With effort, she had trained herself to stop putting her hand to her heart, a gesture that alarmed Duncan so much and felt, even to her, melodramatic. But sometimes, when her heart rustled so queerly in her chest, when it seemed to pause and lurch, she held her breath and tried to prepare herself for it to cease altogether. The sensation, she imagined, would begin with a terrible pain, but she hoped it might then give way to an almost pleasant release, as if the earth had been tugged away slyly from under her feet, leaving her to bicycle slowly in air before beginning her slow revolutions downward. Claire did not imagine dying in the presence of anyone she knew. She believed, instead, that it would happen when she was alone. They would come upon her later, fallen in the garden like a bewitched child, or crumpled by the bed, her cheek bruised, after it was too late. She imagined the toes of Duncan's black shoes staring into her face.

Now her heart fluttered and knocked within her, so chaotic that she felt a rush of anger, sure that now, just as they had arrived, her heart would fail her at last, cheat her of this final reward. But Duncan stopped the car and turned off the engine. And as they sat there for a moment, Claire listened to the ocean, surrendered to its massive sway over her, and felt her heart calm. It was, as she knew it would be, perfectly quiet except for the sound of the waves breaking rhythmically upon the shore.

CLAIRE HAD NOT seen the house they would be renting except in photographs, pictures in which it appeared to tilt, as though the arm of the person taking the photographs had been jostled just as he snapped the shutter. Claire had spread the handful of photos out on the dining room table back home in Providence, trying to piece together what the house looked like from the jumbled details, but the fragments did not seem to fit exactly; the perspectives were different, frame to frame. The pieces overlapped in maddening ways.

Still, she liked what she saw, a runaway rose of Sharon growing by the front door, the folded shutters punched with half-moons, the terrace with its low stone wall, the sky flying up over it all like a tablecloth snatched and shaken, billowing up into the air. The house was set in a grove of pines, a short walk from the beach—a path led over the dunes. In the distance rested the ocean, a straight edge of blue and silver, brimming at the horizon.

Extracting Duncan from their house in Providence had
been exhausting for Claire. In his mid-sixties, a mathematics professor at Brown, and more than a decade older than
her, Duncan was not a man who had ever liked traveling. A
year before, Claire had gone away for the first time without
him, on an Alaskan cruise with an old college roommate
who had married a man from Fairbanks after her first husband drank himself to death. Claire had not enjoyed her
friend's company very much—Leigh drank too much herself and was boring and embarrassing after dinner, and de-
pressed and contrite in the morning, so that Claire felt it
necessary to be very kind—but in every other way the trip
had met and then surpassed her expectations. She went to
every lecture, signed up for every walk, and saw at least one
whale, and usually more, every day. She had brought back
photographs to show Duncan but was disappointed to recognize that the pictures conveyed nothing of the whales'
enormity, their thrilling size. "I wish you'd been there," she'd
said to him as they looked over the photographs together,
Claire trying to match up the creatures in the pictures, small
and insignificant as pencil erasers, with the animals that had
inspired in her such intense happiness. Standing at the railing of the Alaskan boat, when the first whale of the trip
broke through the waves in front of them, she had felt a
wild, hysterical joy. The sensation was both completely
novel and yet vaguely, achingly familiar, as if it resided as
only a faint, disappearing essence, a memory of a memory,
in the cells of her fingertips. She had wanted to clamber up
on the railing and fling out her arms and shout with triumph, a primal salute to this mighty beast, its back long and
rigid and dignified as an aircraft carrier. But she had not said

or done anything, of course, and the disappointment, the actual physical difficulty of having to choke back such an impulse, had been so powerful that it had brought tears to her eyes. *How few such occasions are,* she had thought hopelessly, as that first whale disappeared from sight. And later she had been rude to her friend, ignoring her at dinner in favor of the company of a retired female botanist from Edison, New Jersey, who had worked for Du Pont and was self-congratulatory but fascinating on the subject of arctic flowers. Claire had not felt herself all evening, though. "You must come on trips like this all the time," she had said fiercely to the botanist as they left the table, expecting a recital of itineraries. The woman had looked at her shrewdly, but not unkindly. "I'm trying to spend all my money before I die," she said. "I have only one son to leave it to, and he's an utter pig." And then she swept away, leaving Claire breathless with shock.

The year's rental in Newcomb had come about through a colleague of Claire's. The young woman hired as the new architect for the Providence Preservation Society, where Claire was the administrative secretary to the president, had an aunt with a small beach house in Newcomb. The aunt was eager to find someone to look after her house for several months, as she wanted to spend the year in Phoenix with a daughter who had just given birth to twins. Once apprised of this opportunity, Claire, who had lived her whole childhood on the Rhode Island shore, had persisted with Duncan to the point of anger, telling him finally that she would leave him alone for a year and take the house by herself if he wouldn't come with her. She wondered whether she would actually have done such a thing, if it had come to that, but he had finally agreed, and so she had never had to find out.

"It's right on the ocean, Duncan," she had said, hardly able to contain her excitement at the prospect of it, once he'd agreed to come along. "It's on the next beach down from Matunuck. It's a beautiful place. Remember?"

"Of course," he had said. "Do you think I am losing my mind?"

Now she did not wait for him. She got out of the car and advanced toward the house. A small flagstone path led around the side through a narrow gate fitted between a crabapple tree and a crumbling stone post. Claire unlatched the gate and walked down the path to the back of the house, to the terrace, with its wooden chairs and table, its row of pots on the ledge, the sea spreading out before her. She stood there, looking out over the water. And then, because no one was watching, she put her hand to her heart. But it was not a gesture of fear. She lay her hand there as if to comfort it, as if her own heart were a small child made to see the light, surfacing at last through disbelief to happiness after a great disappointment.

She turned at the sound of a door opening behind her. Duncan stepped out onto the terrace, a piece of paper in his hand.

She felt so glad to see him there suddenly, as if he had just arrived after a long separation between them. She smiled at him. "Isn't it marvelous?"

He squinted into the sun, put up a hand to shield his eyes.

"What's that?" she said, looking at the paper he held.

"Instructions. Tablets for the water, trash pickup, that sort of thing. Power goes out, of course, in a bad storm. She keeps flashlights in the kitchen." He hoisted one, leveled it at Claire like a gun.

Claire recoiled. "Duncan!" She had spoken before she could help herself, and she knew her tone was one of accusation and reproof and bewilderment, as if he had really shot her, put a bullet into her heart, and was now watching her bleed to death before him.

Duncan stared at her. "Also in the kitchen, a case of wine, as a gift. Mixed years. Mostly reds," he said quietly. He frowned, looking down at the paper in his hand again; she saw that she had embarrassed him, that in saying his name in that way she had upset him. Why had she done that? Recovering, she stepped up to him, took the flashlight from his hand. "Duncan," she said, standing on tiptoe, wrapping her arms around his shoulders, "I am so *happy*," and she felt an enormous relief as their bodies met. What a thing her foolishness was, a thing to be borne all her days, like a hump on her back.

He bent his face toward her, allowed her to kiss him.

She tugged at his hands. "Come with me."

Inside, they passed through the small kitchen, through a dining room dim behind long drapes, through the front hall, and into a bedroom. The double bed was stripped. A coverlet and a quilt were folded at the end; the pillows, stained and slightly damp, were stacked at the head. Claire pulled Duncan down beside her on the bed, unbuttoned his shirt, tugged her trousers down over her feet, working fast, kicking her shoes to the floor. And when he rose over her, his jaw grinding into her cheek, she squared her hips beneath him, looked up briefly for a view of the world thatched through the black-and-gray scrim of Duncan's hair.

Duncan did not speak when they made love, but he made noise; a dead language, she thought of it as—the words Descartes might have used if mathematics had not only its own rigorous language of symbols and effects but also an accompaniment like a musical score to a ballet, or something even less graspable, a dark and scrabbling sound like the murmurs of a strange, secret life behind the walls of the Pyramids.

"What did you say?" she had asked once when they were first married, pushing away from him and laughing, looking up at him. But it had so embarrassed Duncan that she had never mentioned it again. He was not entirely aware of it, she believed, and she herself almost didn't hear Duncan's low accompaniment to their coupling anymore. The pressure of their two bodies together over the years had become so exact, so precise. Yet now, when she least expected it, she was surprised to find her own desire suddenly flagging in her, falling away like a candle flame extinguished by a distant breeze.

She lay still, disappointed, feeling Duncan sink into her, relaxing. And then, quite unbidden, she thought of Vikram, the Indian archaeologist who had pursued her so ardently that fall more than fifteen years before. He had been on a semester's exchange at Brown, roving the streets of Providence like an exotic, slender and handsome in his immaculately cut suits, though he made Claire think of a dancing reptile trapped in a room and reared up on its hind legs to survey its surroundings. Vikram had strolled into the Providence Preservation Society one afternoon to find Claire down on her knees poring over a set of blueprints. He had hovered there silently behind her, but she had somehow felt his presence, his eyes exploring her backside, her hiked-up skirt and unseemly position, and she never forgave him for embarrassing her so much.

That fall, he had pursued her so relentlessly, so extravagantly, with such wounded accusation and, finally, such seething anger, that she had been forced finally to tell Duncan about it and ask for help. She'd been afraid Vikram would actually appear at their door one day, armed if not literally then with some strange logic with which he would bombard Duncan, eventually vanquishing him by the force of his heated insistence that he, Vikram, and Claire were meant to share a season of voluptuous rapture. She imagined Duncan waving his hands in protest, clapping his hands to his ears, withdrawing to the dining room and closing the French doors, leaving her there in the front hall to defend herself. She wanted Duncan to be prepared for Vikram's insinuating reason.

That first afternoon, unaware of what she was beginning with her customary politeness, she had shown Vikram nervously around the building, explaining their current project to him—the restoration of a house in the Portuguese section of the city that had been, briefly, the home of a minor poet. When Vikram had returned the next day, closeting himself in her office with a bouquet of roses, which he pressed into her protesting hands, and engaging her in a conversation so lengthy and abstruse that she could scarcely follow the logic and innuendo of it, she had felt positively terrified. It became a bit of a joke among her colleagues, who, conscripted to protect her from Vikram's lugubrious advances at the office, were nonetheless helpless to prevent him from surprising her as she walked home in the evenings. Appearing at her side from one street corner or another, he had talked incessantly —about his home in India, about his family and wife and children, about his political difficulties at the University of Calcutta.

"Women in this country have such freedom," he told her. "Not like in India. Here, you can do anything you want. Am I right? A beautiful woman like yourself? You could have anything you wanted."

She had murmured, demurred, casting desperate looks around her, both hoping to see someone she knew and could signal for help, and wishing at the same time to pass unnoticed along the streets, this ardent man's arm linked through her own, his voice in her ear, his hands gesticulating wildly. Passing by the Blue Point, a seafood restaurant and oyster bar frequented by students, he had stopped her under the neon sign, caught her arms with hard fingers.

"You are so afraid," he had whispered then, pressing her up against the wall, where she could feel his erection against her thigh. "Why are you so afraid?"

That night, after the children had been put to bed, she had told Duncan the whole story.

At first he had not seemed able to grasp her sense of terror, though she had tried to be plain about it.

"Duncan," she had said finally, after he had suggested that she simply speak firmly to Vikram, tell him she did not care for his company. "I'm not afraid he is going to rape me. Or—" She had shaken her head, trying to sort out the sense of sexual threat she felt from Vikram from this other, greater threat. "I'm afraid he's going to kidnap me. I'm afraid he's going to kill me."

She could not explain why this should be, she realized.

The words sounded foolish, though the feeling was strong, unmistakable. She wondered, still, what had prevented her from pushing Vikram away, why she had seemed unable to summon words to explain what she had felt. "I am married," she had whispered, pinned up against the wall of the Blue Point. But she had said it as though it were an apology, an excuse.

"I'll speak to someone in Ryder's office," Duncan had said finally, referring to the dean. And after that, though she had passed Vikram a handful of times, he had crossed to the other side of the street when he had seen her coming, had pointedly averted his gaze from her, a prophet punishing a disciple.

"Why is he doing this to me?" she had asked Duncan.

He had shrugged. "He's crazy," he had said, and she had felt wounded, as though Duncan could not imagine that a sane man might fall in love with her. But that night he had held her very close to him, stroking her hair, his leg crossed over her thigh.

Still, over the years, the image of Vikram's glittering eyes and licorice breath continued to occur to her, haunting her, as though he had in fact raped her, as though he had laid some stain upon her soul. In truth, apart from one unsatisfying early sexual encounter with a boy she had known in college, Duncan had been her only lover, and she could not exactly imagine sex with anyone else. It angered her that Vikram had stayed with her, like a virus that appeared on her lip with a telltale blister. He had robbed her of even harmless imaginings of infidelity, her occasional appreciation for men other than her husband, their shoulders moving beneath the cloth of their shirts, their hands flexing, their eyes meeting her own. Vikram stayed there in her memory like a caution, a dead crow strung up on a fence to warn off other crows from the garden.

Now, sinking slowly into the downward spiral of her own unfulfilled desire, she closed her eyes against the image of Vikram.

Duncan reached up, blind, felt her face, tucked her hair behind her ear. His fingers, soothing, played over her temple, her brow. She fell asleep.

WHEN SHE WOKE, the bedroom was shadowy and she was cold, chilled as if a faraway breeze had been blowing over her body. She lay still a moment, trying to get her bearings. Gradually, the fact of the new house and their presence in it came back to her. She listened for a moment for a sound from elsewhere in the house, Duncan moving around, acquainting himself with their new surroundings. In hotel rooms, Duncan could never resist moving the furniture around, even if only slightly, adjusting the position of a table or chair, nudging the nightstand a little closer to the bed, moving a lamp from one surface to another.

Claire listened carefully. From another room came the distant sound of a radio being tuned from one station to the next, static interrupting the music, a surge of voices. She sat up and looked out the window. The beach grass lay flattened along the dunes in a stiff wind, its spines washed red and gold in the setting sun.

Her trousers felt too large when she pulled them on. She tucked her shirt inside her waistband, wriggled her feet into her sneakers, and then rose, quietly opening the sash and climbing through the window, dropping to the grass below.

Standing there a moment, feeling her collision with the soft ground in her knees, she felt like a teenager again, on the nights she had eloped from her own bedroom window to the roof of the toolshed below, hurrying across the dark lawn, fragrant with glass clippings, to the sandy lane that led to the beach. Night after summer night she had escaped the house to head for the water, where, against her parents' warnings and even the faint admonition of her own better judgment, she had stripped off her clothes and swum along the shore, long, regular strokes that pierced through the waves' breaker line, the cold and salt scalding her flesh.

One night, when she was fifteen, she had been discovered by one of their neighbors, Senator Paulson, home from Washington at the end of summer for the congressional recess. Out walking his dogs in the moonlight, he had seen her dark head bobbing through the waves. Claire saw him stop and then advance down to the water's edge to call after her.

"Hey! You!" he had shouted, alarmed, his dogs surging into the water after her, barking against the spray of surf.

She'd stopped, finding the sandy floor with her feet, sinking on her knees to keep her breasts below the water. "Hello, Senator," she said.

"Claire Hopkins!" The senator had peered in at her. "Is that you?"

"Yes, sir," she replied.

"God*damn* it, girl! Get out of that water! You shouldn't be swimming out here alone at night! Where's your father?"

"He's at home, sir," she said, treading water.

"Well, get on out of there. C'mon. Right now."

Claire had thought a moment. "I left my clothes up the beach," she said. "I'll have to swim back there."

The senator looked down the darkened crescent of sand as if he might be able to see her clothes, a little flag staked over them, perhaps. "Come in closer to shore," he said. "I'll go get your things." And he had walked off down the beach, the dogs bounding after him.

Claire waited, flipping onto her back, watching her white body float to the surface of the water, washed with a bruised light. Her hair drifted around her head like an anemone, her breasts crested the water. She was disappointed to have been discovered. She expected he would tell her parents.

When he returned a minute or so later, he came down close to the gently foaming line of the surf, her clothes bundled in his arms. "I've got 'em," he said. "Now come on out of there. Good God. Your mother'd have fits if she knew you were out here swimming at night."

Claire bobbed in the waves, treading water.

He stepped closer to the edge. "Just how often do you do this?" he asked.

Claire hesitated. "Well, just about every night, when it's warm enough," she said. And then she surprised herself with her boldness. "You won't tell, will you?"

He didn't answer her directly. "Get out of the water," he said after a moment.

She waited. He stood there looking in at her, her dark head disappearing in the surf, her clothes in his arms. The moonlight hit him like a searchlight, his face carved and wooden as a sentinel, a figure lashed to a bowsprit regarding the waves ahead.

When she rose to her full height, the water fell from her; she looked down and saw it spouting from her breasts as though they were uncorked flasks. The man stepped back, but did not turn away. Claire faced him in the moonlight, the warm bath of the sea lapping at her waist. For a long moment they regarded each other.

Finally Claire stepped forward through the surf, through the coiling spray, her toes knuckling the sand, clutching the shifting grains as they sped away in the backwash. When she was almost out of the water entirely, he dropped his eyes from her at last, placed her clothes upon the sand, turned discreetly aside.

She dressed, called to the dogs, threw a piece of driftwood into the waves for them. Senator Paulson turned back then to face her, away from the dunes, the orange lights of the houses there.

"Thank you for getting my clothes," she said. "I'm sorry."

He paused. "Thank *you*," he replied softly.

And then he bowed a little to her, a short, deferential bow, before clucking for the dogs, walking away.

He had not told her parents.

Now Claire walked through the sea grass, its razorlike wands catching her trouser legs. She tried to consider how it could be that she was the same person, the same bold girl. She looked out over the dunes, at the sea like a metallic plate pocked with geysers of flame. For a few years, when their children were small, she and Duncan had returned to her parents' house for summer vacations. Then, she had not really had time to think about her childhood;

she was too busy with her own children, her still-young marriage to Duncan. After a while, the children had other summer pursuits, camps and summer schools, trips with friends; she and Duncan had put her parents' house on the market after her mother died. Her father had retired to a rest home nearby, passing on peacefully in his sleep just a few months after her mother's death.

She knew the Newcomb beach well, though its sliding shape had changed somewhat over the years. The dunes were pinned now behind ribbons of wire fencing, and the arc of the beach had shrunken slightly, like the shape of the moon as it angled through the seasons, bulging and then contracting. The Matunuck beach was the next one over, reached by a breakwater to the salt marshes behind. At low tide, the water there receded to reveal a sunken moat of gray sand.

Sliding down through the dunes, she reached the beach, walked to the near edge of the waves, where the sand was firmer, crisp under her feet. Maybe it was the sea itself, she thought, how the sight and sound of it caught at her heart, that had made her climb out of the window, just as she used to do so many years before. For a second, as she moved down the beach, she considered Duncan, his surprise and consternation when he checked on her, expecting to find her still asleep in the bedroom, and discovered her gone. She was surprised to find herself annoyed at him, as if he had been waiting outside the window for her to jump, stopping her before she had even begun.

But she was distracted suddenly by how familiar everything began to seem. The same shingled houses rising on the dunes, turned and cocked toward the sea as if a child's hand had picked up each one and peered inside it, resetting it on the dunes not exactly straight. At the far end of the beach, in the vaporous early evening air, she could just make out the shape of the lighthouse, the dark, trailing length of the stone jetty. She walked down the beach, glancing from side to side, now at the water, now at the familiar houses, some painted with fresh blue trim, folded umbrellas and beach chairs grouped at the tops of the wooden steps leading down to the sand. There was the Montagues', the Sterns', the Calloways'—or at least those had once been their houses. She imagined they belonged to others now, like her parents' own house, or to the sons and daughters of the couples she remembered, people now her own age or older, children grown to adults whose faces she might not recognize if she met them on the street.

As she drew near to the last house, the dunes of the bird sanctuary flowing away behind it like a rippling desert, she recognized it as the Paulsons'. An American flag still flew from the metal flagpole planted on the dunes in front of the house, just as it had when she was a child, the grommets clanging against the pole with a forlorn sound, like a half-furled sail banging tonelessly against the mast of a lonely boat moored out in the water. She climbed over the sand to stand below the house a moment. There were no lights within; the yellow porch lamp was on, though, illuminating the wooden settee, its rubbery, flowered cushions battened down against the frame with twine, a sand bucket and scattering of children's plastic beach toys by the closed door.

She ascended the short flight of steps and stood on the darkening lawn in front of the house, the hard grass broken here and there by flower beds ringed with stones. The spokes of a metal clothesline revolved slowly in the wind. She moved to the edge of the lawn, in search of the path that led to the old dinghy the Paulsons had towed up to the dunes as a plaything for the children, its rotting wooden hull sunk in sand, the metal oarlocks smooth as polished stone. The old boat had been a favorite place for neighborhood children to play, standing on its worn seat and looking out to sea. They had defended it against enemies, girls against boys, boys against girls, the younger against the older children, or vice versa.

Claire scrambled up through the dunes, following the rivulet of pathway through the bending grass. Soon the path grew wider; someone had spread gravel along its surface and chopped at the encroaching dune grass. She stopped, a little breathless, at the crest of the hill. Where the old boat had rested, a square of metal fence had been erected, its black Gothic spires marking off a cleared patch among the thorny roses and beach plums. A grave marker stood in the center of the enclosure.

Claire stepped forward uncertainly, and then she felt her heart catch, that familiar sensation of shock followed by a blurred moment when the atmosphere seemed suddenly sucked dry. Her hand moved, bewildered, palming the air. But after a moment, her heartbeat resumed, a thick thudding in her chest as her breaths came quickly now, as if she had run a great distance.

She opened the latch and moved to the stone.

SENATOR JAMES CHARLES PAULSON, the inscription read, 1904–1988. SAILOR, STATESMAN, FATHER, HUSBAND, AND FRIEND TO WOMEN. GIVEN IN LOVING MEMORY BY HIS WIFE, MARGERY KIPLINGER PAULSON, DAUGHTERS ELIZABETH, CATHARINE, LAURA, YVONNE, AND RACHEL.

CLAIRE KNELT, OR rather fell, as though a muscled arm had struck her behind the knees. Surely, surely, she knew he had died? It must have been reported in the papers, she thought wildly, touching the stone with her fingers. How could she not remember such a thing?

But what was this sudden sorrow? Why were her cheeks wet with tears?

An image of herself came to mind, rising naked from the waves, the moonlight on her shoulders, the man's steady gaze upon her, his perfect contemplation. She saw the senator's courtly bow, his mannered appreciation; it was as though he had been staring not at a live girl, a child he had watched grow up into a young woman, a child he knew, but at a painting in a museum, a voluptuous rendering on the ceiling of a chapel. *Friend to women.*

Her hands moved over the stone, the reclining bed of earth. She was, at that moment, she realized, the same age that the senator must have been that night so long ago, just past fifty. She saw how formal the contours of her own desire had become, how like his own.

She rose clumsily to her feet and stood there a moment, looking around wildly. And then she found the path through the dunes and began to run. She slipped and fell where the path met the beach, rose again, and rushed to meet the water. When she was knee-deep, she stopped to strip off her clothes, waded heavily into the surf, and sank.

She thought she would die. *The cold, the cold,* she thought, surprised, as if water were not like this, as if the thing she knew as water were a different property altogether, something calibrated at the sink, an adjustment of the faucet. But when her head broke the surface, she realized it was not the water that was cold, but the air, as though in seconds her body had perfectly acclimated, as if the sea itself had flowed into her veins, replacing the thick, slow blood with something clear and cold, arresting and wakeful, something that flooded her heart.

She sprang from her knees, her arms describing wings of beaded light, thrown water sparkling in air. She swam, the defining strokes of her youth, straight toward the horizon of black, a relentless surge through the water.

When she opened her eyes at last, she realized how far she had come. The beach was distant, the sound of collision more than a sight; the papery light at the horizon had grown fine, translucent. She made of her body an arrow, forced it downward but encountered no resistance, no sandy floor. Cresting again above the water, she relaxed, rested, buoyed on salt and sound.

When she climbed from the water at last, rubbed her sandy shirt over her body, she felt tired beyond all imagining. The moon and stars had risen in the sky. The houses along the dunes were lit like jack-o'-lanterns on a fence, eyes and mouths, grimaces and expressions of surprise. She dressed, gathered her socks and shoes, stood, and turned for home.

I loved him, she thought. And for a moment she rested her head on the senator's sleeping chest, his dignified shirt-front, his arms crossed there, cuff links glinting.

SHE SAW DUNCAN before he saw her. His eyesight was not very good, especially at night, when there was no light to throw shapes into relief, which defined one thing from another, distinguishing the man from the hat rack, the shadow in the mirror from the thing itself. She knew it was Duncan by his great height, the trepidation of his step, the wagging head. She slowed to encourage the distance between them, postpone their meeting.

But her heart, as though receiving some delayed signal that, for waiting and wanting, acquired a terrific and unjustified force, shook as though an electric current had been administered to her body. Her heart was failing.

Not here, she thought. *Not now.*

And by sheer resolution, by the force of her own refusal, she waited it through, waited for it to pass, for it all to pass. And then she waited until Duncan was nearly abreast of her before reaching out her hand to stay him, say her name, say, *Duncan. It's me.*

Miniature Man

For fifteen years, Gregorio Aruña worked among us, building his museum of miniatures here in our village of Monterojo, high in the Sierras de las Marinas, and in all that time, no one was allowed in the door of his museum. Fifteen years is a long time to work at something that no one is allowed to see, you will admit. Not even his mother and father had been inside the building, and naturally over the years there had grown up a suspicion that Gregorio's strange museum was destined to be a failure. It is difficult, after all, to believe in something you have never seen that presents you all the time with a locked door, and paper over the windows, and a secretive host.

Still, for all those years, he worked more or less peacefully among us, and then at last the time came when there was to be an unveiling. One night in the café, Gregorio announced that his work was nearly finished, and he ordered several pitchers of *tinto de verano*. This was proof of his intentions, at least, because Gregorio was very close about money, wearing the shabbiest of clothes and always asking for yesterday's bread and the scraps off your plate. But that night, glasses in hand, we forgot his foolishness for an evening and raised a toast to him and his museum. Soon he would open the doors at last, and we would see what all his years of toil amounted to.

The next afternoon, I was taking my customary siesta on the examining table in my office when I was awakened from my dreams. Gregorio was standing beside me, and his face was dreadfully white. "Dr. Xavia," he whispered, "help me."

He held out his hands. They had been crushed as if an anvil had been dropped on them.

I sat him down right away and turned the fan on him and poured a brandy down his throat and then another. And then I checked to see that I had film for an X ray and enough gas to keep him comfortable. While I got things ready, he talked. It had happened, he explained, like this: a marble lintel over a window in his museum had split inexplicably and fallen across the backs of his hands while he was installing the glass in the frame below.

"Don't move," I said, and took a picture of one of his hands and then the other.

While I developed the film, he kept talking. He told me that in the second it took for the rock to crack and fall, he looked up and ascertained, first, that he had done a poor job of plastering around the marble, and second, that his reflexes were inadequate to the task of removing his hands in time.

I did not say so, because only a cruel man would have pointed it out, but I guessed that he had been reckoning the cost of the glass he held in his hands, too. Gregorio is like that—we accuse him of foolishness, but it is true that only an idiot would refuse to let go of a piece of glass and allow his fingers to be crushed instead.

"What happened to the glass?" I asked him, beginning to scrub.

"I dropped it when the rock hit my hands. It sounded like a lot of money when it fell, too."

It was a terrible job to fix him up. I extracted shards of bone no bigger than fish scales from the backs of his hands. A good number of the metacarpals had been broken, and in one or two places they had been crushed like pieces of chalk. I could not offer him much hope that he would ever regain full use of his hands. This news, to a man who has made it his life's work to re-create on a tiny scale a complete village and nativity, enough to fill the rooms of a small three-story house, could not be anything but devastating. So I chose to make no prognostications.

"Be quiet," I told him when I began working. "I need to concentrate." I nodded to Natalia, the silly girl who is my assistant; she had come back from her siesta and gagged at the sight of Gregorio's hands and was now doing the gas for me.

"They look like empty gloves," she whispered over the top of his head.

"Go to sleep for a little, Gregorio," I said. "It will be easier on all of us."

But later, after he was awakened, he had to ask me, our Gregorio. I took his hands, two blunt white cudgels bandaged up like boxer's gloves, and held them gently in my own. Natalia had opened the blinds and gone to wash her face; the sun had moved around the mountain by then, and there was a marvelous breeze. We expect them here around this time of day, coming from the east in the late afternoon. Everybody starts to wake up again, with that breeze stealing over their faces as they lie on their beds.

"Don't talk to me about signs, Dr. Xavia," Gregorio said. "Just tell me the truth."

But I would not punish him with that kind of talk. There would be enough people to say it was bound to happen anyway, and what could you expect from such a crazy endeavor?

"There will always be some stiffness," I said, taking care with my words. "Maybe some pain."

He pulled his hands away and shook them in my face. "Finish your thought."

I put my hands in my pockets. No fighting for me. I am a doctor, and I need my hands, much, I suppose, as Gregorio needs his—for careful work. Gregorio is a thin man, small and wiry, with black hair like a monkey's, which falls over his forehead in a childish way. I think he is thirty-five, maybe thirty-six. I helped deliver him, but I cannot recall the year exactly.

He screwed up his face at me. "I know what you are thinking," he said, but I wonder if that was true.

What I thought was this: why would a lucky boy go away to England to study, win a miraculous if modest lottery settlement while on a single three-day holiday with his relations there, and come home to this mountaintop village in Spain, even if it is the most beautiful place on earth, to spend the best years of his life building this museum, as he calls it, of tiny houses like dolls' houses?

I did not pass judgment on it, you see. I had never been inside his museum. For all I knew, it might have been splendid, or ridiculous, or it might have explained itself perfectly, though it was hard to imagine. He had told me about it when we met in the café from time to time, and he talked like a man who cannot help himself from spilling a delightful but probably untrue secret. He described the tiny churches and houses built from stone, and the electric lights that winked in the windows, and the lakes and rivers with real fish swimming in them, and the train that curled around the mountain, blowing clouds of steam. He told me about a bucket that fell into a well and came up brimming with water, and about a forge from which real sparks flew, and about the tiny fires burning in the orange groves against an imaginary frost. He explained how all these scenes—the mountains and the valleys and the forests and the creatures there—were built upon platforms in the rooms of his museum, how you could walk around them from any angle and see something new every time.

His parents, good people, both of them, despaired over Gregorio. I have known him since he was a baby and can say, with less emotion than his parents, that he is a mysterious person, as all people who are obsessed must be.

But I did not criticize him, though there were many who did. I only asked, in the quiet and thankfully private room that is my own mind, *why*.

"Do you want to call your mother?" I asked him. "I'll dial it for you."

I saw the shock on his face. He could not even dial the telephone.

"I'll manage," he said, but his face was white again, and he stood up unsteadily.

"Let me walk with you, then," I said.

He waved me off, and I thought he looked even more like a monkey, or maybe like a starving, tormented bear, swinging at invisible bees.

I watched him step outside into the bright street. We have no vehicular traffic on these high streets in Monterojo. The roads were built by the Moors in the Middle Ages and they are wide enough for a cart, but not much else—two men standing at either side of the street in their doorways can spit into each other's face without taking a step.

So I did not have to worry about Gregorio being hit by a car.

But I had many other things to worry about, and so did he, only he hadn't discovered them all yet.

HE TOLD HIS MOTHER the same thing when we walked up the hill to see him a few hours later, when I judged the full effects of the gas would have worn off and he would be in considerable pain.

Gregorio had bought both houses when he came back from England, one for his museum and also the house next door, where he planned to live. I'd been in that house, at least, and it looks like all the others here—built of stone, with small windows and cool interior rooms hidden from the sun. Some of us have tiled floors and some of us wood, and some of us have a little stone courtyard or even a fountain to the side, but we are all more or less the same otherwise, as far as our living arrangements go. The houses run next to one another, side by side like pearls on a string, on several terraces carved out of the side of the mountain and linked by narrow alleys with steep flights of steps. At the very top is the castle. From the door of Gregorio's house, you can look down a dizzying slide over the rooftops of Monterojo and down the slopes of the Sierras de las Marinas, etched with the thin, curving crescents of terraces built by the Moors so many centuries ago. The terraces are planted with olive and almond and lemon trees, and *níspero* trees under enormous billowing tents of gray gauze, which protect the fruit against the thieving of the birds and give the mountainside, from far above, the look of a patchwork quilt.

We are used to thinking of this place where we live as beautiful. People come from all over the world and climb to the top of the mountain, to the castle's highest tower, and take photographs of the view. I myself have been asked to pose for some of these pictures, as if I, too, am part of Monterojo's charm. Still, I have learned that if you have lived in a place all your life, it is possible to become blind to it, both its good and bad sides.

It is even possible to stop seeing it entirely.

Gregorio stood in his doorway, blocking our way. "I'll manage," he said to us, but I could see how much his hands hurt him.

"Are you out of your mind? How will you even wipe your bottom?" Celeste stared at his bandaged hands. "Look at you! You can't do anything. Come home. Come home, Gregorio."

"No. I'll manage."

"Dr. Xavia says you should come home," Celeste said, though I had offered no such advice.

I stepped forward. "I've brought you something for the

pain," I said. "Let us come inside and get you something to take them with, at least."

I found a glass in his kitchen and some bottled water. "Open your mouth and I'll put them on your tongue. You might drop them trying to hold them."

I put the pills on Gregorio's tongue and held the glass to his lips. Celeste watched. It is terrible to see your children suffer, I am sure. I could see what she was feeling. And they have never known how to talk to Gregorio. None of us has.

He would have a very bad time of it here alone, I thought, looking around. He might possibly turn on the tap by using a wooden spoon or something as a wedge and manipulating it with his elbows, but it would be very hard to turn it off again. He could not cut open one of the oranges from the bag on the table, nor break off a hunk of bread. He could lap at a dish of olives like a dog, and he could finish off some beans by putting his face into the bowl, also like a dog. But he could not unzip himself to take a piss, and his mother was right—how was he to wipe his ass? I could see how this night would go for him.

"Come," I said to Celeste, and led her away weeping. "Come, come. Shhh. He is upset, you can understand that. Give him time."

I stopped her, though, at the corner. "Wait here a minute." I went back to the house, knocked on the door, and let myself in without waiting. Gregorio was standing in the kitchen, looking dazed. I went up to him quickly and unzipped his fly. He gave out a cry as if he were a child and I had hit him, a cry of outrage and disbelief and pain.

"You'll thank me later," I said.

That night, as I lay in my own bed, I thought about

Gregorio and tried to imagine what he must be feeling. I was not worried about him so much for that one night—he knew where to find me if he wanted something more for the pain, and he knew I was used to being woken in the middle of the night by someone calling my name from outside in the street. It was the question of his future that troubled me—that, and the sorry condition of his hands. Surely, with the museum set to open, he must be almost finished with his work there, I argued to myself. Perhaps someone else could finish up whatever details were still left. Yet these thoughts did not comfort me. I felt restless and worried, and when I fell at last into sleep, it was fitful. I dreamed of Gregorio's museum, and I seemed to see it all as though I were a child passing slowly before the displays—every black eye in every motionless painted face, every terra-cotta tile on every roof, every humble creature waiting endlessly at the manger, the miniature garden of cactus rosettes, bristling with eternal dew . . . even the miraculous baby's tiny toes and nails.

When I woke in the morning, I said my prayers, as always, kneeling beside my bed on the hard floor and thanking God for giving me one more day. And then I added a question. *Why are you punishing him, Padre?* I asked. *I never thought you had such a mean streak.*

I WAS AT BREAKFAST with Celeste and Carlos, Gregorio's parents, when he appeared later that morning at the back door. The bright light behind him made him appear almost translucent. He'd had a very bad night after all, I thought.

Celeste greeted him with a cry of joy, but I caught her pinching him on the back of the neck when she pushed him into a chair. He winced under her fingers. "You smell," she said, bending close.

He sat down hard, his hands held before him like a begging dog's paws.

I looked at his face, which was drawn and pale. "How is the pain?" I asked him.

He shrugged.

"I can give you more pills. I'd be surprised if you didn't need them."

He nodded his head. I found the pills in my pocket, leaned near to him, and put them on his tongue, which this time he stuck out obediently. I held my coffee cup to his lips.

"It's very bad luck." Celeste sat down across from us at the table and shook her head at Gregorio. Her face was shining with sympathy and rage. I thought it had looked like that, so far as Gregorio was concerned, ever since he'd been a little boy, but it had been worse since he had come home from England with all that money and announced his plans to build his museum. This morning her face had a special brightness as if vindication, now that it had come, was aflame inside her, burning up her heart on a fat pyre. Had none of them wanted him to succeed?

Carlos growled at her. "Don't talk about bad luck. It's bad luck to talk about bad luck."

For a moment there was silence. Carlos picked up his knife and began spreading honey on his bread.

"Give that to him." Celeste gestured toward Gregorio.

Carlos hesitated, looking back and forth between his wife and son.

She half rose out of her seat, threatening. "Can't you see he's starving?"

"I'm not," Gregorio said. But I watched his eyes follow the dark honey melting into his father's bread, falling onto the plate in thick, slow, black drops. I come for meals with the Aruñas several times a week—Celeste is my cousin, and I have no wife to cook for me anymore—and it is established that we all have our favorites among the honey Carlos makes. Celeste likes the lemon, Carlos prefers the oleander, but Gregorio and I ask for the lavender, which has a mysterious, complex flavor. Carlos harvests each batch separately, removing the hives from one location to another under cover of darkness while the bees are sleeping, a practice that beekeepers in these mountains have observed for centuries. It is the only way to keep the flavors of the honey pure. Every summer, the Aruñas send a mixed case to England to their daughter, Mercedes. She is eleven years older than Gregorio and married an Englishman she met while working as a waitress at the tourist beaches in Benidorm. The Englishman—Nick, as they must call him now— brought her back with him to England. A beautiful girl, Mercedes.

Carlos reached out and offered his bread to Gregorio.

"Idiot!" Celeste snatched it away and came to sit by Gregorio, the bread cradled in her palm. "Can't you see he can't do a thing for himself?" But she was looking at Gregorio, not at Carlos, and her voice had become gentle and full of tears.

Gregorio opened his mouth, poor boy. He couldn't help it.

"He's like a baby again," Celeste said, and she sounded

almost satisfied with this terrible turn of events, her grown son eating from her fingers.

Carlos stood up as if he'd had enough, and I, too, felt eager to go. This was not a place I wanted to be, I thought to myself.

"He may be a baby, but he's getting bald," Carlos said. He towered over his son, looking down at the crown of his head, the thinning hair there. "You have less hair than anyone in the family now, except Dr. Xavia," he said. But then he stooped down and kissed Gregorio quickly, once on each narrow cheek.

"Don't let her kill you with the kindness," he said quietly, and brushed at what was left of Gregorio's hair with his fist before leaving the room.

At noon, Celeste came to find me at my office, where I was examining a wound on the head of Vicente Delgado's cat. If I am not busy, I agree to look at the animals of my friends. I am not proud about such things. May I be of use, is all I ask. And when that day comes when I can no longer be useful, may I suffer a massive myocardial infarction and pass from this world to the next in my sleep, in the midst of a happy dream. I have seen too many other kinds of death, and I should prefer this one.

"I want you to come with me," Celeste said. "You can make him see reason."

I did not reply to Celeste right away. She is a woman who will take a mile if you give her an inch. It is best not to jump too quickly to obey Celeste, lest she think she has you in her grip. I gave Vicente back his cat, rubbing the animal's ears under my thumbs. "Bathe the wound three times a day with warm water," I told him. I found in a drawer some ointment against infection. I put the ointment in a paper bag and gave that to him, too. "How many has she left now, Vicente?"

"Only two lives," he said proudly.

"That is a very fortunate cat," I told Celeste as I got my hat.

"Don't talk to me about cats. Please. I'm in no mood."

We climbed the hill to Gregorio's house.

"He insisted on coming back here after breakfast," Celeste said as we walked. She put her hand to her side as we slowly began to climb the steps. "It's a tragedy, what has happened to his hands, no doubt. But there is a way to see it as a blessing. Maybe it will be the end of his crazy museum. Maybe he will grow up now."

"But he was so close to finishing." I gave her my arm.

"Yes? And then what? Every day he could sit there with a roll of tickets and wait for the king to come so he could give him free admission? Tell me, Tomas. Who is going to come and see this thing Gregorio has made? Who is going to pay money to see it? No one, is who." She made a noise of disgust.

We arrived at the door to the museum. Gregorio had painted a sign for it several days before. MUSEO DE MINIA-TURAS. VISITAS: TODOS LOS DÍAS DEL AÑO. Open every day of the year.

"Tell me the truth," Celeste said quietly. "He will never work on his miniatures again, am I right? It is only a matter of time before he sees this for himself."

I hesitated. The man's injuries were very bad. Certainly

he would lose significant dexterity and mobility. I would be surprised if he could write his name well, when all was said and done. But I did not make this pronouncement to Celeste. "It is early yet. We will see."

We had stopped at the museum door. Paper was still tacked up over the windows so that no one could see inside.

"What do you suppose it looks like in there, really?" Celeste stared at the door.

I thought of my dream. "Both familiar and strange," I said after a minute.

Celeste seemed struck by this. "That describes Gregorio himself."

WE FOUND GREGORIO at his long worktable on the shaded terrace next to his museum, a tiny paintbrush clenched between his teeth.

"Look at him!" Celeste stopped up short and put her hands to her cheeks. "*Dios mío!* You're like a saint!" She threw herself over his neck, weeping.

When his mother collided with his back, Gregorio's brush left a large, disfiguring smear on the tiny tile he was painting. I winced; the man had been painting with his teeth, after all. It was not hard to imagine how difficult it had been.

He shrugged her off with a violent motion and looked down angrily at his ruined tile. "See what you made me do?"

"Oh, sorry, sorry, sorry." Celeste sat down beside him, wiping her eyes with the backs of her hands, like a child. She did not sound very contrite. "Mama's sorry."

Gregorio moved his work away from her with his elbow.

"We've brought you lunch, your good friend Dr. Xavia and I," she said.

"I'm not hungry." He sat morosely at the table, his bandaged hands resting on his thighs. A fly landed on his forehead; when he raised his arm to brush it away, I saw him grimace with pain.

Now he is learning, I thought. *Now he is learning that without his hands it is as if he is a prisoner in his own body.* It is strange how we cannot help moving our hands. A person moves his hands a thousand times a day. No, more, a million times, all in response to the world around him and according to his own humor—little twitches and twinges and sweeping gestures and rude flicks of the fingers and caresses and blows and gestures of prayer or benediction. Our hands are the dancers at the end of our arms, and we employ them when we cannot find the words and when we can, as if our hands perform an accompaniment to the voice.

When Gregorio spoke now, I knew he had discovered that he had to be conscious of not moving his hands at all, for the pain would be very bad. "You can go away," he said. His hands lay like deadwood on his thighs.

She ignored him. "You need to pee-pee?"

He jerked his chin in the direction of his fly. He was unzipped, of course, for no one had done him up since I'd assisted him with that problem the day before.

"Oh!" Celeste made a noise of impatience. She leaned over swiftly and zipped him up. "People will talk if they see you this way!"

"Let them talk. If they thought about my predicament

for even an instant, they would see that it is kinder to me just to let me stay unzipped." He frowned down at himself. "Now what will I do?"

"Let us eat," I proposed, "and then we will see."

Celeste got up with a sigh, as if none of this were to her liking, but she opened her bag and brought out bread and grapes and a tin of mussels. She and I took turns tearing off bits of bread and wrapping them around mussels and feeding them to Gregorio. Soon our fingers were soaked with the orange oil of the mussels. I went inside and found a bottle of wine, uncorked it, and brought it out to the terrace with three glasses.

Too late, I remembered that Gregorio could not raise his glass. My own glass halfway to my mouth, I stopped. I caught Celeste's eyes, and she stopped, too. There was a moment of silence between the three of us, and I thought that we were, each of us, calculating not simply the change to Gregorio's life, but also the terrible familiarity of accidents, as if trouble has a way of seeing exactly what will not only disarm us but ruin us entirely. After all, he could have lost both feet, and it would not have been such a catastrophe, in a way.

But I was also thinking about Gregorio's museum. For many years I had sided, at least privately, with his parents —Gregorio *was* a bit of a fool.

Here is how it happened. Fifteen years earlier, Mercedes, the older sister, had called her parents from England. I happened to have been there that evening, because it was my birthday and we were celebrating.

"Send Gregorio," Mercedes had said. "Nick and I are going to have a baby. We will help with an education for

Gregorio and he can help with the baby and then he can go into business."

At the time it seemed a fine plan, and we were ready to celebrate again. But Gregorio had left the room and did not come back for a long time. Finally, about midnight, he appeared in the doorway. He was very agitated, as if he had been thinking over his words carefully but was afraid to speak them aloud. "Please, Papa," he said quietly, "I am no good at business."

Carlos is not a violent man, you must understand. But he has his limits, like all of us. He stood up. "You will go to England, to your sister's," he shouted.

Gregorio trembled, but he stood his ground. "I want to be an artist," he said.

That was the wrong thing to have said. Carlos sputtered his disdain. "You are an artist inside a matchbox," he thundered. "That is not the work of a man. That is a mouse's business."

Gregorio flushed violently and then he turned and left the room. Carlos was referring to the little scenes of rural life that Gregorio built inside matchboxes, tiny houses and roads and trees, and the tiny paintings he executed on the tin circles that were the tops and bottoms of cans. Once, Celeste had confided to me that he had embroidered three little canvases, about two inches by two inches, with threads unwound from his socks.

"Are they any good?"

She looked shocked. "They are made from *socks*," she repeated, as if I had misunderstood.

• • •

I WAS NOT SUCCESSFUL at persuading Gregorio to
return home to his parents' house that night. In truth, I did
not really try, even though Celeste kept unsuccessfully trying to elicit my support. I listened to them going back and
forth about it. Sooner or later, I thought, he would have
to ask for their help. It was best for me not to become too
involved.

But that night, I had another dream. Again I was in
Gregorio's museum, but this time I was moving around inside it with a torch, stealthily, as if I were a thief, my light
shining over the surfaces. And yet it was not exactly as if I
were a thief; it was more as if I were discovering this place
after many, many years during which it had been abandoned, for here and there I could see that something was
awry: The tiny senora who stirred her pot over the fire held
no spoon, and her face was cracked down the center. A
flock of white plaster geese with red eyes were upended in
the sand by a small pond. A wagon listed in a plaza, one
wheel missing. When I bent close to the stable that housed
the Holy Family, I seemed to see a tear in the dull eye of the
Madonna, and an expression of pain on the faces of the
Magi. Everyone in this world of Gregorio's seemed to be
growing older and more weary as I examined them—the
man bent over his forge with an aching back, the farmers'
wives exhausted under their baskets of fruit, the grandmother sleeping in the four-poster bed, the mask of death
across her face. Dust had settled in the valleys like the fine,
silken hairs that web the cactus when it is nearing bloom. It
was as if the smooth and infinitely loving hand that hesi-
tates over the world had withdrawn itself and gone away to
other business.

And who knew if it would ever come back?

When I woke that morning, I felt a chill, and when I stepped outside to examine the sky, I paused in a way I had not in a long time to look at the view. For the first time, it struck me that one day I would not be here anymore to take in this sight. And yet, how I would miss it. That was the first time I had felt that: that I would be sorry to die.

WHEN GREGORIO HAD returned home from England fifteen years before, his lottery winnings in his pocket, his dreams of his museum filling up his head, his sister, Mercedes, had accompanied him and brought the baby, Patrick, with her so that his grandparents could see him, presumably, and so that she and her mother could share their outrage.

Gregorio was in disgrace, of course. He had not offered to share his lottery winnings with Mercedes and Nick, though I don't think they needed the money; Nick is a restaurant supplier and quite successful. And though Gregorio did eventually help his parents—he bought Carlos a new truck, and he paid to have his parents' kitchen modernized (now Celeste has a microwave oven)—his apparent selfishness, and the reports of his silly impracticality over this dream of a museum of miniatures, earned him no love among his neighbors and relatives.

During her visit, Mercedes closeted herself with her mother so that the two of them could discuss Gregorio's stupidity at length, and they sent Gregorio and the baby out to walk. Sometimes they tried to enlist me in these discussions, but it is easy for a man to tire of such conversations, and I kept my distance, pleading the needs of my patients, though even then there was not much business beyond the usual digestive discomforts and skin ailments and emotional maladies of our villagers. Instead, I used to watch Gregorio from the window of my surgery. Patrick was a fat, red-haired infant, a little over a year old, the sort who writhes with fury and discomfort most of the time, and it was easy to see that Gregorio was miserable looking after him. He bounced this furious, pale-skinned British relation of his up and down the steps of the alleys in Monterojo in his baby carriage, girls looking sympathetically after them from shop doors. Still, no one ever came over and smiled and said what a pretty baby Patrick was, or how good it was to see Gregorio again, or that they were happy he had come home, or asked what he would do with himself now. Word had gotten around already, you see, and no one was supposed to encourage him.

For the month of Mercedes' visit, Gregorio had nearly full charge of Patrick. I suppose this was his mother and sister's way of punishing him, giving a grown man a baby to see after. (In any case I have always distrusted Mercedes, as one instinctively distrusts women who are so beautiful. I suspected that she had found the determined Patrick rather a shock.) Over the weeks, I watched Gregorio and Patrick go up and down the streets of Monterojo, in and out of the café, where I suspected that Gregorio consoled himself, and perhaps Patrick, too, with an occasional grappa, and I closed my shutters so as not to hear Patrick wailing outside my window. Gregorio sometimes parked him there deliberately, I thought, perhaps hoping that I would lean out and offer a sedative.

But after a while I realized that I heard the sound of Patrick's wailing less often. Whole days would go by, and apart from one glimpse of them heading up the steps by my office in the morning, there would be no sign of them for the rest of the day. Late one afternoon when I had neither heard nor seen them all day, I closed the door to my surgery and went looking for them to satisfy my curiosity.

Gregorio had not bought his buildings yet, of course, and his museum was then a thing made only of air and dreams, but I had a feeling that Gregorio would not be at his parents' house under the disapproving noses of his mother and sister, who in any case had little tolerance for the unhappiness of the male of the species at that time.

And now you will be waiting for me to relate that I came upon something terrible when I went to find them—Gregorio drowning his difficult nephew in a well, or pitching him over the ramparts of the castle, or smothering him with a sheet. Tensions were running extremely high at that point, after all. Or perhaps you will expect the reverse, something sentimental to make your heart swell—Patrick and Gregorio sitting under the shade of a tree, the baby gurgling with pleasure on his uncle's knee, the still-boyish Gregorio suddenly charmed by his little relation. But I found nothing like any of those scenarios. Indeed, it was not an ending at all that I witnessed, neither tragic nor heroic, but a beginning of sorts, a beginning that was aborted by Mercedes' departure for England a few days later.

If I had to say exactly what they were doing when I found them, I would have to say that they were working.

Of course, not many people would use that word to describe what I saw, but I had the feeling nonetheless that

that's what they were doing, each in his own way. I found them up at the castle—my own worst instincts had led me there, I confess, for enough people had been pitched off those walls, or had jumped from them of their own volition, for me to consider the castle a dangerous place, its height rather tempting, I suppose, for the weak of heart who imagine death to be both a thrill and a comfort.

I found them in one of the half-ruined open rooms near the top. Most of the top of the castle is open now to the sky, having been worn away by centuries of wind and rain, and the rooms are mostly shallow depressions in the rock. Still, it is a safe-enough place, really, with railings and supports and signs and binoculars mounted on steel posts from which one can look down into the valley below. There is a good deal of small, loose rubble, pretty white stones you can hold comfortably in the palm of your hand, and piles of sand, and soft, smooth, low steps worn from years upon years of pacing. If you are the sort of person who can entertain himself, it is a fine outpost, really, with the shapes of clouds rushing overhead, and the wind making music in your ears, and plenty to occupy your hands, if you are accustomed to making something of nothing.

And that is child's play, is it not, making something out of nothing? For there they were, Patrick freed from his carriage and tethered to Gregorio's ankle by means of a long rope, happily crawling about or playing with the stones or the sand, filthy, of course, but completely occupied. I imagine no one had ever let him get so dirty or have so much self-determination. And there was Gregorio, paper on his knee, charcoal in his hand, drawing his baby nephew in various attitudes, drawing the castle, drawing the clouds, drawing the rooftops of the village below.

I called it child's play then, but I think differently now. There is a genius to the human being, and not just in the *form* of man, though that is astonishing enough. Any fool could have seen that they were working. They were working, each in his own way, to discover the world.

I crept away before they could see me.

THREE DAYS AFTER Gregorio's accident, I went to take my dinner with Celeste and Carlos. Celeste had made a *tortilla de patatas,* potato omelette, one of my favorites, though it is a simple thing, and *cochifrito,* lamb with lemon and spices.

Celeste had a sly look in her eye when I arrived. Gregorio came in just after me, as if he might have been waiting around outside for reinforcements before entering the house. I can't say I blamed him, but of course it only contributed to his air of doom and hesitancy. I was rather sorry I had come. We sat down at the table.

"You haven't heard our news," Celeste said. "Patrick is coming for a visit."

With Celeste's news that Patrick would be returning to Monterojo, I saw Gregorio look up warily from his place at the table. Celeste was watching him. When he raised his head, she gestured for him to open his mouth. He leaned forward and she put a swift forkful of tortilla into his mouth. "Yes, our Patrick is coming for a visit," she said. "He is seventeen now. Not a baby anymore."

Gregorio swallowed. Celeste beckoned for him to lean forward again and take another mouthful. I thought to myself that when Gregorio's pain was better, I would try to arrange some kind of clamp or hook for the bandage on his hand so that he could spear his own food somehow. It made me lose my appetite to watch Celeste feeding him.

"So, Patrick will stay with us for a little while. Mercedes says he thinks he is a great big boy now and will go off and travel by himself, but we are not to let him do that. She says he is a good boy but not completely to be trusted. So we must find him something to do while he is here. Tomas—"

I raised my head.

"He can watch you?"

"What?" I had a sudden, unpleasant image of myself asleep on my examining table, mouth open in a snore.

"Being a doctor! You know. Teach him about medicine."

I paused a moment. "Certainly, if he is interested." But I thought it was a very odd thing to propose.

"And Gregorio—" She paused. "Gregorio will be his tour guide."

Gregorio's head shot up.

"You can take him all over. He can drive"—she made a dismissive motion at Gregorio's bandaged hands—"and you can tell him where to go. Take him to Seville. Take him to Madrid. Show him Spain."

Gregorio held up his hands and shook them at her. "Have you no eyes? No brain at all?" he shouted at her. "What are you thinking? What about my museum?"

"Oh." She waved airily and began to eat again. "It will be a nice distraction for you." Then she slammed down her fork. "You're always mad at me! I try to help you, and look how you treat me!"

Gregorio stood up suddenly, knocking his chair over. "You think I am going to give up," he said fiercely. "I need your help, but instead you are going to use this to try and kill me." He was white-faced. I had never seen him so up-set. He left the room.

Carlos had not lifted his head during all this, and I confess that I did not know where to put my eyes. I am not a fam-ily man, after all. I am ill-equipped for disputes such as this. Celeste took another bite of her tortilla, but her face was twisted as if she was trying not to cry. "I wanted to open his eyes," she said after a minute, speaking bitterly to the table. "I want him to see that there is more to the world than Monterojo and his museum—his museum, which he will never touch again anyway, because now he is a cripple."

"Celeste," I began.

"What?" she said angrily, interrupting me. "What can a man with no hands do with his life? What will he do when we are all, even you, dead and gone? Tell me what will hap-pen to him then, Tomas. Tell me."

"Perhaps . . . it will not be so bad," I said gently.

"We should never have encouraged him." She wept now, her head down on her arms on the table.

I stood up from my place. "This is a family matter," I said awkwardly.

You can see what a coward I was.

FOR ALMOST TWO WEEKS, I stayed away from Celeste and Carlos. This was the extent of my discomfort and temerity. I told Celeste, when she came to see me one morning, that I was purchasing some new things for my of-fice and would be spending my evenings in Alicante for a little while, inspecting X-ray machines and other kinds of equipment to see what I liked best.

I do not think for a moment that she believed me. After all, I am seventy-seven years old; how much longer did I think I would be practicing medicine, anyway?

After a couple of days, however, troubled by my inattention to Gregorio, I walked up to his house late one afternoon and knocked on the door. When no one answered, I let myself in, for the door was not locked. I left a bottle of the painkillers on the table in his kitchen, as well as a note telling him that Natalia would come and help him if he wanted assistance dressing or bathing or cooking. He had only to call me and I would arrange it. But he did not call.

I did not go back to Gregorio's for several days after that, arguing with myself that I had done what I could. Gregorio would have to find a different way to live in the world, I thought. He would not be much good for fine work, of course, but there was no reason that he could not turn to a sort of labor that would require less exacting skills — driving a farm vehicle, he could probably manage, or even packing fruit.

This is what I told myself, but at night I did not sleep well. I was troubled by images of Gregorio's museum or of Gregorio himself. One night, I dreamed that I was a giant, walking through the village of Monterojo, stooping over to peer in the windows. In the last house, I had to reach in with my finger to pull aside a curtain, but as I did so, I clumsily caused the wall to break, and when I attempted to withdraw my hand, the stone and plaster of the wall fell away entirely into the street as if a bomb had gone off, exposing the interior of the house. Inside, Gregorio was lying on a little bed, curled up, his back to me. Suddenly I was filled with a terrible dread. When I reached for him, meaning to hold him in my palm and bear him away to safety, he was cold and stiff, and at my touch he fell apart like a dry leaf.

After two weeks, Celeste came to me at my house early one morning.

"Patrick arrives tomorrow," she said, sitting down when I pulled out a chair for her. "I hoped you would come and eat with us."

I made her coffee, but she did not lift the cup to drink. I could see she was embarrassed. I passed her the sugar. "How is Gregorio?" I asked instead, sitting down across from her.

She did not say anything for a moment. I looked up from stirring my coffee. Celeste's face looked very old and tired, and for a moment she reminded me of somebody, though I could not think who it was. Then I saw it—hers was one of the faces I had seen in my dream of Gregorio's museum, an old woman sitting alone in a plaza beside a church, a flock of pigeons at her feet. In my dream, the woman's face had been terribly sad.

"I feed him," she said after a minute or two. "I bathe him. How he is inside, in his heart . . . I don't know." She paused. "It is just like always."

She looked up at me. "I will be ashamed in front of Patrick," she said then. "He is my only grandchild, and I do not know him. No one speaks at the house. Not Carlos, not Gregorio. Please, Tomas."

I was overcome with confusion. I did not want to find myself there in the middle of that trouble again. And I was ashamed of something else, too, though I could not have said then precisely what it was. Sometimes, I now understand, it takes a dangerously long time before we see clearly how things stand with us.

That night, I walked up to Gregorio's house again. No one answered the door, so I walked around to the side of the house, where he kept his worktable on the terrace. A utility light had been strung up in the branches of the almond tree that overhung the marble flooring. Gregorio sat at his table, fast asleep, his head resting on one arm. The bandages on his hands were filthy and torn. But his face was the face of the child I suddenly remembered, the boy Gregorio at six, perhaps, with soft black curls and shy eyes.

Quietly I backed away, down into the street. I stood before the door to his museum for a moment. Then—I don't know what made me do it—I reached out my hand and tried the door. It swung open easily, noiselessly, under my fingertips, as if the hinges were oiled. I stood there, shocked. It was completely dark inside the museum. I could not see anything. And then I realized that it had always been this way, unlocked all this time, all these years. Any one of us could have opened the door and gone inside and seen what there was to see.

Maybe you will be surprised to know what I did next.

I closed the door and walked away, back down the street to my surgery, where I poured myself a grappa, and then another, and then one more, before lying down on my examining table. You see, I was not ready yet to go inside. I was not yet ready.

PATRICK ARRIVED THE next afternoon. When I went by the Aruñas' house, he was standing in the kitchen, a pair of headphones hooked around his neck. He was as pale as he had been as an infant, like a piece of wood stripped of its bark, but he was no longer fat, nor red-haired. He had the emaciated look of some teenage boys who are so impossibly thin that it hurts to look at them, and his hair had turned an unexceptional brown. He had not inherited Mercedes' excellent good looks.

Carlos, who had come home from work to welcome his grandson to Spain, had changed out of his work clothes and poured everyone a glass of muscatel in the kitchen. Carlos speaks no English at all, but he held out a glass to his grandson, smiling and making smacking noises by way of encouragement.

"Thanks," Patrick said. "Cool."

"What is all this you have brought with you?" I asked Patrick, gesturing to the bewildering array of electronic equipment on the floor by the door, along with a suitcase.

"Can you believe it?" cried Celeste. "He is so clever!"

Patrick was happy to explain to us how all these many devices worked. He had a laptop computer, and a CD player, and some handheld device that he said was a game, and a huge video camera that was also a projector, he informed us. "I can show movies anywhere," he said, "on an old sheet or a wall or wherever you like. That's what I want to do. Make films."

Celeste brought her hands together. "I *love* the movies," she said, enchanted.

At that moment, Gregorio made his entrance.

He looked pretty awful, I must say. It was easy to see the shock on Patrick's face that this unkempt and angry-looking man was his uncle.

Introductions were made, after which Gregorio sank into a chair as if exhausted.

Celeste threw me a look of desperation.

"Would you like a little tour of Monterojo?" I asked Patrick. "Though I can't say it has changed at all since you were here before. Come on," I said, pulling on the back of Gregorio's shirt as I ushered Patrick out of the kitchen. "I need to attend to your uncle's bandages, too, so we can do both at once.

"First, we have a stop to make," I said, and a few minutes later I pushed both boys ahead of me into the cool interior of the café. "You must drink a great deal here in Spain," I told Patrick. "You are not used to the sun or the heat, and you will become dehydrated easily." I brought three gin and tonics to the table.

"Cool," Patrick said.

"Drink up," I told the two of them. "*Salud.*"

After three gin and tonics, I thought Gregorio was ready to face his hands.

On the way to my office, Patrick asked Gregorio, "Is it true what Mum says? That you won the lotto when I was a baby?"

"Yes."

Patrick looked impressed, but it may have been the alcohol. I put a hand under his arm to steady him as we went down the steps.

"And you've built a museum?"

"Yes."

"But you've never let anyone inside?"

Gregorio didn't say anything.

"That's crazy," Patrick said gravely after a moment.

"Here we are," I said quickly, reaching for my keys.

But Gregorio stopped and turned to face Patrick. "Didn't they tell you?"

Patrick looked blankly at him.

"Didn't they tell you I was an idiot?"

Patrick's mouth opened.

"You were a disgusting baby," Gregorio said then suddenly. "Always crying. I remember you."

Patrick took a step backward, as if Gregorio had hit him.

I made a noise of remonstrance and glared at Gregorio, but Patrick put up his hand. "It's OK. Really." He reached up and carefully took his headphones from around his neck and hooked them over his ears. Glancing down at his waist and frowning, he adjusted the dials of his CD player. His face took on a slightly foolish, dignified look, as though he were listening to something important about which he had been asked to give his considered opinion.

"Go ahead," he said to me after a minute, his voice unnecessarily loud. "I'll wait here."

IN MY OFFICE, I turned on the gooseneck lamp by the examining table, as it was almost dark by now, and pulled up a stool for Gregorio. "Sit here," I told him, pushing down hard on his shoulder, because I was angry. "Put your hands on the table."

It took me a few minutes to gather the things I needed and put them on a tray—sterile scissors, tweezers, fresh gauze, alcohol—and then I sat down across from him.

"I know," he said. "You don't have to say it."

"All right."

But still I did not move.

"I don't mind," he said. "About the pain. Just go ahead."

Somewhere over our heads in the night sky I heard the distant report of firecrackers, their dull, thudding fusillade. I am old enough to remember the Spanish civil war, you see. The sound of fireworks—even a truck backfiring—can still make my hands tremble. In the square of the window, a phosphorescent light bulged for an instant and then went out. I removed my glasses and cleaned them, but my hands were shaking. It seemed to me that it was I who was drunk, and not Gregorio, though I'd had only one gin and tonic to his and Patrick's three. I should never have let Patrick drink so much, it occurred to me. He was only a boy.

I thought I knew what we would see when I unwrapped the bandages, but it had been a long time, years, in fact, since I had treated an injury as severe as Gregorio's. Most of my cases were rather insignificant, things that probably would have taken care of themselves if simply left alone.

Gregorio closed his eyes when I picked up the scissors and began cutting through the gauze, which was stiff with grime and blood. At last his hands appeared, the flesh greenish and swollen unrecognizably and in places nearly black with bruising, like spoiled fruit. In truth, they looked no worse than I expected, but when I heard a gagging sound and looked up quickly to see Patrick standing by my shoulder, I saw Gregorio's hands, lying there on the table under the circle of white light, as Patrick must have seen them: they did not look like hands exactly, but were strangely, sorrowfully familiar, something we might once have called our own but could no longer recognize as part of who we once were.

The boy was dreadfully sick.

I held his head over the basin while he spat and heaved into it.

"What happened?" he said at last, taking a shuddering breath. "What happened to him?"

I helped him to the chair at my desk, handed him a cloth to wipe his face. I glanced over at Gregorio, who was staring straight ahead into the dark corner of the room.

"He has suffered a great loss," I said, as quietly as I could. "Life is unfortunate."

BETWEEN US, WE GOT Gregorio back to his parents' house an hour or so later that evening. I'd had to sedate him finally while I resplinted his hands and changed the dressing, and it was all we could do to get him upstairs and tumble him into his bed. Before I turned off the light, I stopped in the doorway. Gregorio's childhood bedroom had been stripped of everything but the bed itself and a small chest of drawers—I was reminded of the cells of monks, where earthly love has been put away. And yet I would not have called Gregorio either a penitent or a martyr. It was more as if Celeste and Carlos had banished him, scrubbing his old room free of any traces of the boy who had lingered there over his tiny paintings. In that way, at least, he was an outcast among us.

When Patrick and I came back downstairs, Celeste and Carlos were sitting together at the cleared kitchen table, the clock ticking over their heads in its place against the wall. They looked up at me with stricken faces.

"He will feel better after he sleeps," I said.

After a minute, Celeste nodded. Carlos looked down at his hands.

I put a hand on Patrick's shoulder. "I am borrowing Patrick for a little while," I said. Patrick looked up at me, surprised. "Can you bring your movie camera?" I asked him. "There is something we need to see."

IT WAS A RISK, of course, and at first I thought it was my own. But now I understand that it was all Gregorio's risk, not mine. And not just fifteen years of risk, which would be enough for any man, but a whole lifetime, in fact.

The next evening, I arranged with Celeste for Gregorio to go with Carlos when he went to move some of his hives. This task he performed often in the summer, moving his bees from one location to the next after darkness had fallen. In his condition, Gregorio could not be of much assistance, but it was an activity that he had helped with in the past, and I thought he would not refuse if Carlos asked for his company.

After they left, Patrick removed the pictures from one white wall in the living room—a large framed photograph of Mercedes and Nick and the baby Patrick taken at a portrait studio, a rather contrived landscape painting of a long sweep of mountains, some holy pictures. Patrick moved the items with care, stacking them neatly against the wall, I noticed with approval, and then he set up his equipment. After a while, Celeste came into the room. Patrick was fiddling with his camera and the lights. She sat down quietly on the sofa, her hands folded in her lap. I put my hand on her shoulder, to comfort her. She put one hand up to cover mine briefly, and then Patrick turned off the lights.

"Now we wait," I said into the darkness.

We three sat in silence for a long time, but it was a restful silence, I think, as if peace had come at last after a long war. It seemed to me that we were like figures in Gregorio's museum of marvels, three small people sitting there, still as stones. After perhaps a half hour, we heard the sound of Carlos's truck returning. I felt Celeste stir in a frightened way beside me. The headlights raked once across the empty wall. We heard the doors of the truck slam shut and then the sound of two sets of footsteps approaching the house.

"Now?" Patrick was standing at his camera.

"Now," I said.

And then the wall flickered to life before us. The camera's eye, coming in close to the little scenes, had the effect of removing all scale from the images. I had not expected that. Suddenly, it was all amazingly lifelike, the whiskers on the donkey's chin when the camera tilted close and then flew away, the ruffled bunting on the gypsy caravan stirring under the bright, false light; I almost expected the lifeless figure at the reins to raise the whip held in his hands and shout a command. The camera panned over the mountains, over the small train with its plume of smoke and startling whistle, mounting a hillside and disappearing; it moved over rooftops and lakes and waterfalls and forests of palm trees. It hovered close beside the windows of the houses; inside, a woman bent over a baby in her lap before the glow of a fire, and a man sat at a desk, lost in thought, a scroll of paper before him. There was a man on a hillside, his hands on a white beehive, fields of lavender flowing away beyond.

There was a stout woman, the exact shape of Celeste herself, even to the tilt of her head, standing in a kitchen, her hands on her hips, her mouth open wide in laughter. The camera found us all. I recognized many people from the village, even myself, the stiff figure of an old doctor in a white coat, looking out the window of his surgery, a tiny stethoscope in his hands. There was no sound except that of Patrick's and my distant breathing, a faint cough, someone's feet scraping against stone. Someone whispered something in the background—it was my own voice, I recognized. "Over here," I had said. "Over here. Look. It's him."

I knew that Carlos and Gregorio had come into the room then, though I did not turn my head. Beside me on the couch, Celeste's fingers found my own for a moment and held tight. I saw the shape of Carlos sidle in quietly against the wall nearest the door. Gregorio slid in beside him and then stopped suddenly. I held my breath.

"Fantastic. It's absolutely fantastic." That was Patrick's voice, loud but a little distant, the way voices captured on tape sound. But you could hear the awe in it. "He's amazing, isn't he? I can't believe no one's seen this except us."

The camera bounced wildly. "Ooops. Sorry." Patrick's voice again, tinny and unnatural.

"Over here." That was me again, though I sounded like a ghost of myself, someone who had once known the world and loved it dearly, more dearly than he had known at the time.

And then the picture settled. The camera had stopped moving and hesitated at the door of a tiny white three-story building backed up against a mountain, a miniature model of the very house we had been standing in. I noticed—for the second time now, for I had noticed it the night before, of course, as Patrick and I had wound our way through the museum—that in the window on the second floor above the door, the little square of glass no bigger than a postage stamp was safely in place. The camera waited there a moment, as if lingering in sorrow—"That's the window?" Patrick had whispered—and then began to move slowly along the face of the building to the house next door and the screen of tiny cypress trees. The hand holding the camera was tired now, perhaps, and the image bounced, wavered, tilted, held, and then moved up swiftly with a jerk to reveal the hidden place behind the trees, Gregorio's secret place in his museum of miniatures—the marble-floored terrace, the littered worktable, the almond tree with a lantern caught in its branches, the tiny, bent, balding figure of Gregorio himself, sitting at the bench, his hand holding a paintbrush.

Beside me, Celeste gave a cry of surprise and recognition.

But Carlos had moved into the center of the room, blocking the ray of light from the projector for an instant.

"Bravo!" he cried, and I saw the shine of wetness on his face and knew he had been brought to tears. He began to clap wildly. Patrick, grinning, brought his fingers to his lips and whistled. And then Celeste, too, began to clap, and rose to her feet to face her son. She lifted the hem of her dress to climb up onto a chair and brought her hands together, and between her and her husband there was no pause in the sound of their hands meeting.

I looked at the wall behind them, at the image there. The night before, I had noticed the marvelous details of the small figure that was Gregorio's self-portrait—the trousers and the white shirt, presumably made out of fabric snipped from Gregorio's own clothes; the wisp of hair cut from his own head. The likeness was remarkable. But what had impressed me most was not this ability to capture us all so exactly. It was that despite everything, all along we had been his inspiration.

Carlos and Celeste remained on their feet, bringing their hands together again and again. Patrick came forward to join them, whistling and clapping and whooping. And on the wall behind them, the tiny man at the worktable, fashioned out of clay, remained bent over his task, intent only on the work before him.

The Correspondent

All her life, Lettie thought it remarkable that two little girls should have begun and then maintained such a long correspondence, an exchange of letters that was to last into their adult lives. Occasionally, many years after the first letters had crossed between Fanny and Ginger, many years after the letters became no longer necessary, in fact, someone would ask Lettie about her relationship to Fanny. People were often curious about the intimacy between them, which was not exactly that of mother and daughter, and yet was something more than that of friends, too. Lettie would fumble around for the words, smiling helplessly in that old way of hers. But if her listener was persistent, Lettie might, for lack of any other explanation, be persuaded to tell the story of how she and Ginger first met Fanny, when the girls were no more than eight years old.

It was, she would say, the most astonishing aspect of their relationship—not that it lasted so long on only the strength of the children's letters, but that it grew originally out of a chance encounter, no more than half an hour's meeting.

Of course, there were lapses over the years, periods of silence when Fanny's letters would cease altogether, and then Lettie and Ginger would assume they had heard the last from her. But eventually another envelope would appear in the afternoon's mail, and Ginger would take it happily from Lettie's hands and shake it to release the sheet of writing paper and its inevitable accompaniment of picture postcards or other offerings.

"Look, Mother," she would say. "Look what Fanny sent." And Lettie could hear the relief in Ginger's voice, echoing her own. For over the years she had become as interested in Fanny's correspondence as Ginger herself.

Recently Lettie had collected all the letters, nearly two hundred of them, sorted them by date, and stored them in a box. Among the papers covered with Fanny's uneven script were some of her childish gifts, mailed along with the letters over the years: a postcard made of two thin slices of birch veneer glued together, a trillium etched on one side; a window ornament of crimson oak leaves, pressed between two sheets of waxed paper and now turned dull and brittle; a nightgown for a doll, sewn clumsily with yellow thread; a key chain with a tiny straw medallion in the shape of a star. There must have been many others. She supposed they had been lost over the years.

She thought often about the first time she and Ginger met Fanny. She never forgot the mere happenstance that lay beneath their relationship; in light of what has become of them all, one would not forget such a thing. Years and years later, she still found reason to marvel at the accidental way in which things happen and at the bewildering extent to which lives can be determined by what appear to be, at the time, the most glancing and insignificant events.

Once in her life, a long time ago, she was tempted to view their first meeting as something orchestrated by mystical forces, a conspiracy of events. She believed, then, that people were placed in one another's path for a particular purpose, that no one crossed into someone else's galaxy without somehow altering the shape and direction of both individual orbits. She had always loved looking at the stars, loved to watch the shapes of the constellations emerging in the night sky, and so she knew that Fanny appeared in their lives that summer along with Sagittarius, the roving archer aiming his arrow at the shoulder of the filmy virgin fading from the dark sky, aiming his arrow as if to fix a companion there a moment before she disappeared into the darkness. For years, Lettie believed that this had been a kind of sign, one that she had ignored, and she blamed herself for what she saw as a failure of conscience.

The summer they met Fanny, the summer of 1955, Ginger was eight years old, and Cleo a baby of ten months. Lettie had taken the girls on a car trip that July to visit her husband's parents in Natchez; she took them by herself, although the reckless, even desperate quality of the enterprise did not occur to her until later. Eben, who claimed to be overwhelmed with affairs at the bank, saw them off early that morning from the window of their New York apartment. Standing on the sidewalk, waiting for the doorman to bring their car from the garage a few blocks away, Lettie had

looked up and seen Eben framed in the window of their dining room. She raised her hand to him, but there was a frac-
tional delay—just a few moments—before he waved back.
Many times over the next few months, and sometimes even
years later, with a pang that scarcely receded in its impact on
her heart, she was to recall that pause. At the time, she did
not fully understand the significance of his hesitation, but as
she waited there that pretty summer morning, in her yellow
coat and brown hat, holding Ginger's hand and looking up
at Eben from the sidewalk, she felt in his delay what she had
begun to feel more and more often in his company: that she
was perpetrating—by her departure? by the manner of her
departure? in the quality of her farewell to him? by her very
life?—a crime against their marriage and, in some way,
against herself.

Eben's parents were in their advanced years by then—
Eben had been a late child of a late marriage—and Lettie
had always felt fondly toward them. They were soft-spoken
people, courteous and slightly formal. Their lives had become diminished by age and infirmity; yet with their afternoon naps and gentle walks and punctual meals, they seemed
to Lettie content in an old-fashioned, trusting way, and
unsurprised by their contentment, too, as if a more uneven
life—a life of mysterious failures and disappointments,
a troubled life—was unimaginable to them. Earlier that
spring, Eben's father had taken a fall down the stairs, and
Lettie knew then that they would make no more visits to
New York. Yet she wanted Eben's parents to see the girls
again, to remind herself, perhaps, of what beautiful children
she and their son had produced together. Sitting at the pretty
wrought-iron table on their porch, participating in calm and

pleasant conversations, pushing Cleo up and down the sidewalks under the afternoon shade of the oak trees, she imagined that she would remember what made a satisfied life, what made a life happy.

She planned to make the drive herself in eight days, with plenty of time to stop along the way, and almost as soon as she had driven across the Hudson River and into New Jersey, she began to enjoy herself. With the help of guidebooks from the library, which she had carried home one day in a teetering tower, she had planned the places they would stop overnight, hotels that seemed to promise some particular pleasure—a swimming pool in a palm court, baked Alaska in the hotel dining room, a library with volumes signed by the authors who had stayed there, a famous Great Dane who prowled the lobby of one hotel, welcoming guests with a paw raised solemnly for a handshake. Each afternoon, she and Ginger unpacked their belongings in a different room with the pleasurable sense of setting up house. They rolled with Cleo on the wide beds and splashed together in the bathtubs. Sometimes they ordered room service, and at night they curled up together, after returning the dishes to their room service trolley and replacing their gleaming silver dome hats, and fell asleep with the windows open, listening to the sound of waltzes and fox-trots and rumbas being played below in the hotels' ballrooms.

It was a relief to be away from Eben and his dissatisfaction with her. Though she felt she had not changed at all since their marriage, she understood that she had failed to live up to his expectations in some significant but unstated way. Eben had plenty of money, enough for her to amuse herself in any manner she chose, but after a time, she could

see that her long walks through Central Park, her appetite
for books and novels, her tendency to daydream at the window, piqued him.

"What do you do with yourself all day, Lettie?" he would
ask, at first with genuine curiosity, but later, after Ginger
was in school, with irritation. She would shrug and smile
helplessly, unable to describe her day to him, how she passed
it gently and easily as a leaf falling to the ground. She could
not explain to him that she, too, felt as if she was waiting for
something, though she longed to be able to say such words
to him, to have them wonder together what lay in store for
her. Perhaps he might even help her discover what her future
should be. Because she did believe, at least for a while, that
she had a future. One day, she imagined, she would find herself suddenly aroused by life, instantly certain of her aim and
purpose.

But she had never said anything of that sort to anybody,
and she could not imagine confiding in Eben in that way. Instead she had Cleo, in an effort to make herself appear le-
gitimately occupied in his eyes. She told herself, and it was
true, that even if Cleo had not been so instantly and irre-
sistibly lovable a child, she would never have regretted her
birth anyway. There were some lines from Shakespeare's
The Winter's Tale that she liked, Polixenes speaking of his
son Florizel: "He's all my exercise, my mirth, my matter; /
Now my sworn friend, and then mine enemy; / My parasite,
my soldier, statesman, all. / He makes a July's day short as
December, / And with his varying childness cures in me /
Thoughts that would thick my blood." Her children, Lettie
thought for a long time, were the only really wonderful
thing she'd ever done.

On the last morning of their drive to Natchez, she calculated that they had only four hours or so to go before reaching Eben's parents' house. The weather had been fine for most of the trip, and Lettie had boldly taken various detours from time to time, always managing to wind her way back on course before becoming hopelessly lost. These deviations had thrilled her, and Ginger had enjoyed them, too, sitting on her knees on the seat beside Lettie and looking out the window. Ginger was a good child, observant and imaginative. As they passed houses by the side of the road, they would try to imagine the lives of the people who lived there —what they ate for supper, what they named their pet dog, what songs they sang in the bathtub. Cleo, always a contented baby, slept for hours in her car bed in the backseat, and Ginger would clamber back to sit beside her when she woke, to sing to her or play games. In those days, many hotels would pack a picnic for guests who wished one, and sometimes Lettie and Ginger spoke to the kitchen the evening before and enjoyed a fine lunch the next day at a table beside the road.

All in all, Lettie was sad to be setting off that morning. A pleasant string of days was coming to an end, and though she reassured herself that they would enjoy their time in Natchez and could look forward to the trip back home, too, nonetheless it felt like the beginning of the end.

That morning, they set off from Jackson along the last leg of the Natchez Trace. Lettie left the main road rather quickly, eager for an interesting detour that might prolong their drive a little. She struck off blindly onto a narrower road that led away like a pencil stroke into the Mississippi swamp and surrounding forest.

Years later, she could still recall the quality of the light in that forest, and though she had tried, many times since, to reproduce it in her photographs, she was never successful. Many years later she had taken a series of pictures from the top of the Empire State Building, and something about the flickering light in the sky that morning had reminded her of the light in that Mississippi forest. Still, she knew that she had never seen anything exactly like it since that day so long ago when Fanny first appeared to them.

Both Lettie and Ginger were struck to silence by the silvery luminescence of the air that morning, the way the long velvet leaves of the magnolia and the moss stirring in the branches of the live oaks glowed in the soft light. The spaces between the trees, full of a vaporous summer haze, beckoned them into an indeterminate distance and more than once drew Lettie's eyes dangerously from the narrow road, its dry, sandy shoulder just a few inches, in some places, above the shining water of the swamp.

She drove for a long time in a state that was almost a doze, neither consulting the map nor speaking to Ginger, who had slumped sleepily against Lettie's shoulder and watched the road ahead through slitted eyes. Not until a dog ran out suddenly across the road—a low brown dog streaking out of one invisible place and into another as if pursued by demons—did Lettie come fully awake and happen to glance at the gas gauge.

They were dangerously low on gas. Lettie sat up straight in the seat. She thought of her children, their lovely, innocent heads, and realized she had put them at risk by her foolishness, wandering off into the middle of nowhere. They might be stranded here, stalled by the side of the road with the swamp to every side. And there was something disconcerting about the silence around them, and about the light, and the way time itself seemed to be slowing down, as if the world were losing strength and breath and will. She didn't know where they were anymore, though she had a vague sense that they had been drifting southwest along the dropping contour of the land. She had seen nothing along the road that made her think they were nearing civilization.

Now, at last, she saw the untenableness of her position— a young woman traveling alone with a child and a baby at a time when few women did such things. This was 1955, after all, and the South was, though courteous to women in general, full of difficulty between the races, silences and confusions that made her feel shameful and uncertain. Seeing herself in that light, she began to wonder at the kindness of various employees at the hotels where they had stopped, and she realized that their pleasant manners with her had not been, as she had supposed, a shared jocularity at her adventure— for she had chattered away cheerily about their trip while checking in—but rather a performance as calculated to deceive as her own. She had been running away, and they knew it; and even as she had tried to seem the spirited traveler, she had been aware of the falseness of that position.

She knew that when they returned to New York her life would have changed beyond her wildest speculations, and the prospect, when she addressed it fully, terrified her. And yet they had known it, too, somehow—all those doormen and bellboys and concierges into whose palms she had pressed generous tips. They had known that she was a woman whose life was in disarray. A woman who was in danger of drowning.

She had no choice but to keep driving, but as she tightened her hands on the steering wheel, she felt the entire arc of their voyage collapsing around her. At that point, Cleo woke up in her car bed and began to cry, the first sign of unhappiness from her in the entire trip.

They had not gone another two hundred yards, however, when around the corner appeared a small gray building with a sheet metal roof and a single, battered gas pump in front.

Lettie pulled the car onto the turn of packed dirt in front of the pump, relief flooding through her, and opened the rear door to extract the wailing Cleo. The baby opened her eyes wide in the bright air as Lettie pulled her from her car bed, and stopped crying.

When Lettie turned around with Cleo in her arms, a small, thin child, a girl perhaps eight years old, stood before her, looking worried. "Is your baby sick?"

Blue veins at the child's temples showed through her pale skin. Her light hair was silvery blonde, straight as pins. She wore a yellow printed blouse, misbuttoned, and a red skirt that had been rehemmed several times to lengthen it. The ghosts of former folds showed along the bottom of the material.

Lettie turned Cleo with her damp, pink face to show her to the child. "She's fine," she said. "Only hot, like us all." She smiled down at the little girl, exhilarated by her relief at finding a gas station. And Cleo, too, cooed and laughed delightedly and waved her little hands.

At Cleo's antics, the girl's face flickered into a sudden, willing smile, involuntary and shy, and then became serious again. She stared up at Lettie.

It was odd, how the place seemed to have appeared out of

nowhere. There were no other buildings to be seen; a perimeter of quivering, sparkling swamp surrounded the small store, the light-filled forest closing in from behind. Lettie had the sensation that it had not been there before and would vanish after they left. It seemed to have materialized out of the swamp itself. And yet it was real enough, the crop of waist-high weeds growing around the building, the stained gravel before the pump, a rock by the dark screen door. But there seemed to be no one else there except for the child. There was no noise except for the roaring and sawing of invisible insects in the bushes close by.

Then the screen door suddenly clattered shut, as if someone standing inside had been holding it slightly ajar, watching them, and had then turned away abruptly. Lettie stared at the door, but she could see nothing through the dark opening. Yet the thought of Eben rose in her mind then, as though it might have been Eben himself inside, waiting for her. He had not discouraged this trip of hers; indeed, he had offered no comment on it at all, except to say he knew his parents would appreciate her trouble. And now, as if he were standing before her and she could freely accuse him, she was angry. So many terrible things might have befallen them. Was it not as if he had abandoned her to this fate? He had never once mentioned concern for her, never mentioned all the possible dangers. He had never even spoken to her about the car. She had no idea how to change a tire—she doubted if she could manage such a thing. But he had never told her to take care, never told her not to stop in strange places, nor how to protect herself. He had sent her off without any advice at all, almost as if he felt himself beyond responsibility for her.

She looked down at the girl, who stood there as though she was waiting for something, and Lettie had a sudden, ashamed awareness of herself, in her stockings and crumpled lavender dress with the narrow white belt, discreet damp stains under her arms from her fright earlier at being lost.

Once, in an effort to explain her long walks to Eben, she had told him that she felt sometimes as though she were an invisible figure moving around on a stage. She had tried to explain how fascinating it was, how she felt she could come up close to people without their seeing her. And often they really didn't see her, she'd noticed. She was an unusually small woman, with a delicate, dark prettiness, and she supposed that she was, in fact, small enough to be overlooked, or even taken for a child.

It was not like being a sneak, she had wanted to explain hurriedly, not like a voyeur—for something in Eben's expression had troubled her. It was more, she had wanted to say, like admiring a painting, trying to determine the marvelous trick of making a flat surface contain so much depth and light. She often saw things in terms of light, and her moods were sensitive to it, rising at the unfurling of a clear morning, sinking to a pleasurable sadness on rainy afternoons. Sometimes she had to stop and simply stare at the way things looked when they caught the light in a particular way that moved her and that made them feel significant.

Eben had raised his eyebrows at her. "But you are not invisible, Lettie," he had said. "You're perfectly real." And he had reached out and touched her cheek with the back of his hand, as if she were a child and he was sorry for her. It was one of his last acts of tenderness toward her. Later she thought it was the moment at which he felt he had said good-bye to her, and so could justify his abrupt departure.

But she knew she was not invisible. Eben hadn't needed to say such a stupid thing to her.

The child stared up at her, and Lettie felt her face burn with a sudden embarrassment, as if the child were seeing Eben's neglect, the casual way he had sent her off, washed his hands of her. How unprepared she was. It was ridiculous. She was ridiculous.

Lettie shifted Cleo to her other arm. Well, she must find out where they were, at least. Any fool could read a map. "Do you live here?" she asked the child, attempting a smile.

The girl shook her head and pointed down the road, to a fork dividing off into the forest. "Down that way. In Grandy."

Lettie managed another smile, bigger and more jocular. "Well, we are certainly glad to see you and your pump. We were just about out of gas." She turned and motioned to Ginger, who had slid over into the driver's seat and was regarding them from behind the wheel.

When Ginger climbed from the car and the two girls stood facing each other, Ginger raised her hand slowly.

The child Fanny, for it was Fanny, raised her hand in reply, a sober expression on her face, as if she knew that with this first gesture something significant was beginning in her life. The girls were about the same age, Lettie judged, though Fanny was the smaller of the two, despite an air of determination that suggested she was already used to making her own decisions about things. Later, because Fanny herself had seemed so thin and underfed then, Lettie was surprised to discover that one of Fanny's first impressions of them was that they were unusually small people, tiny and foreign-looking. Once, when she was eleven or so, Fanny sent them a length of yarn that was exactly as long as she was tall. Lettie and Ginger had pinned Fanny's yarn to the wall and measured themselves, too, mailing back their corresponding lengths in ribbon. But Fanny was to outgrow Ginger in a few years and, soon afterward, Lettie herself, becoming a rangy woman, almost six feet tall, with arms practically as thick as Lettie's legs. Lettie sometimes thought of sailors when she considered Fanny. There was a kind of towering loneliness about her, as if she were accustomed to long days and nights out of sight of land.

Ginger reached for Lettie's hand. "I'm thirsty."

"We have soda pop in the cooler." Fanny looked from Lettie to Ginger and back again, and Lettie smiled at her.

"That would be nice."

Inside the store it was so dark that for a moment Lettie could see nothing at all, though there was a bad, powerful smell—of some kind of wild animal, Lettie thought, a bear or a fox or something. She stopped just inside the door, unwilling to venture much farther. Gradually, as the room came into focus, she made out three or four low shelves with ordinary sorts of goods stacked on them: boxes of flour and tins of fruit, packages of crackers and canisters of soap powder, small tiers of matchboxes, a basket of corncob pipes, a jumble of spring-loaded mousetraps. At one end of the room was a makeshift counter—boards laid over sawhorses, with a piece of printed fabric as a curtain—and behind it a woman seated on a tall stool. She was perched with her legs gathered up high, as if she wanted to keep her feet away from the floor. She appeared ready to spring at any moment.

"A baby!" She slid down from the stool and approached Lettie sideways, as if she had an injury, with a sly, beseeching look. She held out her arms. "Come on to me, sugar. Come on."

The woman took Cleo from Lettie as though she, Lettie, were only a nursemaid who had been minding the baby for its real mother. Lettie felt foolish; she could not struggle with the woman over the baby—that was ridiculous. But an alarm had begun to grow in her.

The woman's manner changed abruptly when she held Cleo in her arms. Suddenly she became peaceful, her whole body relaxing, her eyes closing as she brought her cheek to Cleo's soft head. It was hot and close in the room, intensifying the strange odor; it was even hotter than it had been outside, though it occurred to Lettie that it should have been cooler there in the dark, out of the sun. The woman's neck was wet with sweat. Lettie realized that she was a large person—her cringing manner had prevented Lettie from seeing it before. Her skin looked loose on her big bones, and she gave the appearance of filling out after an illness, as if she might once have been much larger, heavy and padded with flesh.

The woman tilted Cleo back to look at her face and croon. "Beautiful. So, so precious."

Slowly she began to turn away, and Lettie saw with alarm that the woman was acting out an almost comic parody of criminal intent, moving on tiptoe as if not wanting to alert anyone before she made a mad dash for the door.

It was ridiculous. They were all standing there, watching her; what on earth did she think she was doing? Lettie felt pained, inappropriate laughter struggling to escape.

Ginger, who was used to people exclaiming over Cleo, stood open-mouthed. Her little hand came up to find Lettie's, and Cleo herself began to cry in a startled way.

But before Lettie could do anything, Fanny hurried forward out of the dark. "Give her to me, Mama," she said quietly, hoisting the baby expertly and handing her back to Lettie quickly, as though she did not care for the feeling of Cleo in her arms. She turned abruptly to look at Ginger. "Do y'all want a root beer?" Her face had flushed red.

Ginger nodded mutely.

"And we'd like to fill up the car," Lettie said, finding her voice. She stroked Cleo's head to quiet her wild sobs. "There, there. Hush." Who should she address now? Lettie worried. Was the child in charge?

"Suit yourself," the woman muttered, turning away.

Fanny shifted uneasily. In the dim light of the store she seemed to waver, unsure. "I'll help you," she said then, as if she'd decided something, and escaped through the screen door.

Lettie glanced at the woman's back. She had climbed up ponderously onto her stool again. Lettie was reminded of a monkey she used to watch sometimes at the zoo, a mournful, erratic creature that would bare its teeth and rush the bars for no apparent reason; she had felt afraid of the monkey and painfully sorry for it at the same time.

Outside, Fanny had started to fill the gas tank, holding the hose in both hands.

Lettie watched her thin back with dismay. "I can do that," she said, hurrying forward. Was there no man about?

But Fanny shook her head.

Ginger climbed hurriedly back into the car. When Lettie

bent to resettle Cleo in her car bed, Ginger scuttled over on the seat and sat close beside her sister, looking down at her, her hands clasped between her knees.

Fanny replaced the cap on the gas tank and wrenched it into place. "Just a minute," she said, and ran back into the store. After a moment, she came back outside, carrying two root beer bottles, straws stuck in their mouths. "Five dollars for the gas," she said. "The drinks are on the house."

"You're so kind," Lettie said. The thin little child holding up the root beer bottles was breaking her heart, she realized as she stared at her, with blows so soft and deadly she'd scarcely noticed the pain of them at first. But now she understood better. There was no one there to help this child, at least not now, at least not today. "Please let me pay you for the drinks," she said desperately. "You've been so helpful." She opened the clasp of her purse and began to fumble inside it for her wallet, but Fanny shook her head resolutely.

Lettie took a deep breath. She closed her purse slowly. "Well, thank you. So much." She ducked into the car to hand the bottles to Ginger and then stood up again, facing the child. There was something more the child wanted, she felt sure. And there was something she wanted to say in return, she knew, though she had no words for it. Something had happened back there, in the store. They had seen something they were not meant to see, perhaps. "Isn't there something I can give you?" she asked instead, and she thought at first of money, or the box of colored pencils she had saved for Ginger for their stay in Natchez, or a pretty hair ribbon, before recognizing the way those things—any of those things—would be so terribly inadequate.

Fanny paused. Then she glanced in at Ginger in the car.

"*She* can," she said. "She can write her letters, can't she? I'd like to have a pen pal. I've heard of that and I think I'd like it. You're from New York. I looked at your license plate. Are you going home?"

"Well, yes. Yes, we will go home," Lettie said, and knew she had decided it then. She realized she had been fantasizing about going someplace other than New York, anywhere else at all, in fact. "In a couple of weeks. We're on a trip."

"I'll give you my address." Fanny pulled a bit of paper and a pencil from her skirt pocket and squatted down to write on the ground.

Lettie searched her handbag for paper and a pen and wrote their own names and address on a piece of hotel stationery. "This is Ginger," she said, handing the paper to Fanny, and including Ginger in her smile. "I should have said so before." Ginger was kneeling in the seat again, looking out at Fanny. "And I'm Mrs. Ramsey. Lettie. It's a nickname."

Fanny nodded as if she had heard of such things, passing her slip of paper through the window to Ginger. Then she stepped back. "I'm sorry about my mother," she said suddenly. She looked away in embarrassment. "She wouldn't ever hurt your baby."

"I'm sure she wouldn't," Lettie said, but it was insufficient comfort, she knew. It sounded like forgiveness, and that wasn't what she had meant.

"She's just sad," Fanny said, and her eyes slid to Lettie's face and then away again. "For our own baby. She died."

"I understand," Lettie said quickly, though the truth was that she did not understand. She brushed aside Fanny's admission with a freezing, terrified politeness, but she did not

understand at all. And it was that failure—not of not understanding, per se, but of *not wanting to*—that was to tor-
ment her for so many years afterward.

How had she become such a coward?

THERE WAS ONE final exchange between them before Lettie drove away that day, the child Fanny growing
tinier and tinier in the car's rearview mirror, until at last the
store and the gas pump and then finally Fanny herself in her
red skirt became completely indistinguishable from the
world around them, part of the blur that was what they left
behind.

"We'll be certain to write," Lettie had said. "I promise."
And then she reached for her camera on the front seat.
"May I take your picture?"

Fanny stepped back, glancing around nervously as if
searching for a place to retreat. And that was how Lettie first
caught her on film, a look of surprise on her face as though,
glancing behind her to the dark doorway of the store, she
could not believe she had come from there, could not believe
that she found herself in that place, could not understand
how, when the curtain parted, this should be the stage upon
which she stood. It was the look of someone much older, the
look of someone who understands that her circumstances
have only an accidental relation to her essential self and yet
knows nonetheless that her essential self will be forged inevitably by the accident of her birth. Fanny Sims was a child
born into a trough of misfortune, and somehow, even at a
young age, she knew that it had something to do with her,
but not everything.

Lettie took other pictures on that trip, of course. But when her film was developed, the one of Fanny leaped out from the others, more-conventional arrangements of the children, of Eben's parents holding Cleo, of empty scenery.

Lettie felt, as they drove away, a terrible, aching sadness, as though she were leaving one of her own children behind. She wanted to take Fanny with them, to bundle her into the backseat, to spirit her away from the danger and sadness of that place.

But of course she could not. And so they left her.

FANNY'S FIRST LETTER was waiting for them when they returned to New York a few weeks later. Enclosed with it was a label from a soapbox, carefully steamed off and pressed flat, a painted picture of a pretty little child sitting beneath a flowering tree, her dress spread over her lap, bluebirds fluttering at her wrists as though they held her arms aloft in a posture of innocent helplessness.

> I hope you all are home safe. It has been very hot here. My mother has been sick, but I am learning the store, as you saw. I am eight years old. Ginger, how old are you? I have a dog. Sometimes he growls, but he is a good watchdog. Can you tell me about New York City? So, you know how this place is. You can think of me here.
>
> Love, Fanny Sims
> P.S. Please write back.

Lettie read the letter over Ginger's shoulder that evening, fussing over her as she helped her get ready for bed, delaying the time alone with Eben.

"I'll write her back right away. Tomorrow," Ginger said.

Lettie sat down on the bed and put her arms around her daughter. She smelled the good, clean scent of her after her bath. She would have liked to stay there, holding Ginger, but she knew Eben was waiting. Still, as she drew the curtains in Ginger's room, turned on the night-light, she did just as Fanny had suggested. She thought of Fanny in that place.

The afternoon they had driven away, they had passed a sawmill and timbering operation a few miles down the road, a couple of raw, scraped-out acres and some long open sheds, and beyond that, through a scrim of thin, sickly trees knocked askew but left standing, she had made out what must have been a massive area that had been logged. The light across those devastated acres had the scalded, endless quality of desert light. Suddenly, the narrow road behind and ahead of them had been full of trucks stacked high with the giant trunks of trees, rocking from side to side and hurtling down the road with their enormous cargo.

Yet, standing at Ginger's door that evening, looking at the pretty drape of the curtains in shadow and the soft curve of the upholstered slipper chair across the thick, patterned rug, she remembered Fanny standing resolutely beside the gas pump as they had driven away from her. It was as if they had left her on an island, the forest falling around her, a ruin of toppled trees and broken branches and terrified birds screaming a chorus of warnings.

Eben was waiting for her in the living room. He was staring out the window at the lights of the city, his hands clasped behind his back. He turned when she entered the room. "Lettie," he said. "There will be some changes here."

And then he outlined for her what he wanted, which was to take his leave. He promised to maintain them as they

were, though he did not exactly do so. Lettie would continue to receive an allowance from him to run the household, he said; he would visit with the girls from time to time.
Should Lettie need anything from him, she could reach him
at the bank. He had taken an apartment close by.

Lettie could not speak. Theirs had never been a marriage
of many words, those few trickling to almost nothing. Once,
she supposed, she had seemed promising to him, a slender,
sweet-tempered girl who looked good on his arm, who
charmed his associates and friends with her innocence and
pleasure at the world's festivities, all apparently arranged for
her enjoyment. But as she aged, though she was not so very
old even then, she imagined she had lost the quality that had
once seemed so appealing to him. The tenderness and vul-
nerability of her early youth had been replaced, not with the
admirable control of a mature, confident matron, but with
a sort of helplessness.

She knew that Eben did not understand how she was
waiting, how she felt that at any moment she would find a
foothold in the rock wall of her life. But staring at Eben's
face that night, at his expression of uncomfortable remorse,
she understood that she had waited too long, that she had
somehow missed her cue, that her life would simply continue as it was, though without Eben's presence in it—a
slowly unwinding pattern of events in which nothing would
change, no great moment would announce itself, no door
would open.

She did not mind Eben's departure exactly. She had married as a function of her habitual willingness to take whatever was offered to her without discrimination. They had
enjoyed many conventional forms of happiness, she supposed

—the dinners, the tennis games, the exhibits and concerts the city offered in such abundance. But she knew, had known all along, perhaps, that there was no real love between them, nothing powerful enough to become its own force steering them through life. So she bowed her head like a child when Eben spoke to her, and she saw him to the door with his suitcases, which were already packed.

He stopped, shrugging into his coat. "I tried to tell you," he said, and a note of anger crept into his voice. "But you never seemed willing."

The accusation hit her like a blow, as if he had made a fist and struck her in the face. Willing to do what? She had been so willing, she had wanted to say to him, so exactly willing, to take her place in the world.

It had just never happened.

EBEN'S EXIT FROM HER LIFE, though she continued to see him and make her life known to him over the many years that followed, was the beginning of a slow change in Lettie.

That night after Eben left, she walked around their apartment, an unfamiliar anger burning in her chest. From the windows it seemed she could see the entire city, its mass of lights, the hectic moaning and colliding of traffic on the streets below, the scream of brakes. Standing there above the roaring and mashing of the world, she understood for the first time that nothing was waiting for her, that she was not going to step, as she had imagined, onto a threshold that would usher her forth into her future, a future in which she could only vaguely imagine herself, anyway. The world beneath her windows was incalculably unaware of her, and she was ashamed that she had ever imagined it to be otherwise.

Yet she thought of Fanny again that night as she stood there at the window. She thought of Fanny's aggrieved face, and Fanny's mother's neck wet with sweat, and the suggestion of the dead baby, and the foul stench in the store. She thought of the forest and the child growing smaller and smaller, and in her mind she put out a hand and touched Fanny's shoulder.

She did not know what made her think, at that moment of her own reckoning, that she could be a help to Fanny. It was part of her presumption, she supposed, a last breath of hope that even Eben's defection from her life could not extinguish, that made her feel Fanny needed a protector, and that she should be the one to step forward.

After all, when she looked closely at her life at that moment, it was she who was in danger. It was her own poor excuse for a life that was flickering then in a cold and unfamiliar wind.

IT IS A LAW of the universe that the object at the front of a train, the first car, should be the one most vulnerable to derailment, the propulsion of the weight behind it testing the conviction of its course. This is how Lettie thought of herself after Eben's departure. For the first time she stood at the head of the line, with neither parents nor husband before her, and behind her, pushing her on faster and faster, was the whole wasted weight of her life.

For a while she exhausted herself with the effort to behave

as though everything were completely normal, completely the same. The children had never seen much of Eben, who had always been busy at work anyway, and they had depended on Lettie completely for the structure of their lives and its comforts and obligations. Yet where the leisurely business of attending to her children had once seemed easy and pleasurable to her, she now felt worn out by it. Without the construct of a marriage around her, the demands of life with small children, which make a woman's world so terribly busy and so empty all at once—shopping and fetching and cleaning and sewing and cooking—began to seem preposterous to her, a kind of universal joke. It wasn't that she minded the work of it, nor did she love her children any less; she loved them more, perhaps, for giving her life a purpose it so desperately seemed to lack. It was that everything else, everything that had been rendered proper or meaningful before by virtue of her marriage, was now revealed to her to be utterly pointless. Suddenly it was no longer enough simply to walk, to doze in the afternoons, to read and reread Turgenev or Chekhov, the Russian writers she so loved. Though she was spared the burden of financial terror, for Eben continued to provide for them, she could no longer hide behind the acceptable role of a wife with no certain occupation or interest.

It was the humiliation she minded most. The realization that she had led a pointless, trivial life. The realization that she was a pointless and trivial woman.

It became clear to her after Eben left that she had no friends. Those with whom she and Eben had enjoyed a superficial social exchange heard quickly enough of the change in their circumstances, and Lettie understood that a single

woman, unlike a single man, was nothing but a social lia-
bility. Lettie suspected that Eben had gone to the considerable trouble of changing his address with all their creditors
and friends, and for months after he left, there wasn't even
any mail for her, just the letters to Ginger from Fanny, and
occasionally something from Ginger's school. She imagined
—though perhaps wrongly, she thought later, more kindly
—that people did not blame Eben for deserting her, and she
herself made no effort to keep up relationships with friends
in their old set. Soon all her exchanges in the world, other
than those with her children, were reduced to conversations
with neighbors in their building or shopkeepers. If the children needed something, she would send Eben a note at the
bank, asking him for the money. For herself, she asked nothing beyond what he had estimated she would need to maintain the house for the girls, which he sent her promptly at
the first of every month.

In October it was Fanny's ninth birthday. Lettie and
Ginger sent her three books—*Gulliver's Travels,* and Louisa
May Alcott's *Under the Lilacs,* and *Swallows and Amazons*
by Arthur Ransome—a set of colored pens, and, at the last
minute, a beautiful and extravagant sweater of soft, rose-
colored wool. Lettie sent Eben the bill, a carefully worded
note that did not make clear exactly for whom these things
were intended, and for weeks afterward she worried that
he would call her to ask about it, but he never did. Once a
month he came and took Ginger off with him for a day,
but Cleo was still in diapers and could not go with him, of
course, and before long she was frightened of him and clung
to Lettie when he came for Ginger.

At home, Lettie took her photograph of Fanny and taped

it to the window over her desk. Each time she looked at it, whether in the fisheye of the leaden morning sky or the blaze of a cloudless dawn, or at night against the black sky above the gaseous light of the city, she saw Fanny's image, world within a world. On the weekends, she and Ginger took Cleo with them to the zoo or to museums or to Central Park, and she and Ginger wrote to Fanny about their excursions. Fanny wrote them back, asking question after question.

For Christmas, Lettie sent her a set of encyclopedias. She charged them to Eben.

NOW SHE CANNOT even remember when she began, nor what prompted her, that first day, to bring her camera with her, but in spring—late April, she thinks it was, because she remembers how the light changed when the trees in Central Park lost their winter sharpness and were all over filmed with the most delicate green—she began taking photographs again. She'd used to carry a camera around with her quite often. Eben had thought it fetching, once, his little wife darting around on her dainty bird feet, kneeling in the grass and focusing seriously on a flower or something that had caught her attention; she had been so grateful for his admiration that she had not minded its patronizing quality.

But eventually he'd become annoyed by her habit of taking pictures everywhere they went.

"These are awfully odd," he'd said to her once, looking at some of her prints. "They're all of buildings, or complete strangers, or funny-looking bits of things. I can hardly make them out. Why don't you take proper pictures? Pictures of the children?"

She did take pictures of the children. Lots of them. But she'd taken pictures of other things, too. When she picked up her photographs from the camera shop, she was usually disappointed by them—how small and unremarkable they seemed—but she could always remember what had struck her about the original image. Her pictures were like an imperfect set of symbols for something. Sometimes she would look through them and feel puzzled by them, but she did not throw them away, even though Eben frowned at her when she sat on the floor in their bedroom and sorted through her stacks of prints, leaning up against the radiator that hissed and spat in a comforting way.

One day shortly before Eben left them, she came home to find him riffling through a set of pictures she had left carelessly on the table in the hall—she'd put them there for a moment and then remembered something she'd forgotten at the store, and so had run out again. When she came back, Eben was standing in the hall, still wearing his coat, her pictures in his hands. The photographs were of people walking in Central Park. Lettie remembered the day exactly—it had been just a few weeks before, near Christmas, and quite cold. Several inches of snow lay on the ground. A very few people were out that afternoon, wearing heavy, dark coats and walking in pairs or alone on the path ahead of her. The long boughs of the evergreens bending over the path were layered with snow, which fell silently to the ground on occasion, sending up plumes of snow fine as smoke in the frigid air. An older man, some twenty feet ahead of her on the path, had stopped once and taken off his hat to pass his hand over his head of thinning hair, as though he'd suddenly become hot, as though something had caught up with him at that moment and had overtaken him with its weight of sadness. The man had stood alone near a bowed-over fir tree at the intersection of two paths, the park cold and formal and austere around him, the long lines of the paths running away from him into the piercing whiteness of the empty, snow-covered field. It was the image of him there, taking off his hat to wipe his head as if it were an August day and as if he were troubled, that had interested her.

"Do you *know* him, Let?" Eben had turned to her, dismayed, as she came in breathlessly with her parcel.

"I thought he was someone famous," Lettie had lied. "A general. You know."

THE SPRING AFTER Eben left, she began to take pictures almost every day. She walked Ginger to school in the mornings, and afterward, while Cleo was still young, she took Cleo out with her.

She had no idea how many photographs she took that way, Cleo riding ahead of her in the stroller. They could take only short trips, to the Cloisters, or to Greenwich Village, or to Central Park, sometimes to Brooklyn if Ginger had a piano or ballet lesson after school and they could come home later than usual. She photographed indiscriminately — people, the buildings of the city, its landscape of stone and water and man and machine, all of it like a force of nature that was taking her by the shoulders, shaking her, turning her upside down.

She spent months haunting the city's piers, shooting the

great boats and pleasure liners as they breasted the dock—
the *Queen Mary,* the *Queen Elizabeth.* She photographed
the groaning chains and cables that secured the boats to
land, the mad activity at the pier, people parting and re-
uniting. The churning water, the sailing trapeze of the
George Washington Bridge, the ravenous flocks of gulls, the
wide sweep of the gray Hudson River, the weeping of those
left behind, and the excitement of those under sail—before
long she had hundreds of photographs of it all.

She did not try to explain to herself, at the time, why she
was so interested in the docks, but she understood later that
it was the presence of change there—the enormous size of
the ships, their vast weight, and the way they broke away
from the land with such purpose and power, their engines
deafening, the water roiling. They backed away from the
shore like giant landmasses breaking loose, almost like ge-
ologic events, tectonic ruptures. It was the sheer force of
their withdrawal that she wanted to study. Or not their
withdrawal, she corrected herself later—their reinvention.

When she looked back on those years, she was mostly
amazed at how without incident they were. "You must understand my great sense of shame," she was to say later, explaining herself, "to be a woman without a husband." As
time went by, she began to see that it was common enough
to be divorced, a woman alone with children, and there
seemed no particular shame in it. But back then she didn't
even have the freedom of being divorced. Eben never raised
the matter, though she understood from Ginger after a while
that he had a lady friend who sometimes accompanied them
out to lunch or to the zoo. Once, when Ginger was still quite
young, she asked Lettie, "Why do you and Papa not live together anymore?"

Lettie thought and was forced to say, somewhat lamely, that they were happier this way. "We are not divorced," she said quickly, as though this would make it easier to understand, but of course it did not. From time to time she thought she should ask Eben for a divorce, but whenever she imagined how this conversation might go, she realized that she wouldn't know what to do with her freedom, even if she had it. In a way, it would only complicate things. She could still say, if necessary, *My husband will do this,* or *My husband will do that,* or *I'll have to ask my husband,* and it wasn't a lie.

Through the months, and then the years, they continued to hear from Fanny, whose letters contrived to show them, show someone, the fabric of her life. As she grew older, her confidences about her family became more mature. Lettie and Ginger learned that she had a father, employed erratically as a field laborer for a tobacco farmer, and that her grandmother, in the wake of what appeared to be Fanny's mother's evident decline in health and spirit, ran the small store with Fanny's help in the afternoons and on weekends.

In one letter, she wrote:

I enjoyed the books you sent. My mother likes them, too. Sometimes it is the only thing that seems to make her happy, when I read to her. She has been very bad lately. She did not get out of the bed for all of last week. On Sunday my grandmother made her dress and took her to church and she cooked us a dinner that night. I cook for myself mostly, and she sleeps a lot. I can make a sweet potato pie. Ginger, tell your mother thank you for the money and the skirts. They are the nicest ones I have. Sometimes I am angry at my mother, but there is nothing to do about it.

These letters and others like them tore at Lettie's heart. Ginger wrote Fanny faithfully, though Lettie wondered if either of them could imagine Fanny's life in any real sense. More than once she offered Fanny a place in their home in New York, for a visit or even permanently if she wished, but Fanny always declined.

"I can't leave my mother," she always wrote. "But maybe one day we'll see each other again."

For a little while, in her early teens, Ginger kept Fanny's letters to herself and sealed her own replies before giving them to Lettie to mail, not letting her read them. Lettie imagined that the girls exchanged the confidences of adolescents, and she was glad that their friendship, though remote in body, had yet managed to become so intimate. Years later, rereading the letters together, the three of them were moved by the innocence of the confessions exchanged and by the reminder of who they had once been and what they had lived through with their country.

"I will never forget him," Fanny had written passionately about President Kennedy, as though he were a lover.

"I'll never forget him either," Ginger had replied.

Lettie and Ginger continued to mail Fanny books, and money for special occasions, and clothes. At night, staring out the windows at the lights of the city and the rough, dark shoulder of the Palisades, across the river, Lettie thought of Fanny often. It was when she was lonely, when she missed the company of another adult in her life, that she thought of Fanny most. How funny, really, she thought later, that

Fanny should have always seemed to her like another adult rather than what she was—a child.

All the while, Lettie continued to take pictures. She converted the pantry into a makeshift darkroom and taught herself about developing her own film, the sour smell of the chemicals clinging to her hands, drifting through her hair. She had hundreds of photographs, though no notion of what to do with them. They gathered around her like falling leaves around the trunk of a tree; she found them comforting, the way they seemed to constitute evidence of her life, and she would riffle through them in the evenings after the children had gone to bed or while she waited for Ginger to return home from some evening spent in the company of her friends at a movie, or skating at Rockefeller Center, or attending a dance at the Plaza. Sometimes she looked around and realized that their apartment had become shabby—the slipcovers worn, the paint faded and scuffed, the drapes fraying. If she and Eben had still lived together, she would have had it redecorated, probably several times. Instead she filled the walls with her photographs and Cleo's drawings—Cleo had the artist in her and executed long, vivid panoramas on rolls of paper, foxes and lions and stags leaping buildings and mountains, bright fish flying through the air over parks and statues and waterfalls, bullfrogs lurking in plazas and fountains and on the onion domes of churches. She worked on them on the floor, her little elbows and knees stained with greasy smudges of color, and Lettie helped her pin the drawings to the walls, where they wound from room to room, through doorways and across the windows. Eben no longer came to the apartment to collect Ginger; she met him on her own sometimes, after school, though their meetings had grown fewer and fewer over time.

One day, Ginger came home from school and announced, "Today's Papa's birthday."

Lettie, who was helping Cleo unroll one of her drawings, looked up from the floor.

Ginger stood in the doorway, eating an apple, watching them. "He's fifty. Isn't that ancient?"

And Lettie realized two things: that she had not actually seen Eben in over a year, though they had talked on the telephone several times, and that she herself had turned forty-one, three weeks before.

GINGER CELEBRATED HER eighteenth birthday and departed for college. Fanny began to write to Lettie and Ginger separately, letters full of horror and grief over the terrifying newspaper photographs of the war in Vietnam, and frustration at her mother, who was increasingly unhappy and difficult.

To Ginger she wrote, "You're so lucky, about Lettie being your parent. The world can be so ugly and awful that you'd think it would be easier to be crazy, in some ways. I know it's not my mother's fault that she is how she is, but sometimes I want to kill her."

Ginger wrote back, with words that made Lettie wince when she reread their correspondence years later: "I love my mother, but it's so weird, the way she never divorced my father. He's had tons of girlfriends. I don't think Mother's laid eyes on him in about five years, but she still calls him her husband. I've heard her do it. I feel sorry for her."

LETTIE LOVED BROOKLYN for its relief from the scale of the city and went there often to assuage her loneliness the year Ginger left home. On many streets, the buildings were only three or four stories tall, and the trees crowned the rooftops, a rare sight in New York. At the end of summer, in full leaf, the trees gave the streets a comforting, muffled air.

One morning a few weeks after Ginger had left home, Lettie took the train to Brooklyn Heights and walked from there along the sidewalks in the shade of the trees, toward the East River, heading for the Esplanade, where she sometimes paused to sit and watch the passersby.

At the edge of the Esplanade, she took a seat on a bench. She held her camera, her old Leica, in her lap, her fingers resting lightly on it; by now she hardly went anywhere without it. It was a fine October morning; the sun was pleasant against her face, reminding her of the welcome warmth of her children's bodies when they'd been young and she'd held them in her arms. The first hints of red and yellow had begun to color the trees, and their reflections wavered in the river below, a hazy pinkness. Lettie watched the slipping colors, the dancing light.

It was strange that so few people seemed to be out enjoying the day; it seemed to her one of the nicest fall days so far, one of those that balances poignantly between the seasons, and yet she was a solitary soul sitting there. Only a stout woman in a nurse's uniform, holding the arm of an old gentleman, had climbed the steps to walk along beside the water down at the far end of the Esplanade. They proceeded slowly toward Lettie, the woman facing the water and the bright light, and the man looking down at the ground, his chin dropped on his chest.

Lettie's fingers moved on her camera, but the light was behind them, after all.

The pair drew near. "Good for you, sir," Lettie overheard the nurse say. The old man was muttering a long string of words. It sounded as if he was reciting a list of figures or instructions for a procedure, or as if he had lost his understanding of inflection, how it informs conversation. "Good for you, sir," the nurse said again mechanically, not taking into account that he was still speaking, that he did not seem to have finished whatever it was he had to say. The nurse continued to stare out over the water, her face turned away from the old man, who held his arms before him, crossed at the wrists over his chest like a prisoner's. The nurse's meaty little forearm was pushed through his, holding him up against the starched mass of her breast. They passed Lettie, the man shuffling and talking in that low, monotonous way, his eyes on the ground, unfocused. The nurse with her slow steps came along beside him.

As they drew even with the bench where Lettie sat, the nurse turned her head toward Lettie as if she might smile or nod a greeting over the old bare head of her charge.

But the woman's eyes swept over Lettie without any change of expression at all—park, tree, bench, tree, park.

Her chin pointed away again, a watch swinging smoothly on a chain, and her gaze returned to the water.

Lettie felt a cold breath on her neck. The woman's eyes had not registered even the slightest acknowledgment of her presence there. How could that be? There had not been even half a second's lingering in her glance, nor the moment of studied indifference and then self-conscious looking away of a stranger. Yet it was not rudeness, Lettie felt sure. It was something worse.

She rose unsteadily to her feet. Had the woman seen *no one* sitting there?

The trees' reflection in the water below, pink and green and yellow, pulsed and wavered and was broken up in the gray wake of a barge. The sounds of the world drained away.

Years later she remembered that moment with a chill, the moment before everything in her life changed, the moment when she became—for an eternal second—invisible.

SHE ROSE FROM HER bench and left the water's edge, moving blindly toward the street. At the curb she stopped like a sleepwalker, out of habit, her camera held between her hands, the cars moving past her so fast and so near that she could feel the air bulge toward her in a tantalizing, almost playful way. How curiously easy it would have been to step down from the curb then and into the traffic, hardly even a gesture on her part. Yet she did not step down. She waited there, blinking against a grief that felt, for long, shuddering moments, like the final caress from her dearest, most intimate enemy, something that knew her so well it could kill her in just an instant.

And then the acrid smell of smoke reached her.

Her head snapped up as if someone had drifted smelling salts under her nose. That was the smell of fire.

Sirens sounded a moment later, a few blocks away. Lettie looked up and saw people beginning to run on the far side of the street, jogging down the block. The fire couldn't be far away, for fantastic plumes of smoke billowed into the sky almost directly overhead, foamy and dark against the blue. Caught up in the river of people, all of them hurrying toward the blaze, she too began to run, clutching her camera to her side.

A few blocks ahead, the crowd turned and swelled at a side street. Fire engines and police cars parked at angles across the road. As she neared the corner, she could hear the fire and see the ash drifting in the air; and then she saw it—a house halfway down an interior block was ablaze, engulfed in black streamers of smoke, the flames reaching toward the street through the lower-story windows.

Pressing through the crowd, Lettie arrived at a barrier of angled white planks. A furious policeman, red in the face and waving his arms angrily, was shouting at people to step back. Lettie took a half step forward, caught his eye, and almost without thinking, raised her camera, which was still hung around her neck, to show it to him. He met her gaze, thumbed her through with a flick of his hand, and moved on, still shouting.

She never knew what official business that policeman thought she had, trespassing beyond the barrier, or how he even managed to see her, to pick her out of the crowd, so tiny among all the people straining to see. But the photograph she took that afternoon—of a child not four years old flung from an upper-story window by a man in his shirtsleeves, the child's body in its small white nightgown tumbling through the geysers of smoke, the man's arms outstretched from the window, a look of pure anguish on his face as his baby fell toward the street—that was the picture that ended up the next day in the *Daily News*.

She wondered many times how she knew to look up at that moment. How did she know she would see a human body, suspended in air as though flight were a state natural to man, the child's face engulfed with an ecstatic terror? When she developed her film hours later—that frame and the ensuing shots of the child splayed in the canvas hammock held by the firemen, of the man himself jumping heels-first after his child, of the child held in his father's arms, the man's weeping face raised to the sky—she calculated that it had lasted only a matter of seconds, the baby's flight. But she had been there for it.

The breathless man who came up beside her as she stood there taking pictures had been young, not much older than Ginger.

"Who're you working for?" he'd shouted at her over the noise. "You freelance?" He pulled a card out of his notebook, held with a rubber band. "I'm from the *News*. Call me if you got anything good."

That night, having employed a neighbor to come and stay with Cleo while she slept, Lettie looked up the address of the *Daily News* and left the apartment, the photographs under her arm.

The young man she'd seen at the fire looked over her prints at the door to the newsroom and then pointed her toward a glassed-in office. "Great," he said, smiling at her. "These are great. Les will want them."

The first time she saw him, Lettie judged Les Agnew to be some twenty years older than her, in his early sixties perhaps. He had pale blue eyes, and a pronounced Adam's apple that rose and fell in his throat like a cork, and the thick shoulders of a bricklayer. He wore a graying goatee, not at all fashionable, and yet he gave the impression of a dapper man, someone neat and compact, his still-dark hair combed back from his forehead, his pressed shirt rolled crisply to the elbows. When she saw him in daylight for the first time, early the next morning, when he came to her apartment and spent two hours going over her photographs, she realized that he was not as old as he had looked the night before under the fluorescent lights of the newsroom.

He had brought her some extra copies of the newspaper. Her photograph had run inside, on page three, almost as large as the original print she'd made.

As she led Les to the living room, Lettie tried not to look at its untidy condition; if she'd known he was coming, she would have straightened up, but now there was no hiding the state of things. Long ago, she and Ginger had taken down the drapes and cut them up for costumes and dresses and tablecloths, and the room, with its white walls, was filled with bright light, even to the high corners. Cleo's panoramas wound the chair rail, bright as Chinese dragons.

But Les did not seem to notice the state of things around him—the chairs and floor heaped with books, Cleo's art supplies spread over the dining room table, her bicycle parked at the end of the hall, the strings of photographs drying like laundry in the kitchen. Eben's ottoman, the one on which he had once rested his beautiful black shoes, had sprung a leak years before, and Lettie had patched it with tape. When she put down a coffee tray on the table, the ottoman lurked near her ankle, and she moved it carefully with her foot to hide the tape.

Les made a seat for himself on the sofa by unconcernedly moving aside a stack of books. "How long have you been taking pictures, Lettie?" he asked her, accepting a cup of coffee.

She realized she could not answer his question in a simple way, but surely he wouldn't want a complicated answer.

He watched her for a moment over his coffee cup. When she didn't say anything, he smiled at her. "It's a difficult question?"

It wasn't a difficult question, she thought. It was that it forced a reckoning. She blushed. "About ten years."

He pressed his hand against his cheek. It was an oddly feminine gesture from this man who reminded her vaguely of a reformed pugilist. She saw that he was suppressing some surprise. The heat rose in her face again. Of course, he would be appalled. She had little to show for herself, after all.

But Les said nothing more on the subject. "You have children." He picked up a small sock of Cleo's, dangled it gently.

When she realized he was smiling at her, she smiled back. "Two. The older one's at college. Cleo's eleven."

"Who's the painter?"

"Cleo." Lettie smiled.

"Ambitious." Les followed one of Cleo's panoramas around the room with his eyes. "Husband?"

Lettie hesitated. "We have not lived together in many years," she said finally.

Les was quiet for a moment. Years later, she would catch him sitting like that, frowning gently, and ask if he was thinking about his wife and daughter. They had been killed in a small plane accident many years before, on their way to the wedding of a friend's daughter. "Sometimes," he would tell her, reaching for her hand.

But that morning he kept his attention on Lettie for nearly

two hours, looking at her pictures, asking questions. At
10 A.M. he said he had to leave, but as they walked back
through her study to the front hall, Les stopped to look at
the old photograph of Fanny that was taped to the window
over Lettie's desk. "Who's this?" he asked.

And then he turned around and smiled at her. "I'm sorry.
I'm used to asking questions. I'm afraid I forget, sometimes,
how to be a human being."

Lettie reached over and took down the photograph. It
was the only one she had of Fanny as a child, though Fanny
had sent them a photograph of herself the year before at her
high school graduation.

"She's someone we met a long time ago," she began, then
she told Les Fanny's story.

Les leaned against her desk while she talked—more
words altogether than she'd said to any adult in the last
decade—his arms folded, listening.

"So they've written back and forth for all these years, she
and Ginger. Remarkable. And she writes to you now, too?"

"More than ever. She's bored, I think, not being in
school."

"Remarkable," Les repeated.

At the front door he turned around and offered his hand.
"Lettie, do you mind if I call a friend of mine?" he asked.
"He's got a gallery. He'd be interested in your pictures."

Lettie looked at him blankly.

"They're very good," Les said. And then he paused to
look closely at her. "Or didn't you know?"

• • •

TWO DAYS LATER, Lettie was visited by Les's friend David. He suggested shocking prices for Lettie's photos, discussed framing and matting with her.

"Is Lettie a nickname?" he asked, looking up from the floor, where he knelt with a cigarette and a ruler, sliding sheets of vellum between her photos, stacking prints into piles. "Is that how you want to be known?"

What a strange opportunity lay in that question, she thought, looking down at him on her floor. It supposed that she might take another name for herself. Indeed, another identity altogether.

LES INVITED HER to dinner a few days after David's visit to her apartment. He suggested a restaurant on the West Side, the single dining room sunk a half-story below the sidewalk. As Lettie stood in the door unbuttoning her coat that evening, she saw that he had already arrived, and was sitting by himself at a table in the corner. He was wearing his glasses, and a tweed jacket, and was reading something.

She had not had dinner with a man in ten years. Now she had no appetite. She understood it was nerves, but the knowledge only distressed her even more, as if she could not control what might happen. She knew she was dangerously teary.

Foolish, she told herself, gripping her umbrella. *Don't be foolish.*

She could not believe how much she liked this man.

He stood when Lettie reached the table. "Lettie," he said warmly, and his eyes looked pleased. He took her coat and handed her a menu.

But she could not read the menu through her tears. Furious blinking did not help, and in a minute she knew she must give an ugly sniff.

Les looked up.

Lettie put the back of her hand to her nose, but she had to shut her eyes tight, and felt her face contract.

In a moment Les had gathered their things and led her from the restaurant, down the sidewalks with their dispersing passersby, past striped awnings half furled, the whirl of voices coming from within the stores, through the smells of smoke, of singed meat, of wet gutters. She thought, through her tears, how strange it was that the city, with the fields and streams of the country so far away, could still manage to smell like fall, like something remembered from her childhood, the feel of dry grass prickling her back as she lay upon a hill, the thrilling revolution of the globe beneath her body.

They walked in silence, passing down the steps to the dark edge of the river, the lights of the city flickering on its little waves. Walking, she felt calmer. They passed the open mouth of a stone lion, then a graceful stone arch, its keystone poised above their heads. Les took her arm. The kindness of the gesture, his small, wiry fingers on her elbow, made her weep again.

At his apartment, with its rooms unfolding one after another like a telescope's expanding lenses, the pocket doors sliding away, Les led Lettie to his bedroom, tugged her gently down on the bed and lifted her feet to the coverlet. When he lay down heavily beside her, she could smell the cigar smoke on his collar, the scent of cologne in his thinning hair. And when he turned to clasp his arms around her, his hands knotting at the small of her back, it was as though their pressure touched some buried pain, some hard burl of misery grown in her spine. The rooms contained them like a shell's winding structure and glistening walls, the sounds of the city vanishing, the world held at bay by the baffling contrivances that serve to protect the heart, the fragile heart within.

WITHIN A MONTH, Lettie had a date from the gallery for the first show of her photographs, and Les's friend David had bought five prints himself, three from her series of the ships, for his private collection. At dinner with Les and Lettie in a restaurant near the Museum of Natural History, David gave Lettie a check for two thousand dollars and kissed her on the cheek. "Welcome to the world, my dear," he said. And then he looked over at Les. "Soon she'll be famous and she'll forget you ever lived."

"I won't," Lettie said quickly. She wanted to reach out and touch Les's hand, but David was there, and she was embarrassed.

"So, what will you do with it?" Les asked her that night as he walked her back to her apartment.

She hadn't thought about it exactly, but as soon as he said it, she thought of Fanny. "I might see if Fanny will take it," she said. "For college. She wouldn't before, maybe because she knew it was Eben's money. But if I tell her it's mine . . ."

Les stood back and waited while she unlocked the door, but as she was fitting in her key, the door was suddenly flung open from inside. Cleo stood in the hall, white-faced and tearstained. The neighbor who'd come to stay with her hung back, looking worried. "She's been very upset," the woman said. "I'm afraid it was the phone call."

Cleo rushed to Lettie and put her arms around her waist, burying her head.

"What is it? What happened?" Terrified, Lettie looked over Cleo's head. "Is it Ginger?"

"No," said Cleo, her voice muffled. "It's Fanny."

WHAT SHE THOUGHT at first, of course, was the worst thing. That Fanny had died.

But in a way it was the next worst thing, because when Lettie tried to call Fanny back that evening, there was no answer, nor again an hour later, nor all that night, though Lettie picked up and dialed the phone a hundred times.

Fanny had not died, but she had disappeared.

Cleo told them that Fanny had called, very upset, at about nine o'clock. Her mother, she told Cleo, had wandered off into the forest the day before, and now the police would not help them look for her anymore. Fanny had been crying, and it had been difficult to understand her, Cleo had said, weeping afresh as she told Lettie what Fanny had said.

"She wanted us to come and help look for her mother," Cleo said. "She said she was calling everyone. She just left her phone number and I wrote it down."

It was the first time Fanny had ever called them on the telephone. All those years, and they'd never even exchanged phone numbers, Lettie realized that night as she sat on the sofa in the darkened living room, holding the telephone to her ear and listening to the endless ringing, with Cleo's sleeping head in her lap. Fanny must have called the operator to get their number.

Some months before, Fanny had sent them a photograph.

It was a picture of Fanny and her mother in front of the gas pump at the store, taken in late afternoon, Lettie thought, judging by the light. On the back of the photo, Fanny had written, "Fanny Sims, 18, high school prom, 1966. Dress by Celeste Sims."

Lettie had been glad of that photograph, for the hope it contained, and she had marveled over the grown-up Fanny, how the child Fanny was still present in this young woman with the broad shoulders and high, square brow and wide cheekbones. She imagined that the expression of happiness on Fanny's face grew not so much from the excitement of the evening ahead but from the promise of her mother's labor, stitch by painful stitch, on that dress, a sheath of shiny turquoise with a matching cape like a bat's wing.

In the photograph it was Fanny's mother who stood central to the picture; Lettie had been shocked at her obesity — it was the first image she'd had of her since that day so many years before, when Celeste had taken Cleo from her arms. In the picture, it looked as though her very flesh hurt her, as though it were squeezing the breath from her. Fanny, almost as tall as Celeste but only a third of her size otherwise, seemed practically dwarfed beside her. But Fanny's expression was rapturous; she leaned confidently on her mother's arm, though Celeste's baffled gaze seemed blinded, unsure. Lettie had hoped, looking with Ginger at the photograph, that Celeste was perhaps mending at last, after so many years, and that her gift of that dress was evidence of renewed hope. The glare of high noon fell, unflattering, across their faces in the photograph. Yet there was compassion in that hard brightness, Lettie felt, the light so unflinching and steady. As she stared at the picture, which Ginger had framed and set up on her bureau, she came to feel that Celeste was not, after all, the largest figure in the arrangement, or even its central subject. There was something that hovered over them, an invisible presence that Lettie could not identify but which she hoped, as she continued to ponder it, she would one day be able to recognize and name.

IN THE MORNING there was still no answer at Fanny's house. Lettie tried a dozen more times, but eventually she had to get Cleo to school. On her way home from walking Cleo the six blocks to school, she saw Les standing outside her building, obviously waiting for her.

She came up to him, and he took her hands. She remembered the other night, how when she had stopped crying and had rolled over finally to face him, he had looked back at her with a steady gaze. Behind him on the nightstand, along with a clutter of books and newspapers and a dusty carafe of water, stood a photograph of his wife, a formal portrait of her in a wedding gown.

"I'm going to go," she said to him now. "I can't get her on the phone."

"I'll come with you," Les said.

LETTIE SAW SUFFERING everywhere on their trip south—in the clenched whorl of a knot on the trunk of a tree outside her apartment building, in the staggering steps of a drunken man who passed them on the street while they waited for a cab, in the broken legs of a spider, an orb weaver tilting upon the cracked spindles of his limbs in a corner of the ladies' room at the airport, a creature who would perish by starvation, his web fraying overhead. *Everything is lost,* grief says. *Everything is impossible. Everything that is alive now will die. If you want life,* the world seemed to say, *then you will have to have this with it, this outrageous suffering.*

Lettie saw nothing that did not seem to contain a cry, a lost voice hurtling out from within the most common object, the most ordinary view, as if everything were animated by the great, contagious terror of Fanny's mother lost in the woods. They stopped to eat something at the airport before their flight left, and she watched people drinking Cokes and biting into sandwiches. *Fanny's mother is lost in the woods,* she said to herself, the two states—people calmly eating sandwiches, a woman lost in the woods—suddenly forming an awful, irrevocable partnership.

They flew to Jackson, rented a car. Lettie was amazed that she could find her way after so many years, but she remembered that she had taken the first turn off the Natchez Trace after leaving Jackson so many years before, and once on that secondary road, there were no other turns to be taken. They just drove through the twilight and then the first brilliant black of the October night, and by the time they arrived at Fanny's family's store, the moon was high in the sky. In a way, she could not believe that they'd found the place, that it was still there, just as she remembered it, that it was real.

Twenty or thirty people, gathered under the white glare of a light mounted on the sheet metal roof of the building, were being deployed by a man who appeared to be in charge, a character of outrage and furor, his hat smashed upon his head. He was counting off bodies, shouting orders, bustling new arrivals into search parties no matter how ill-equipped they seemed—older, heavyset women in cheap shoes, teenage boys, a man on two metal canes.

An old man stood near the gas pump by his truck, a pack of hounds yelping and snarling in the cab. "I'll go with the dogs soon as someone gives me the go-ahead," he said to no one in particular, and spat into the gravel. "I've come one hundred miles. I'll go one hundred more. Soon as someone gives me the go-ahead."

The local police were noticeably absent save for one cruiser parked a hundred yards down the road, its blue light flashing soundlessly, its interior dark.

Les parked the car.

At the door of the store stood two women. One, in a flak jacket, stepped out to block Lettie's path as she and Les approached. "You from the TV?"

"We're just friends." Lettie saw the woman look at their clothes, the camera in Lettie's hands, and make a judgment about what sort of friends they might be. "I tried to call. Is Fanny inside?"

"There's no one inside but the old lady, honey," the woman said, looking at her in surprise. "We're protecting her."

Lettie knew her face expressed bewilderment.

"Where's Fanny?" Les asked, stepping forward.

The woman jerked a shoulder toward the dark forest. "In there. Been gone since last night, looking. They shouldn't have let her go in by herself like that, should they? They should have made her wait. I told them." She reached behind her head, cinched her hair tighter into its ponytail.

Lettie stared at the woman. "She's gone looking for her mother? She went alone?"

The woman gave her a long look. "Where have you been, honey? On the moon? There wasn't anyone *to* go with her."

There was a silence while Lettie struggled with this, how Fanny had asked for help from everyone she knew, but then had not been able to wait any longer.

"You're friends of Fanny's?" Les asked.

She shrugged. "We're just people," she said. "It might have happened to any of us."

Lettie and Les thanked her and withdrew into the swelling crowd. The land under their feet seemed to tremble as though the store and its gas pump were rooted to an island threatening to snap off and drift away. The man busy organizing everybody was pacing back and forth, shouting into a megaphone. "The name's Celeste. That's what you want. *Ce*-leste. Wearing a red shirt. Red shirt."

A man shouldered past them with a rifle.

Lettie turned to Les, who squinted into the crowd, put his hand to his face. "What do we do?" she said.

"We help," he said.

But the man in charge turned them away. "We've got so many people out there they're going to be bumping into each other right now," he said, and he sounded disgusted, as though he'd expected a trained army to show up for war and had gotten nothing but women and children. "But we're going to need reinforcements when the first parties start to come back. Stick around."

Les dozed for a while in the back of the rented car. Lettie could not sleep. From time to time little bands of people emerged from the woods, their flashlight beams twinkling. Lettie could not help feeling that none of them were getting far enough, that they were all circling, like children lost in a maze—the same routes, the same paths, the same small circumference, tightening like a noose around the island of the store.

After a while, Lettie took her coat and made a cushion out of it and sat on the ground at the edge of the trees. She kept seeing Fanny, though what she was seeing was the child, the child she had seen just that one time. She thought of Celeste lumbering slowly off like a sleepwalker toward that light between the trees—the light Lettie remembered from that morning ten years before—the shape of something Celeste wanted, something she longed for, dancing there in the promising light. She imagined Celeste pursuing her phantom, her lost baby bucking to life in a spasm of death reversing itself, crying for its mother at last after so many years of silence.

At 1 A.M. an older woman appeared from the store. It was the grandmother, Lettie thought, Celeste's mother; she felt she knew her from Fanny's letters, but she did not go up and speak to her. The woman spoke quietly to one of the women standing guard at the door. The woman in the flak jacket inclined her head, nodded, touched the older woman's shoulder with a heavy hand before she disappeared back inside the store.

"Coffee," the woman yelled then, cupping her hands around her mouth. "Hot coffee."

Les was asleep in the backseat of the car, his hands folded under the coat beneath his head, his eyes shut. Moving to the store, Lettie took a cup of coffee and wandered to the edge of the encroaching forest. Ahead of her she could see the flashing lights of searchers, like small eyes opening and closing through the leaves.

She walked slowly, aimlessly, stretching her legs, stopping to sip her coffee. Trees loomed up ahead of her in the dark as if they had sprouted in an instant, an entire forest resurrecting itself out of her memory. She walked as one walks in a dark bedroom after leaving a brightly lit hall, as though the floor might contain a sudden crevice, a fault line opened up in an otherwise familiar place. But there was a path, wasn't there? When she looked up, she saw it in the sky, the deep blue of a wide road massed with stars. Where the trees parted, there was a corresponding alley of light above them, and that was what she followed.

She had no idea how long she wandered. She tried to keep the store and its hectic perimeter of light in sight, afraid that she, too, might become lost. Now and then she realized she had drifted deeper into the woods, and then she would simply stand there, waiting for a sound that would orient her. Time and time again she returned to the arena of light and activity around the store, only to wait restlessly there for a few minutes before setting back off into the woods, into the darkness. Once, she stopped, pressing up close against the trunk of a tree, listening and watching. She sat down finally, reasoning that she could not be more than a ten-minute walk from the store, and rested her head against the bark of the tree behind her.

Perhaps she fell asleep, she told Les later, for she could remember weeping, the bottomless tears of regret and mystification. How little she had done for Fanny, how little she had risked, and now one instant had passed and then another, and after all she understood no more today than she had ten years before. She had watched the world as closely, even as jealously, as a lover watches a beloved sleep, and still she could not name what she saw, could not see how she herself was part of it.

Yes, she must have fallen asleep, for she could remember, later, how the feelings of terror and guilt that had pursued her all day and night ever since Fanny's phone call, the phone call she had missed, began to ease away from her after all the tears, as if she were dying. Such feelings would not matter to the dead. Those were distant things, distant as the lights of the search parties fading into the woods; distant as the memory of Fanny, standing at the gas pump, growing smaller as they drove away; as distant, perhaps, as Celeste herself, pressing on toward the light.

When she woke, the forest had filled with a cool grayness, and the beam of her flashlight, fallen to the soft ground at her knee, was no longer distinguishable. She sat up against the tree, blinking into what she realized was mist, a silky, wet vapor that rose up from the ground to the full height of a man, filling the spaces between the trees, erasing the trees themselves, swallowing the world.

And so it was that she heard them before she saw them, first a coaxing voice, sourceless and far away, as if the invisible leaves themselves held the disembodied whisper of it. And then the shape of them pulsed ahead, wavered, a floating pigment, Fanny's tall form, the hesitant red blur of her mother's enormous bulk beside her, the two advancing slowly through the trees, coming toward her.

Now, YEARS LATER, when she is in her darkroom at night, she thinks of ghosts, of how it has been given to everything trapped within her film to bear a moment of sleep, of hibernation, before the particles of the image re-assert themselves, reversed in a memory of gray against the nothingness of the negative's black background.

All around her hang the dripping papers of developing pictures, the world slowly coming to life again.

Here, tonight, are her latest photographs, a series of Fanny and her mother seated on a wrought-iron bench on the great, spreading, golden lawn of the mental hospital where Celeste came to live after Lettie brought them both to New York, Celeste's care paid for by her work as a photographer and Fanny's as a nursing assistant.

This is her privilege, she thinks.

She touches the papers, flutters them overhead, the sour bath of the chemicals evaporating, the sound of water lapping.

In these pictures, Celeste's face is carved deep, the flesh fallen from it; Fanny's own has acquired substance, as though the blue, spoonlike shells beneath her eyes have filled with water. There are several frames: Fanny and Celeste seated side by side, arms locked, facing the camera, yellow leaves littering the lawn at their feet. Fanny reclined on the bench, her head in her mother's lap, her arms folded over her chest. Fanny mugging, perched upon the backrest, her elbows on her knees, her mother leaning against Fanny's thigh, looking up at her. Here is Fanny, Chaplinesque, at the far end of the bench, legs crossed, yawning an exaggerated yawn, vamping, gay.

There is something wrong with Celeste, of course; you can tell that, looking at the pictures. When Lettie and Les visit, Les says it's as though Celeste is watching not just the world go by—the ordinary passage of birds, a strolling pedestrian, the movement of the dappled leaves—but the substance of the world itself, the atoms and particles of it dancing and colliding in space. It is as though she is eternally distracted by something only she can see.

This is Lettie's favorite picture, though, she will say to Les when she emerges from the darkroom in a few minutes, wakes him from the sofa where he will have fallen asleep, mouth open, head thrown back upon the armrest: Look. Here is Fanny with her arms around her mother, her long legs folded like a delicate insect's over the empty stone pool of Celeste's shallow lap, Fanny's small head resting on the upright of Celeste's shoulder.

Here is the mystery, trapped like a thimble-size bird, holding still for your examination.

Keep looking. For in all the wide, wide world, something has been lost, and something has been found, though they aren't the same thing, aren't what you might have expected. Something happened here. How, you cannot say. You only know that if you wait until rage and grief acquire the long shadow of patience, one day you might see it again.

Wings

She was rinsing her teacup in the sink—still so surprising, that there should be only the one cup —when Frank called.

"There's something in your bushes," he said, his voice close by. And then words failed him. "Go on outside and see," he said.

Lorna looked through the kitchen window to her brother-in-law's house next door. Frank appeared from the screen door and stood on the porch, bending over the railing and peering at the front of her house, the moat of daffodils with their orange centers, the wands of forsythia waving long fingers toward the empty road.

Since Edward's death a year before, Frank had stepped forward to help Lorna with the business of being a widow: first the funeral itself, and then the settlement of Edward's estate, and then the long days that followed. It had been comforting, having Frank next door. He had been unfailingly nice about doing odd jobs for her around the house, clearing gutters and so forth. She was grateful and had therefore tried to understand and forgive him for the one evening he had made a show of staying after the supper they sometimes shared, trying to eat their way through the bounty of the garden.

Frank missed Edward, too, of course. Lorna did not need to be reminded of that, and the lost look Frank had acquired since Edward's death was as painful to her as her own grief. Frank had been older than Edward by almost three years, but it was Edward who had always behaved like the elder of the two brothers—the first one to leave home, for instance, the first (and only) one to take a wife, the first one to buy a house. Even the first one to die, Lorna realized with regret, considering the cruel way certain advantages could swing round to become disadvantages, if you waited long enough. Edward and Frank had shared a bedroom under the eaves as boys and had lived most of their adult lives next door to one another in Charlotte Hall. In some ways Edward's death had truly been harder for Frank to bear than for herself, Lorna sometimes thought, for she at least could still vaguely remember a time in her life before Edward had been in it, quiet, dim girlhood years when she had moved through the days (somehow lighter? somehow less encumbered?) with no notion of what it was like to be attached so intimately to another human being. She could still remember having been without Edward, once, and so she knew it was possible.

But for Frank there had always been Edward—Edward

the optimist, Edward the certain, Edward the choreographer of their lives. It wasn't that Frank lacked for practical skills. He could make bluebird boxes, for instance, and crude furniture and keepsake chests out of wood; he could fix their cars and handle minor plumbing and electrical repairs. He could do a lot of things that Edward could not, or in which Edward at least professed no interest. But Edward had the confidence that Frank lacked. Edward could come home from work and take a glass of iced tea and lie in the hammock, the picture of contentment, but Frank was always looking for the next thing that had to be done, trotting over from his garage next door to show Edward cracked hoses or bent tines or burned-out cylinders, presenting Edward with evidence of the world's inevitable wear and tear with a worrier's fanatical combination of helplessness and vindication.

"Well, you can fix that, can't you?" Edward would say slowly, swinging his legs over the side of the hammock and taking the broken part in his hands. His tone would suggest complete faith in Frank.

And Frank would say that, yes, he could fix it, and then he would describe how he'd go about it, and what the risks and problems might be, and where he might need to go to find the necessary parts, and somehow—somehow, Lorna thought, in that occasionally perfect way people have of meeting each other's needs—Frank would be happy, and Edward would be happy, and all would be well.

But recently, Lorna had found herself turning away from Frank—not answering the door and claiming later that she'd been in the shower, for instance, or taking the car out for long, aimless drives, just to avoid having to look at him. She knew, just as Edward had known, that Frank could fix practically anything, but somehow she lacked Edward's ability to make Frank himself feel that.

Every soldier needed a general, she thought. The problem was that both she and Frank were soldiers, and now their general was gone.

Without Edward between them, neither Frank nor Lorna knew how to behave with each other. Six months after Edward's death, the awkwardness that had flown up between them as Frank had stood there that one evening, waiting uncertainly at the cleared supper table, had frightened them both. From then on he had withdrawn punctually, cracking his knuckles, leaving her alone in the darkening garden or in front of the television, which she watched until she fell asleep.

Lorna put down her dishcloth and went outside. Pink haze rose off the fields beyond the wet grass of her front lawn. The air gleamed and shone in the early sunlight. From his porch, Frank pointed at the azaleas planted before her basement windows. She went down the steps and bent over, but she couldn't see anything in the bushes.

Frank came over to join her. "Look," he said, directing her with his hand on her shoulder. "There."

And then she saw it.

The bird stood as high as her knee, its breast bowed forward wearily to sustain a great train of tail feathers, a cape so astonishing in its range of color that Lorna gasped at the sight. A mane of snowy feathers drew back from the bird's head like a formal wig from another century. The bird's back, mottled in stripes of black and white like a zebra's hide, gave way to the glorious tail. Lorna dropped to her knees on the sopping ground, staring, her hands clasped before her.

"My goodness," she said.

They were silent, regarding the princely bird as he paced nervously before the wet scrim of the azaleas.

"Where did it come from?" Lorna asked finally. "What *is* it?"

"I don't know. I've never seen anything like it." Frank passed his hand over his head, the thinning hair, the red birthmark that mapped his brow in a shape like an unfamiliar continent. "I forgot to tell you I saw it before, a day or so ago, running like lightning up Virlona Avenue. I thought I was seeing things."

The bird stopped its anxious strutting and paused, frozen, against the wall of the house. It stood out like a freak, a riot of color against the cinder blocks.

"It was running?" Lorna tried to imagine it.

"Maybe it's got a broken wing. Or maybe it doesn't fly at all." Frank looked critically at the bird.

Lorna shifted her weight; her pants were soaked through. She glanced down at her kneecaps, circles of damp from the wet ground spreading over them. Inching forward, she tried to get a closer look at the bird. Its wings certainly were no rival for its magnificent tail; they were small and brown, folded against its back. She couldn't imagine they were much good for flying. For balance, maybe. She remembered something she'd seen once on television about birds in Africa. The wings were—vestigial, that was the word: things you had once needed that, over time and in a changed world, had gradually lost their sense of purpose and become stunted, useless.

"What do you suppose it eats?" she said.

Frank gave a short laugh, looking down at Lorna. "You planning to feed it?"

Lorna looked at the bird. It stared off at some point in the distance and then slowly swiveled its small head to regard her, its black eye holding her miniaturized in its iris. She felt the bird's gaze upon her, light and impersonal, like a prince scanning the crowd in the plaza below his balcony. And then the bird withdrew his head. A milky white membrane slid sideways over its eye and then flicked back again, dismissing her.

A little color rose in Lorna's cheeks.

She drew back slightly from the bushes and considered herself—she was sixty-six years old, a widow in muddy dungarees, in a cardigan buttoned up to her neck.

"I just thought it might be hungry," she said.

"Let's get some chicken wire and trap it." Frank began to move away. "Then we'll figure out what to do. We're not doing *anything* if it gets away, believe *me*. That bird can run."

They found a roll of chicken wire in the basement and muscled it outside through the Bilco door. The bird was still there, a vaguely accusatory figure lurking in the bushes. Lorna wedged through the shrubs by the front step and bent the edge of the wire against the house, and then Frank unfurled it clumsily until it formed a wobbly pen around the bird.

Lorna sat down on the steps. The day was already warm, unseasonably warm for May; Frank's shirt had damp streaks across it. Frank was a tall man, the bottom-heavy sort described as pear-shaped; he widened at the hips like a woman. Edward had been the lankier and more athletic of the two.

"Now what?" Frank said, his hand over the birthmark on his face. His hand often found its way there.

"Should we call the zoo?" But immediately Lorna regretted having suggested this. It was only a thing to say, she thought, just something she had said without thinking about it. Because when she did think about it, when she pictured the bird behind iron bars, gawked at by children rushing from one cage to another, she was filled with guilt.

The bird did not look at her again.

EDWARD HAD SUFFERED a heart attack while driving in the car, perishing instantly in the accident that followed. Lorna, a length ahead of him in her own car, had witnessed Edward's car leaving the road through her rearview mirror. A year later, the pain of being alone, without Edward, seemed to have lasted for a long, long time, like something buried at the base of her spine that had been working secretly on her since her birth, preparing her for this, slowly folding her over toward the earth. At home, standing before the mirror, she twisted around, wondering if she saw a hump beginning on her back. Out of the house, on errands into Charlotte Hall, she tried to stand upright, tried to fight against the invisible weight in her spine, but at home she gave in and slouched. It was disturbing to catch sight of her image passing in the hall mirror. She couldn't even meet her own eyes in the glass; she looked out at herself through lowered brows—like a Neanderthal, she thought.

They'd had no children. None ever appeared, and their embarrassment at this failure had prevented them from pursuing the reasons for it. Neither had wanted it to be the other's fault, and so they had preferred not to know why they had been, as they saw it, overlooked. Their childlessness, rather than making them free—inclined to weekend trips or late nights—had woven into their life a long period of quiet penance; they had stayed at home, dutiful to the smallest routine, as if staying there, behaving as though they were needed there, might earn them children. Sometimes now Lorna wondered disloyally whether they had wasted all those years, but she knew that they had chosen freely. No one had made them live that way.

For twenty-five years, Lorna had worked in Charlotte Hall's health department office as a secretary, assisting mothers with infants needing immunizations, and confused old people applying for food and medicines. She had liked being of help to people. But when there were layoffs in the department just after her fifty-ninth birthday, she had felt that perhaps she was too old to go looking for another job.

One afternoon, though, when she went into Charlotte Hall, she saw a sign in the window of Woolworth advertising for a waitress.

She went inside and seated herself at the lunch counter and ordered a glass of milk and a slice of lemon chiffon pie. The place smelled wonderful, full of what Lorna thought of as happy smells—shaving soap, and puppies, and hamburgers grilling, and floor wax, and new fabric still wound in bolts—and the sun streamed in gaily through the big, clean glass windows. The three women working there—two broad and solid as cart horses, and one a quick, thin, sexless little thing with a wide mouth who reminded Lorna of an elf—had appeared to be great friends. They teased and flapped dishcloths at one another as they moved up and down behind the counter, laughing helplessly, in between making coffee and scooping ice cream and serving up hot dogs and grilled cheese sandwiches with a clattering confidence.

But Lorna had not been able to imagine herself in their midst. She was no good at banter of that kind, she judged. Edward had called her shy, and she supposed she was. So she went home from Woolworth and made no other inquiries about jobs. She spent her days working in her garden and cleaning the house and ironing shirts—for herself and Edward, and for Frank, too, because it was silly for Frank to spend the money on dry cleaning when she was right there, getting the ironing board out anyway—and waiting each afternoon for Edward to come home.

Sometimes she thought wistfully about the women at Woolworth. They might have become her friends, she thought now, almost angrily. They might have been a support to her now.

Edward and Frank's younger sister, Mary, dead herself of a congenital heart ailment nearly twenty years before, had been deaf, and both boys had learned sign language as a consequence. After Edward's military service—four years in the navy—he had driven a few miles inland from the naval base at Nanticoke and settled in Charlotte Hall as a teacher at Merrywood, a school for the deaf. Merrywood was a group of prisonlike stone buildings whose severity was partially forgiven by the beautiful apple orchard that surrounded the school on three sides; in the spring, lovely pink and white blossoms from the orchard blew over the lawns and onto the main building's shingled roof. To Lorna the school felt like a place from which an evil curse had been lifted, and she could never quite shake off a sense of sadness

that came over her whenever she was there. She had accompanied Edward to functions at the school, graduations
and sporting events, but she had never felt at ease there; she
could not master sign language well enough to feel confident
using it, and among the silent, milling crowds of children,
she would grow disconcertingly still and alert. She felt like a
lightning rod planted in their midst. Standing there, gripping
Edward's arm, she felt as though she was waiting to receive
a signal, something that might tell her how to proceed. She
imagined that if it ever came to her, a current of fire filling
up her whole body, it would make the doors and windows
to the world fly open, and she was half afraid.

At Edward's funeral, the students from the deaf school
had approached her in pairs, their hands working slowly,
expressing regrets. Her own vocabulary was small, limited
to the language she and Edward had used in the car as he
trailed her to the church on Fridays, when she helped cook
for the Senior Supper Club. *I love you! See you soon! Have
a good day!* He had taught her these phrases and a few others, intimacies they exchanged at home sometimes, or fifty
feet apart in their separate cars, tiny signals viewed in the
rectangle of her mirror and then vanishing like invisible ink.

Edward's funeral had been held in the chapel at Merrywood, and the school's minister had officiated. A fat woman
with a chin that descended straight into the neck of her choir
robe had signed to the congregation the minister's words
and, with a kind of daunting gusto that bewildered Lorna,
the words of the hymns sung by the choir from Charlotte
Hall's presbyterian church, which had been borrowed for
the service. Frank had stood at her shoulder during the service; from time to time she had been aware of his shoulders

shaking beside her with suppressed sobs, but unlike her, he had not made a sound. She had been unable to keep herself from bowing her head and weeping, as quietly as she could. Even the smell of Frank near her, the wrong sort of familiar, had made her weep.

Among Edward's students, Lorna had felt helplessly inarticulate, tense with the effort of fashioning a response with her hands from the few simple phrases she knew. Her whole body tensed with the confusion of trying to translate her thoughts.

Thank you, thank you, she had signed, murmuring the words to the mourners coming up to her one by one or in couples, the men silent and stricken, their wives tense and alert, protective, hands clasped over their husbands' arms. She remembered Edward's fingers tapping against her ribs when he held her in his arms. At breakfast he ate silently, receiving with raised arms the warmed plate she brought him, held in her hands between a dish towel. *Thank you,* he would sign to her. *Hey, have we met somewhere before?*

Frank had driven her home from the cemetery after Edward's burial.

There was to be no supper afterward, he explained quietly to those gathered at the graveside; Lorna wasn't up to it.

At home he made them tea instead and gave her the pills from the doctor, and he stayed with her until she fell asleep, sitting beside the bed, the white of his eye staring out vigilantly from the dark side of his face like a lantern hung on the branch of a tree.

• • •

THE DAY THE BIRD arrived was a Friday, and Lorna drove to St. Augustine's as usual early that evening. Since Edward's death, with so much time on her hands, she had begun taking the long route, winding up and down Lawyer's Hill past the big houses with their deep porches and windows with shades half drawn against the late afternoon sun, which slanted heavily across the lawns. The shadows of the leaves from the trees overhanging the road fell over the tarmac, massive and cinematic, like movie footage of the shadows of clouds rushing over the land.

Lorna had stayed away from the church for a few weeks after Edward died, wandering the house and sleeping a drugged sleep day and night until day and night had no meaning for her anymore, and then she knew she must do something. Frank would come to the porch and ring the bell, but he did not try the door; they would never trespass against each other in that way. But she had heard him calling her from outside on the porch, his voice anxious, and after a while she had hated herself for being the one who lay on the bed and wept while Frank tinkered with things outside and tried to go on as before. She got up, finally, and that night she made lasagna and garlic bread for herself and Frank. He had eaten his two platefuls so fast, hunched over at her kitchen table, his elbow out, that she wondered whether he'd eaten a proper meal at all since Edward's funeral.

The next morning she had taken the car and gone to the grocery store, and to have her hair done, and to the cleaners, where she had left Edward's suits. Moving from the car to the sidewalk to the store and back again, it felt to her that her movements had become smaller, diminished. Always a small woman, the sort people had called a doll baby when she was young, she knew she had lost weight. Somehow, in the span of just a few weeks, air itself had become a constraint, and she was aware of squaring her shoulders as if she must batter at the atmosphere to let her through.

In the car that evening on the way to church, her dreams from the night before came back to her, as they often did while she was driving. She had them all the time now, vivid, dramatic dreams that arrived night after night, full of the archetypes of fire and flood. In last night's dream she had been confronted suddenly by her own figure looming, like the prow of a great ship, in the narrow hallway of her house. The woman (was it herself? It seemed to be) bore down upon her with an unnerving intention, as though it were trying to tell her something. Elephantine and mournful, her great breast bound in widow's black, the figure vanished as Lorna tried to address it from the drugged depths of her sleep. And just before waking, she remembered now, she'd had another dream. She had been making her way across a vast marsh, the charred and deserted buildings of a city towering behind her. Gradually the stinking pools and oily hillocks of fibrous grass had given way to a sweet, uninhabited freshness. At the fragile margins of the marsh, where the sea began, a string of low fires glowed, issuing narrow pinnacles of blue smoke into the clearing sky. She had reached the water's edge, hope rising in her heart, and then she had woken.

Lorna turned the car into the gravely parking lot behind the church. The strangeness of these dreams, which made her feel that she was gradually turning into someone she did not know at all, both disturbed and excited her. She reached into the backseat and lifted out the armload of daffodils she had cut to bring in for the tables. She put her face in the flowers for a moment and breathed deeply. How steadying flowers were.

Shelley was already at work when Lorna pushed open the door to the church's basement kitchen. A handsome girl with thick, auburn hair cut to her shoulders, and a beautiful bright color in her face, Shelley was the paid cook for the program; Lorna and the others only volunteered. Shelley had her back to the door; she was shaking rolls from paper bags into baskets, a fine flour dusting the table. Lorna took in the combined smells of the small room—its damp rock walls, the lima beans and potatoes and beef in the soup on the stove, the cool air from the nearby Patapsco River falling down the stony steps beneath the church, which was poised high on a granite shelf. The back door was propped open to the evening air. A God's-eye, made by a child in the congregation, twisted in the window, its faded yarn fraying.

Lorna advanced to the sink with her armload of daffodils.

Shelley looked up and smiled. "Oh, aren't they *pretty.*" Wiping her hands, she came over to look at the flowers. "They'll love them. From your garden?"

Lorna placed the flowers in the sink and turned to search in the cupboards for a vase. "They're the late ones. The sweetest ones." She handed down to Shelley a vase from the recesses of a high shelf and then stepped down carefully from the footstool. "I'll go get the cakes."

She returned from the car with a shallow cardboard box holding two cakes, both finished with swags of pink icing.

"You're a marvel," Shelley said, looking around as she was putting the last daffodil in water.

After Edward's death, Lorna had taken it upon herself to

bake a dessert for the Friday night suppers. No one asked her to do it, but she liked sweet things herself, and she thought the old people ought to have something sweet after their supper sometimes. She found the work of it was good for her; her heart slowed and resounded peacefully inside her during the painstaking work of fashioning a tracery of sugar roses or a lattice of chocolate. The cakes were strangely flavored sometimes—with honey or anise or cinnamon, odd pairings called for in the old-fashioned cookbooks bequeathed to her by Edward's mother, who had taken what seemed to Lorna a crazy delight in troweling up odd matter from the fields, dandelions and a green she called creecy, and serving it to her family to eat. It was why, Lorna surmised, Edward had insisted with her upon a diet utterly predictable and bland, food separated on the plate in even portions, each serving unto itself.

Now, eating alone so often, she scavenged in the spirit of her mother-in-law, taking a bowl of this or that to the porch and eating haphazardly as she watched her neighbors go about the business of the evening, shutting up sheds and calling in their dogs, bringing a load of wash in from the line, the low light falling gently like palm fronds over their properties, which were tethered loosely together by ribbony hedgerows wild with forsythia and rose of Sharon. She watched, eating slowly, and rinsed her bowl in the sink afterward, using it again in the morning. Sometimes, it seemed, she hardly used anything at all. She had Frank to dinner a few times a week, though, and she noticed that when she tied on her apron now after supper, he would rise to clear his own plate from the table and bring it to the counter for her. When Edward had been alive, she had always stopped him and Frank from getting up to help her—she'd liked hearing them talk at her back while she did the dishes. But now there was no one for Frank to talk to, and no one for her to listen to, and so she took Frank's plate from him. He always cleared just his own plate, never hers or any of the serving dishes, as if he honestly had no idea that all of them would eventually need to be washed. Sometimes that was the worst moment of the day for her, when Frank handed her his plate.

Shelley began laying out bowls on the trays, and Lorna ladled the thick soup into them. When the first tray was full, she hoisted it and backed through the swinging door into the church hall, where the assembly of old people had taken their seats at the tables, the women with their purses beneath their chairs. The lights overhead flickered, an electrical problem no one had ever been able to fix, which gave the room an unstable air, as though a storm were about to hit and plunge them all into blackness. The old faces in the room turned when she came in, looking toward her with varying degrees of recognition. Some of them didn't seem to know her from week to week.

A woman named Nadine leaned over her bowl and sniffed. She was wearing the same ugly orange pullover over her dress that she'd had on last Friday. Lorna couldn't imagine how she'd managed to get it on. She imagined someone trying to pull it over Nadine's fragile-looking head with its splotched scalp; she hoped that someone had helped Nadine bathe, at least, since last Friday. It was too awful to think of her trapped inside that sweater for a whole week.

"It smells wonderful," Garnet Osborn said, his old hand reaching up to catch Lorna's arm as she bent over him with the tray. Garnet lived with his son and daughter-in-law.

They took good care of him, but he liked to come to the suppers and talk to people and spare his daughter-in-law the trouble of cooking for him. She was a police officer.

"How are you?" Lorna smiled at Garnet.

"I am very well, considering my age," he said, winking at her. Lorna watched him take a mouthful of the soup, his lips closing unevenly around the bowl of the spoon. His hand shook.

Shelley backed through the door and began setting down bowls, chatting cheerily to the group.

Suddenly, Lorna remembered something. "Garnet, you don't still keep your pigeons, do you?" she asked.

Garnet reached into his pocket for his handkerchief, a vast affair in red silk. Trembling, he wiped his mouth. "Had to give them up." He paused. "I was sorry for that."

Lorna sat down in the chair beside him and put a roll on his plate and then began spreading it with butter. "I've a funny bird in my yard," she began, pushing the plate close so he could reach it. She set down the knife slowly. "It's amazing, really, a million colors and big as a . . ." She faltered. "A turkey. With a white hood and a long tail and wearing a coat of feathers like nothing you've ever seen."

"Sounds exotic," Garnet said. "Where'd you get it?"

"I didn't get it. It just appeared. I don't know what it is. Or what to do with it," Lorna said. "I've trapped it. Frank and me, with chicken wire."

"Sounds like someone's fancy breed. Try Seth Lewis," Garnet said. "He lives up on Lawyer's Hill. Used to know him from the pigeon-racing trade. He's got all sorts of birds. Of course, I haven't seen him in years. He's older than I am, I think. Might be dead, for all I know."

Lorna stood up and reached for Garnet's bowl. "Well, I can try," she said. "Will you have some more?"

"He hasn't got a phone," Garnet called after her. "You'll have to go up there yourself and ask for him."

THAT NIGHT, AS SHE and Shelley were cleaning up the kitchen, Lorna stood at the sink, scrubbing slowly at old stains. From time to time she looked out through the window. The moon was a flat white coin high in the sky, pinched by purpling clouds at its edges.

After dinner, Shelley had sat down with some of the old people while Lorna cleared away bowls and plates. Shelley sometimes read their palms for them. It was a joke, really; they understood that. Lorna had stood for a while by the table and watched. Shelley was wonderfully tender with them, stroking their hands so softly; Lorna could see the old peoples' eyes close a little, enjoying the feel of Shelley's warm fingers. She had felt her own palms tingle, and pressed her hands together under her apron.

She had liked listening to Shelley, too. It was astonishing, she thought, that even with their lives so fully spent, the old people were still quickened by the prospect of the future, as though anything might yet happen, as though hundred-dollar bills might be discovered folded inside an old night-gown, or a suitor suddenly appear at the door, bearing armfuls of lilac. Listening to Shelley talk, she realized that she had stopped imagining her own future. Or if she had thought of it, it was only in a bleak and uneventful way, like a flat line; her death would be only a little falling off from that straight edge, a barely perceptible decline.

Shelley flattered the seniors, told them their hands were interesting, yielding story after story. It was just a way of getting them to talk; Lorna saw that. Shelley read Garnet's quavering hand, holding it gently between hers until the trembling ceased, and pretended to be shocked by what she saw, averting her eyes. "I see the past, too, you know," Shelley said. He loved that.

"Don't worry over that old sink," Shelley said to Lorna now, coming back into the kitchen with the broom and dust-pan. "It'll *never* be white again. You go on home. I can finish up here."

Lorna looked quickly out the window, as if her attention had been caught by something out there in the darkness. A weight of tears, hot and embarrassing, pressed behind her eyes. She didn't want to go home, she thought.

There was an awkward moment. "Oh gosh," Shelley said at last into the silence. "I'm sorry, I always—look, honey, would you like to come out with Tim and me sometime? We'd love to have you come with us. You know, there's a whole crowd of people using Feaga's dance hall again. They fixed it up and it's really fun."

"Dancing?" Lorna was surprised that Feaga's was back in use. The old dance hall hadn't been open in years, as far as she knew. She thought of Edward, the lovely vise of his grip on the dance floor, how fortunate she had been to drift into it, snagged there like a straying thread and woven tight into his life. She'd loved dancing at Feaga's on the smooth, old wood floor, the doors open to the moon and stars and the dignified black shapes of the fir trees at the end of the field. Edward had sung to her while they danced, and held her against him with authority.

That was it, she thought. She had been *happy*.

"Do you like to dance?" Shelley was smiling at her.

Lorna imagined, for a moment, dancing with Shelley herself. She knew young people did such things nowadays, girls dancing with girls, or whole crowds jostling on a crowded dance floor, no one dancing with anyone in particular. She thought of Shelley's arms around her, the sweet scent that emanated from her some nights in the hot kitchen, something floral to it, the same scent that rose from the crushed stems Lorna braided in her garden after the flowers were spent. She saw herself with her head falling to Shelley's shoulder, remembered for an instant her own mother's distracted embrace, and then Edward again, the arc they had spun, a galaxy of dancers on the floor of Feaga's dance hall, each couple orbiting slowly in its own delicate pattern like stars in the milky sky.

Had she known it at the time? Had she really known, in an important way, that she was happy?

Lorna looked up. "I'm all right," she said.

There was Shelley's face, anxious, kind, bending toward her.

Lorna looked around vaguely, as if something might have happened just a moment before that she had somehow missed. She had the feeling that she had walked away into another room for a moment, summoned there by someone or something, and then come back. Here she was, but she could still remember it—the scent of the corsage she had worn, the cool night air on her flushed cheeks, the secure feel of Edward's arms around her. Yet she had invented something, too, out of that memory, for the bird had been there, the amazing bird she and Frank had trapped—it had flown past her deliberately, its tail brushing her lips. And then she had been out among the fragrant black shapes of the fir trees for a moment, and then she was back here.

"I remember Feaga's," she said slowly, looking up into Shelley's face.

Shelley came forward, took her arm, and squeezed it. "You're a *lovely* person, Lorna," she said urgently, as if Lorna had disparaged herself in some way. "Tim and I would be happy to have you come with us. Honestly. Please."

"I *will* come with you," Lorna said. "I'd like to see it again."

"OK. You've promised." Shelley looked around the kitchen. "Look, we're done here for the night. It's always cleaner after you come and help me than any other day of the week, anyway." She smiled at Lorna. "I can do the rest of this in the morning."

The women gathered their things. Lorna waited at the door, holding it ajar for the trapezoid of moonlight falling to the floor, while Shelley turned off the lights. They made their way up the steps together, arm in arm in the darkness, the sound of the river accompanying them.

Mares' tails, white and wispy, leaped across the graying night sky, like a breath blown across the level in a teacup, frilling the surface.

Lorna thought, *This is what it would have been like if I'd had a daughter.*

WHEN LORNA TURNED onto her lane, she parked the car down the hill by the mailbox, worried that the glare of the headlights sweeping over the face of the house might panic the bird. She hoped now that it was still there. Driving home, she'd had a sudden fear that it might have escaped.

She felt her way forward on foot in the dark, struck by the unexpected stealth of what she was doing, as though she were a stranger creeping up on her own house. Walking carefully up the driveway, eyeing the house, which floated above its invisible foundation, pale and unsubstantial, her eyes gradually became accustomed to the dark, and she could make out the shiny planking of the front steps, the crouched shapes of the shrubs, the glittering prison of wire around the bird.

It was still there, huddled against the house, its eyes open. It twitched at her arrival, a shudder running down its elongated back, its tail feathers lifting slightly and brushing the dark ground. Lorna knelt down and made a clucking sound with her tongue, a noise intended to sound comforting, and felt instantly foolish. She and Edward had never kept a pet, but it seemed wrong to think of the bird in that way, in any case. She felt its wildness and strangeness; its size made it seem vaguely threatening.

"Here," she said. She reached into her coat pocket and withdrew a slice of cake wrapped in wax paper. She unfolded the paper and lifted the chicken wire an inch or two, nervously, to place the cake neatly on a napkin inside the enclosure. The bird edged backward against the wall at her intrusion, averting its small head.

"I'm sorry," Lorna said.

The bird shivered, lifting one foot delicately from the ground and then replacing it tentatively.

"I'm trying to help you," Lorna whispered to it.

But the bird sank its head onto its breast.

It's dying, Lorna thought. *It's dying of grief.*

Inside, in the darkness, she felt her house breathing around her, the cushions on the couch in the unused living room exhaling slightly as if someone had just stood up from sitting there. She had let the mail collect in the bowl on the chest in the front hall; it seemed as though she had been away for a long time. She closed the door quietly behind her and listened for the distinct click of the lock. It struck her at that moment that she was less locking out intruders than locking herself in.

Then the phone rang, frightening her.

"Something the matter with the car?" asked Frank.

Lorna hurried to the window, carrying the receiver. Her heart was racing. She never could get over the nearness of Frank's voice; it was as though he were speaking right at her shoulder but were invisible, like an echo.

"I didn't want to scare the bird," she said.

"Good news on that front," Frank said brightly.

Frank had never been in the military—he had very bad eyesight—but he had worked as a bailiff at the courthouse and had adopted over the years a manner of speaking that sounded vaguely military. Never married—Edward always said Frank was too ashamed of the disfiguring birthmark on his face—he had always appreciated the sense of family Lorna and Edward provided him, Lorna thought, and they in turn liked the way he enlarged them, someone else to consider, someone else to consult. He and Edward had played cards together in the evenings sometimes, or chess, and he helped Lorna in the garden, lending his tilting weight to projects too cumbersome for her uncertain strength— excavating for the fish pool, digging post holes for the arbor, forking over the compost. Between them they'd made a splendid garden.

"Got a nice young woman from the nature center in Baltimore," Frank said. "They'll come get it in the morning."

"In the morning?" Lorna said.

"Said they'd be here around eight," Frank said. "How was dinner?"

"Oh, the same." Lorna frowned. "What will they do with the bird?"

"Well, I don't know, honey." Frank's voice receded slightly, as though he had turned his face away from the phone for a moment to address someone, his eyebrows lifting. "The lady said they're a sanctuary. They have injured ones and so forth. Maybe they try to find homes for them. Maybe they teach 'em tricks. I don't know."

"But . . . is that the best place for it?" An unaccountable irritation had gripped her across the shoulders. She straightened her back, looked over at Frank's house, his dark windows.

"Well, it's a hell of a sight better than camped out by your basement wall." He laughed.

Lorna said nothing, imagining the bird prodded to stand atop a bucket, its neck outstretched for food, a ring around its foot.

"You going to sleep now?" Frank asked in the pause.

"Yes," Lorna replied, short, sounding angry. She relented, though. "Well, come and have breakfast, Frank, before they get here. I'll make us something nice."

"That would be fine," he said, pleased. "Make us some of those blueberry pancakes."

Lorna hung up the phone and yanked down the window shade. She had a sudden, unpleasant picture of Frank, lying in bed with the phone, hooking aside his curtain with one finger to look at her house.

What business did he have making those arrangements?

Who knew where that bird had come from, what he had left behind, what he had lost or sacrificed.

She stood there for a minute in the darkness of the bedroom. She had given away almost all of Edward's clothes, everything except his naval uniform, because it had seemed somehow unpatriotic to throw it out. Otherwise, there was nothing left of Edward in the room except his trouser press, which had belonged to his father. It stood facing her, a short, headless, truculent thing, with squared-off shoulders and two blunt feet pointing straight ahead at her. She went over to it now and turned it so it was facing the wall, like a reproved child.

When she stepped outside to the porch again and leaned quietly over the railing, she could not see the bird at all, but she knew it was there. She could smell it, she thought, through the familiar scent of wet earth, a strange, foreign scent, like nothing she'd ever known. Before she closed the door and went to prepare for bed, she caught the flash of its eye within the egg-shaped clasp of skin. The eye held her momentarily and then vanished.

IN THE MORNING, after breakfast, Frank patted her hand and pushed back from the table, saying he would wait out front. Lorna rinsed the dishes and then stood at the screen door that opened onto her back garden. Edward's roses, and the perennials and annuals and vegetables, grew in beds perfectly described in a pair of interlocking diamond shapes created by Frank, who had painstakingly drawn the design and then lined the beds with white rocks ferried from the quarry in the trunk of his car. The garden's arrangement had always secretly bothered Lorna, who had discovered, after it was all laid out, that she had to do a little jump over the outer beds to a narrow strip of grass inside in order to reach the interior plants. A nuisance, she thought at the time, though she didn't say so, not after all that work.

Stepping outside, Lorna drifted over to the roses. Absently, she touched her finger to her damp brow and then ran it over the leaves, polishing them slowly and carefully. She heard the voices in the front yard but stayed where she was, obdurately polishing the roses' leaves. Then she heard Frank calling her.

"They're here," he said, loping around back to where she stood, her back to him, dreamily touching her forehead and then the leaves, polishing and polishing. "He's all ready to go. Didn't put up any fuss at all. C'mon around." He was enjoying this, Lorna saw, as if he'd made a kind of valiant citizen arrest, or had recovered something valuable that had been stolen from an important person.

Lorna moved slowly, like a sleepwalker, following Frank. Out front, a huskily built young man with a face that managed to be both earnest and slightly foolish, his hair in a ponytail, stood by the bed of his truck, his hand on the cage.

"Hi there. Tom Iannuzzi," he said pleasantly, extending his hand.

Lorna ignored his hand and advanced to the truck. The bird looked very small in the cage, as though it had shrunk overnight.

Tom glanced at Frank, who looked at Lorna, puzzled.

"This here's a kind of Asiatic pheasant," Tom said brightly after a minute. "They're pretty rare. Somebody's been missing *him*, I guess."

Still, Lorna said nothing.

Tom cleared his throat. "People keep them for show, of course. They make quite a picture, don't they, with that tail?"

"Sure do," said Frank heartily, when Lorna didn't answer.

"How much?" Lorna said.

Tom looked puzzled. "Uh, how much do they *cost?* Is that what you mean? Well, I'd say somewhere around a thousand, maybe. Maybe less."

"And what do they eat?"

He looked at her. "Same as the others," he said slowly. "Same as the other pheasants. We've got one—he's been with us about fifteen years. He's just a common field pheasant. He lost an eye to infection, but he gets around." He cleared his throat. "We have a nice arrangement, you know, if that's what you're thinking. We've got a buzzard, Captain Nelson, we call him—he just walks around like he owns the place. Comes on into the office, drinks coffee right out of my mug. Ha!"

"Do they fly?" Lorna was still watching the bird.

Tom said nothing for a moment. "No," he said at last. "They leap, sort of, but they can't really fly, not for long distances, anyway. They can really run, though." He said this last somewhat aggressively, as if it were a warning.

"Well," Lorna said then, "I think I've found his owner."

Frank, startled, stared at her.

"I'm sorry to put you to the trouble, Mr.—Mr. Tom," Lorna continued, "but I've only just found him, you see. The owner. Just this morning. He feels certain it's his. He's missing one. They don't bite, do they?"

"*Bite?*" Tom looked confused. "No, no they don't."

"Well then, I'll just run him on over there."

And then Lorna surprised herself by opening the cage door and reaching in with both arms. She had to bring her face close to the bird, and she saw her own image looming in its black eye, like the tiny secondary shape she saw in the viewfinder of Edward's fancy camera, a ghostly double.

She bundled the bird up awkwardly into her arms. It didn't protest at all, but under her hands, its breast throbbed wildly. She felt its neck shudder with a swallowing reflex.

"Open the car door for me, Frank," she said.

Frank stood stock-still. "Lorna," he said.

"Get the car door, Frank," she said over her shoulder, heading down the driveway with the bird cradled lightly in her arms. She couldn't believe how little it weighed, as though its feathers encased nothing at all, all that beauty over a puff of air, a feather of a soul. She carried the bird like a baby, its head over her shoulder by her ear, its long tail sweeping down to brush her thighs as she walked, its taloned feet pinched to her belly, its heart pressed to her own, the two hearts racing.

Frank hurried down the driveway behind her. "Lorna," he said. He sounded panicked, and for a moment she almost

stopped and turned around. If there was going to be any
point when she might be able to stop, she recognized, this
was it. "Lorna!" Frank said again. "Lorna!"

She gripped the bird with one arm, and it struggled briefly
against her. And then she wrenched the car door open. She
bundled the bird inside and took the seat next to it, starting
the engine.

"Lorna!" Frank was outside the glass of her window, bending down to look in at her, his face crumpled with dismay.

But Lorna wouldn't look at him then, suddenly terrified
at what she had done. She stood on the accelerator and
drove off hard down the lane, branches scraping her window as she came too close to the edge, her tires rocking in
the rut. Glancing up through the windshield, she startled at
a branch sweeping over the glass and panicked for a second,
seeing again the dark, smoking hole in Edward's car, the
front of it smashed accordion-like up against the tree.

But she righted the wheel, took a deep breath. The bird
fluttered awkwardly on a misstep and fell to the floor, scrabbling against the mat, its tail bent at an awkward angle.

"OK," Lorna said shakily. "OK. Everything's going to be
all right."

But as she drove, her dread grew. What had she done?
There were consequences, she thought in a panic. There
were the two men behind her, awash in her preposterous
wake. There was the bird itself.

The smell inside the car was surprisingly strong. She could
not tell whose scent was filling the space, the bird's or her
own. The glands beneath her arms prickled at a surge of
adrenaline, scratching at the surface of her skin. The bird,
tumbled to the floor, was still, its eye averted.

The car climbed the washboard of Lawyer's Hill, past mailboxes and newspaper boxes sunk into the swale of the gutter, past the knee-high figures of jockeys standing with their empty lanterns at the foot of the driveways, the white houses appearing here and there through the trees. She believed Seth Lewis's place lay at the top of the hill. One year, Frank and Edward had volunteered with the census, and some days she had taken the drive with them. The house was, she thought she remembered, an old stone lodge for the wealthy men from Baltimore who'd once built country homes in Charlotte Hall, as there was good duck hunting in the marshes east of town. She recalled suddenly that a dead man had been found once on the property, a vagrant who'd wandered into the woods from Route 1, become lost, and died of alcohol poisoning.

She searched her mind for what Garnet had said about Seth Lewis—that was why she was here, after all. She felt steadied by the logic of this; it was a thoroughly reasonable thing she had done, after all. She could just explain it to him. She could make it clear. And wouldn't he be happy to have the bird, even if it wasn't his? Anyone would, such a beautiful bird.

She glanced up through the windshield at the blue sky but shrank back in her seat as she felt Edward's face taking shape there, his familiar features elongating as he tended toward earth and searched for her, the growing smile on his face stretching too wide, hammocklike, threatening to take her in, swallow her up. How had Edward's face become so menacing? As though he'd caught her in a terrible act of betrayal.

She righted the wheel with a jerk. There was the drive to

Seth Lewis's house. She glimpsed the house, high ahead of her among the trees, and steered an uncertain course through the sudden shade that engulfed her as her car left the brightness of the main road. There seemed to be a terrible shouting up among the branches, the deafening voices of cicadas and birds hurled branch to branch.

She arrived at last; the car stopped. But it was all apparently empty, no one home at all, no sound anywhere. Seth Lewis must have died, she thought sadly, just as Garnet had said. She stared straight ahead of her, into the still, absolute air of the clearing. This is what it had come to, all her happiness, she thought, and she did not know how to go on then, for it could only be her fault that she was, having been so blessed once, now incapable of any real charity, incapable of any lasting gratitude. Or not gratitude, exactly — she lacked the significant and necessary power to live at all, as if with Edward's death she had died, too, a passing she herself had been almost unaware of. She raised her hand to strike the steering wheel, but her hand fell slowly, coming to rest again as if she had never made any gesture of refusal at all. Even that, she noticed, was beyond her.

And so she believed that it was in a dream that he approached her, opening the car door, pulling her from the seat with one arm, bending again to retrieve, surprised, the huddled bird. The sweep of its tail feathers spreading in the sunlight blinded her, as the gentle hand led her to an old folding chair in the center of the clearing, waving aside a swarm of insects, the air crackling with sparks of light and dark. Her head throbbed in response as his hand came to fall upon her shoulder; the smell and taste of cistern water steeped with fern and dirt rose on her upper lip. She drank, raised her eyes, and in the ring of light saw the dark shape of the man, his bottomless face, the cuffs of his trousers pooled at the ankle, his long feet planted, his whole tall body a column of cloud that soared upward, blocking the light, his hands at the end of his wrists flapping, some gesture, some question—she could not make it out.

Where is the bird? she wanted to ask. But she did not ask, or there was no answer, and in the shocking silence she threw her arms wide to catch it all back, every moment, every shape of every word, and opening her eyes, she saw the bird rising on air, a lighted window in the sky.

The hand on her shoulder tightened, withdrew, fell again, tapping lightly. She inclined her cheek toward it, grateful.

"You all right?" The man stooped before her. "This your bird?"

She looked up at the man and then beyond, to the glowing crescent of emerald lawn that spread from his shoulders like a cape. There was the bird still, standing a few yards away, its long tail lashing the ground, waiting for her to claim it.

Father Judge Run

Someone was shouting, one of the young lady guests at the inn, from the top of the stairs.

"Water!" she cried, and he knew if he went into the front hall full of the early hour's light, he would see one of the girls leaning over the banister, her wrapper closed over her collarbone, the pitcher dangling from her hand, her hair in two long, dark ropes down her back, like his mother's. They were all Bradshaw cousins, come for the town's August picnic, but there were so many of them they could not all be put up out at the Bradshaw's farm below the Peaks of Otter.

He looked out the kitchen window. The sun was up, white and round and hot, clearing the oak trees at the end of the inn's long garden, with its parallel rows of boxwoods and its sundial standing alone at the end on its bed of flagstones. He tried to imagine his mother, all the way on the other side of the mountains in West Virginia, sitting up in her high white bed in the sanatorium at White Hall.

"My room here is bright as heaven, Lucullus," she had written him. "The sunshine makes me better every day."

The voice called again. "Lu-*suh*-lus! The pitchers are empty! We need to wash!"

In the dining room the iridescent parrot swayed on its perch in the black iron cage suspended over the sideboard. "Water, water, water!" it shrieked in a high, effeminate voice. "Fishers of men!"

Lucullus hardly ever recognized the source of the parrot's utterances, but Signora Adelphi, the black cook who'd raised Miss Massie Rivers and now ran the kitchen at the inn, could almost always place the fragment correctly in the Book of Leviticus or in Proverbs or Revelation. He knew this one, though: "I will make you fishers of men." He leaned into the dining room from his place at the kitchen table, where he had been sitting and polishing the copper, and watched the bird pick up a piece of apple in its claw and look at it sideways. Lucullus put down the polishing rag. Were the parrot's odd associations of language deliberate? He could never be sure. It made him wary to contemplate the possible depths of the parrot's intelligence.

The parrot belonged to Miss Massie Rivers's brother, Charles, who had been a missionary in Darkest Africa. He had died, Lucullus had heard, of a disease that ate up his skin. When word came of his death, Miss Massie Rivers had left the inn in Signora Adelphi's hands and had gone all the way over to the African continent to fetch her dead brother's body and his possessions, though there couldn't have been much left of either, people said. She had come back three months later with nothing but trunks of books and the parrot. The books she put in the inn's shadowy library, where the men guests sat after dinner, smoking in cane chairs.

She had arrived home on the train on a hot, overcast afternoon, clouds of gnats hovering in the trees. Lucullus had been dispatched to meet her train by Signora, who told him he could help carry things along with Marcus, the narrow-shouldered, quiet man who was a cousin to Signora and worked sometimes at the inn.

He had worried at the time that he might be asked to carry Charles the missionary brother, or what was left of him; he supposed Miss Massie Rivers would have had him burned to ash and bone, reduced to a manageable size. But when she descended to the platform under the depot's green tin roof, in a long black skirt and a black-and-white-striped blouse that made her look like a pirate, Miss Massie Rivers had handed Lucullus a parrot's cage instead, draped with an odd, fringed cloth the color of verdigris. There were dark pouches beneath her eyes.

"Careful, Lucullus," she'd whispered, as if she'd lost her voice. She had not asked him how he'd been.

She must have stayed awake all night that first day back, unpacking the books, for she was still there when Lucullus had come to work the next morning. She was sitting on the floor surrounded by books, still in the same skirt and blouse, her black hair in two wild wings. The room smelled of mildew and cold ash. She had not looked up from her book when Lucullus opened the door to the library.

She had been crying, though; he could see that. It made her uglier than usual. Behind her back, some of the boys in town called her F.O.P., for Face of a Pig. She had no husband. They said it was because she was too wretchedly ugly, with a pasty face the shape of a turnip. Her cheeks looked as though she held something there inside them, a nugget of gold or a bone; a man would have a heart attack waking up beside her, the boys said. Lucullus thought she wasn't at all pretty, not anything like his own delicate and beautiful mother, who sewed such lovely clothes and now was "wasting away," people said quietly, in the sanatorium at White Hall. But after Miss Massie Rivers's missionary brother had died and she had come back from Africa, Lucullus was struck less by her blank, heavy face than by the great difficulty she appeared to have in accomplishing things, as if she could not remember how to lay the table or beat the carpets or twist a chicken's neck.

He'd watched her standing in the yard, leaning on the ax as if she were out of breath, chickens fussing around her feet.

"What's she doing?" Signora Adelphi would say from the stove.

He'd wanted to go outside and put the ax into Miss Massie Rivers's hand. Something about her immobility, her vagueness, made him feel frightened. It was as if the whole world—first his mother, now Miss Massie Rivers—was succumbing to an indefinite and invisible enemy. She should get on with things, he'd thought anxiously, watching her through the window. But he could not voice such thoughts to Signora, much less to Miss Massie Rivers herself. He hardly knew her, really, and he was just a child.

"Nothing," he'd told Signora instead. "She's not doing anything."

Beautiful dreamer, his own mother called him, but now he

had only letters from her once a month, saying she longed for him and would be well one day soon, she was sure. They'd promised the consumptives sleigh rides in the winter, she wrote, groups of them bundled in furs and taken out to fly like wild geese over the frozen lakes. But she would be home long before then, she was sure. The air was better over there on the western side of the mountains, she said, and he'd wondered at that, wondered if the air he breathed now, the familiar air of his birthplace, was somehow of poorer quality, thin and without substance. Miss Massie Rivers, he thought, was failing. Maybe they would all sicken and die. Maybe it was the air.

Miss Massie Rivers had inherited the inn from her father, Randolph. There was a photograph of Randolph Massie Rivers and his brother in the front parlor, taken in 1861, Signora told him, before they went off to the war. Randolph and his younger brother, Frederick, sat side by side in their drab militia uniforms, Randolph's hand resting on his younger brother's knee as if he knew that Frederick would not live long and wanted to touch him one last time while they sat there quietly together like that. Frederick was killed his second day in battle, but Randolph came back and built the Inn at Coolwell after Appomattox.

The morning after Miss Massie Rivers's return home, when Lucullus had found her in the library, he had waited for her to speak to him. There were guests to be fed and watered, as Signora said, but Miss Massie Rivers seemed to have forgotten that her house was full of strangers. All that day and the next and the days after, she had moved around the inn as if she didn't even see the people who came and went. He had the feeling that she was hoarding something inside herself; she looked like someone who was trying to take stock of a complicated and elusive store of supplies, items she had to hunt down over and over again, for they would not stand still for inspection.

"Should I start the fire?" he'd asked at last, shuffling at the doorway, and she'd raised her head at the sound of his voice.

It was barely light out, but he had come to work early, wanting to show her that even while she'd been away he had kept to his duties; she owed him twelve weeks' wages, all the weeks she'd been gone, but he hadn't known how to ask for it.

Signora Adelphi was nowhere in sight yet. Miss Massie Rivers glanced over her shoulder at him, her eyes like two tiny black coals ringed with fire. She sat back on her heels, her hands spread on her thighs, and looked down at the carpet as if the answer might be found there. Finally she had said something inaudible, and eventually Lucullus had closed the door and gone to start the fire himself.

How strange she was. Had Darkest Africa done it? He had knelt by the fire in the kitchen, feeding it slips of wood. When the door swung open, he heard himself cry out in alarm, an embarrassing, girlish sound. But it was only Signora Adelphi, coming into the kitchen to begin her day over the stove. She stood blinking in the door for a minute. Then she took off her hat and set it on the chair and put on her apron.

"Don't say a *word* to her," she had told Lucullus, commencing to crack eggs for the guests' breakfasts. "She's got a broken heart. You don't want to bother her." She had heaved a globe of risen dough out of the bowl, and it fell on the table with a fat sound. "Now she's got nobody in the world. And she wasn't ready. Got to be ready, I say."

In Signora's hands, the dough became four loaves, speckled brown. "And that bird . . ." She went on dividing the loaves. "Now, he's going to test my patience."

No one knew the parrot's name. All it could say were fragmentary verses from the Bible.

"What's your name?" Lucullus had tried that first morning. He'd stood by the sideboard, looking up at it in its cage, fingering the inlay under his hands, a chain with yellow links like tiny, ivory dominoes. The fragile pink teacups had shivered in their saucers on the table. Feet pounded overhead; there were eight people at the inn that day, on their way to Richmond. He'd brought them chipped ice and mint the night before, and one of the ladies had pinched his cheek and asked if he was Miss Massie Rivers's son.

Lucullus had looked up at her, shocked. "No ma'am," he'd said, and had gone away downstairs on watery legs. His own mother, he wanted to say, was a beauty. His own mother drank a cup of milk with a raw egg in it every day and lounged in fields of daisies. His own mother was over where the air was better. "There is a fine class of people here, Lucullus," she'd written. "And many priests and sisters."

His own mother, he'd wanted to shout, was with the best people.

HE HADN'T KNOWN ENOUGH, at first, to be frightened of the parrot. "Hello. Hello. What's your name?" He'd tried over and over again that first morning, waiting stubbornly by the cage. He touched his finger to the bars.

The bird screeched. "Pluck it out! Pluck it out! Pluck it out!" It followed this command with a high, forlorn noise ending on a quaver that made the hair on Lucullus's arms stand up. He had jumped away from the cage as the parrot leaned toward him. This was a terrifying creature, with its tone of judgment, and echoes of the jungle, and menacing eye.

In the kitchen, Signora screamed with laughter over her pots. "Watch your eyes, young Lucullus," she called.

He'd hurried away fast from the bird then, over the floors he'd polished so painstakingly that they shined like ice. There were potatoes to peel, and steps to be swept, and he wanted to do his job well. He would write his mother to tell her that he had earned enough to come and visit her in White Hall and see how she was getting along. *No one will need to worry anymore, Mother,* he would write. *I'm making money.* And his mother would read his words, sitting up in the bright light in her high bed in the sanatorium, sunlight and fine air all around her like in heaven, and be happy.

"Ask and it shall be given," said the parrot in a sad voice, as Lucullus went away.

The table in the dining room had been laid with place settings for the twelve jurors who would be sequestered there for lunch that day, each plate rimmed with crimson, a cluster of dark grapes painted in the center. A black man was on trial for stealing apples and pigs. The jury would convict him unanimously later that afternoon, after a heavy dinner of mutton and gravy, stewed okra with pimientos like bits of red flesh—Lucullus was afraid to touch them with his bare hands when he scraped the plates—roast potatoes, and quince pie.

"Pluck it out, pluck it out," the bird sang merrily. But no one was listening.

THERE WAS THE voice again.

"Lu-*suh*-lus! Can't you hear? *Water!* We need to get ready!"

He put down the rag with which he'd been polishing the copper and hurried now to fill the bucket from the well at the end of the stone path between the banks of daisies. He pumped the rusty arm; did all girls want to wash so often? He peered over the edge of the well, down into the mossy murkiness. There was nothing to be seen there, no end in sight, but the water in the bucket was black and bright and swayed against the sides.

Going through the dining room on his way to fill the girls' pitchers so they could wash and make themselves pretty for the picnic, Lucullus glanced at the parrot. It was murmuring something to itself in a tender voice, fishing in its rainbow of feathers for lice. Lucullus had come to feel that the parrot's presence was like having a ghost in the house. He was eleven and did not think he believed in ghosts, but Miss Massie Rivers frightened him with her silent ways and distracted manner, now that she had come back from Darkest Africa, and the parrot frightened him when it screamed, "Cloud of the Lord, cloud of the Lord!" as if the cloud that had lain upon the Tabernacle were hovering overhead, tangling in the branches of the oak trees that grew close around the inn. And when he had to go home in the dark now, down the alley behind the inn and then along the edge of the tobacco field, splashing through the cold waters of Father Judge

Run, he was frightened and thought of his mother. *Help me. Save me,* he prayed incoherently, tripping over stones, his heart pounding.

Sometimes it seemed to him that Miss Massie Rivers's dead brother was actually inside the parrot, had somehow inhabited its muscular body. He thought Miss Massie Rivers believed so, too, for sometimes he'd find her standing in the dining room, staring in at the bird, and one afternoon he'd come through with a load of polished brass for the fireplace to find her poised, very still, by the window under the Boston fern, the parrot sitting calmly on her shoulder.

"I've made a friend, Lucullus," she said, smiling for the first time since she'd come home. "What do you think?"

But he didn't like the bird. Its head swiveled round quick as a wink to catch you at something. And if Charles the missionary brother was there, what kind of man had he been?

"Behold," the parrot would call from the dining room. "Behold, behold, behold."

And Lucullus heard the missionary's weary voice as he bent over a guttering candle in a tent, the yellow eyes of lions burning through the bush.

But Charles couldn't have been all holiness, for the parrot had a repertoire of disgusting noises to go with its Bible verses—belches and snorts and other indiscretions. It made Signora Adelphi clutch her sides with stifled laughter to hear the parrot silence conversation in the dining room with a series of escalating explosions.

Lucullus, plucking chickens or splitting wood at the back step, would hear the parrot's ugly noises and see Signora's shaking back, and an unpleasant, giddy feeling would come over him. He wanted to stop it, or else give up somehow—

though what was there to relinquish?—and let things take their inevitable course; he had a sense that terrible forces were gathering around them, a feeling the parrot's insane exorcisms exacerbated. *Why doesn't somebody shut it up?* he wondered fiercely. But he would laugh meanwhile, and the two feelings—of horror and helpless mirth—would grow unbearable, as though he had swallowed something solid, a rock or a spoon, its handle tickling his throat. He would throw down the little hatchet, hard, into the sparkling dust, tears in his eyes.

"Shepherd of Is-ra-el," the parrot would say complacently, after a satisfying belch, and sometimes then the guests would finally explode into laughter after an awful, embarrassed silence.

"She wants a change," Signora said when he came back from delivering the pitchers to the girls upstairs. She was splitting lemons for the lemonade jugs for the picnic, spooning in glistening hills of sugar. It was a month after Miss Massie Rivers's return from Africa. "Mark me, Lucullus," Signora said. "She's going to shut down this old inn and go away. You and me and Marcus going to have to find a different place."

Lucullus stopped up short at the table.

Signora tossed the lemon rinds in a bucket. "Get me that ham."

He fetched it for her, the dead weight of it in his arms, and heaved it onto the table.

"She's just weary," Signora went on. "She's had a long life of weariness. Even as a little baby she was weary already.

She said she might go back where Charles was, but I don't think she'll do that." Pink slices of ham fell away from the knife. "I could go cook for Mrs. Fletcher," Signora said after a moment, plucking up a little shaving of meat and tasting it. "She's only asked me a hundred times." She sighed. "One time ending, another beginning."

Lucullus blinked. "What will I do?" His thoughts came slowly, but they were immense, too big, as if he were coming up into the air at the top of a mountain after being in the clouds and was seeing at last the terrifying slide away down into nothingness below him. This was what had been in store, the bad thing he'd felt, listening to the parrot. He'd never make his money now. He'd never get to White Hall.

"Be a little man," his mother had written. "Help your father in every way."

Six months before, on a bright March morning, she'd been carried away in a chair to the wagon that would take her to the train and then to the sanatorium. He had not been allowed to go; his father had hardly even seemed to notice him that morning, and his mother had only opened her eyes once, a look of fear on her face, when the chair was tilted into the wagon. Lucullus had waited awhile and then had walked down the road where the wagon had disappeared. In the place where the tracks ran among willow trees, after crossing the pebbled, shallow bottom of Father Judge Run, he had seen a short trail of drops of blood and had followed it a few feet, trying to decipher its sudden turns, until it gave out. The beads of blood, dark and no longer wet to the touch, had filled him with dread. He'd knelt in the cold water of the stream and scrubbed at his hands until they were raw.

Signora glanced over at him now. She held the knife toward him, a splinter of ham speared on the tip. "Plenty of jobs for boys like you," she said, wagging the knife at him until he took the ham. "You'll be back to school in September, anyway."

"There's not jobs!" he blurted. "Not good ones, anyway. No other boy has a job earns him so much money as this one! They're all jealous of me!" But he did not know if this was true. Since he'd started at the inn that June when school had let out—it was a job arranged for him by his father, who helped Miss Massie Rivers with the inn's business affairs from time to time—he had hardly seen any of his friends. He had not really wanted to play with them. He could not stop thinking of their mothers.

He worked seven days a week, instead. He wanted to have lots of money by the end of the summer, enough to go alone to White Hall and climb the long hill to the hospital where his mother rested, and then enough to help his father, a lawyer with a sad manner and a reluctant voice who never seemed to get paid in anything but fish on a string or chickens or jars of honey. The people at the sanatorium would not take good care of his mother if they were not paid, Lucullus sensed. They might even send her home, not yet well, if the bills were not settled. *Out you go!* they would say, pushing her in her chair to the gates.

And now he would have nothing, or not enough. And it was all because of Miss Massie Rivers and her—what was it? Her *unwillingness*. She had no right! She was ugly and no one liked her except Signora, who had taken care of her when she was a little girl.

"She should do what she pleases," Signora said then,

scooping up the stack of ham slices and putting them on a plate. "She's never hurt anybody. Ugly people like her should get to do what they like at the end."

At the end? The end of what?

The parrot was exhorting them from the other room. The girls were calling for more water. Doors were slamming overhead. Lucullus saw his mother, her dress plucked up by crows, lifted into the ether over the mountains. A flock of birds darkened the kitchen as they sank into the magnolia tree by the window.

THE YOUNG LADIES, the Bradshaw cousins, came downstairs finally at about ten, after hours of washing. Laughing and smelling of soap, they formed a flotilla of flounces and whispery hats. Signora and Marcus and Lucullus loaded the hampers into the creaking wagon when it stopped on the ring of grass between the oak trees in front of the inn. Carter Lovingston's two gray mares stamped in the harness. Boys in white shirts, and women in broad, shallow hats, little girls in sausage curls, and young men with pink cheeks leaned out over the sides and called to the girl cousins. "Come on! Hurry, hurry!"

In the kitchen, Signora sat down in a chair. "Enough," she said aloud, and quick as a wink began snoring.

The parrot called out, "Deliver thyself!" in a cheerful tone, and then cackled like a lunatic. It flung heaps of seed on the floor, using its beak like a shovel.

Lucullus edged past the bird and sidled into the kitchen, softly clinking two pennies in his pocket.

Signora opened her eyes. "What are you doing?"

Lucullus stopped by her knee and shrugged. "Working."

"Go on," she said. "Go catch up with them. A picnic is for young folk. I can't sleep with you working around me all the time. Don't you know when to rest?"

"Give me a job, Signora," he pleaded. "I don't want to go to any picnic. Want me to wash out these bowls?"

"Take off my shoes for me," she said instead.

Lucullus knelt at her feet to unlace her shoes. Her legs grew out of her brown shoes like two tree trunks. Her toes were little brown burls, curled over atop one another. Lucullus thought suddenly of Finn the mortician, who laid out people's naked bodies on a stone, and he felt strange. Signora's feet were so hard worked and sad.

Signora leaned back in the chair and closed her eyes. "Away now." She waved at him.

Lucullus lingered. "Somebody spilled the pot of violets in the hall," he said, standing up. "There's dirt all over. One of them did it with her umbrella."

Signora waved at him again, her eyes still closed. She had made six coconut cakes for the picnic. Lucullus walked over to the stove and looked at the coconut shavings left in the bowl.

"Where's *her?*" he said after a minute.

"Sent her down to see about some ducks," Signora said, still with her eyes closed. "Give her something to do, get her some air. She can pick out some ducks."

Lucullus tried to pull out a chair quietly so he could sit down. He was suddenly afraid to leave the room, leave Signora.

But she opened her eyes and glared at him. "I don't like being watched while I sleep," she said. "Bad things can happen."

Lucullus stood up.

"There's a piece of cake for you in the dining room," she said, leaning back again and closing her eyes one last time. "On a nice plate. You go eat and let me rest."

LUCULLUS ATE HIS CAKE, sitting alone at the end of the big table that shone darkly like a pool of water. Then he went and stood in front of the parrot's cage. The bird tiptoed over on its perch to look at him and then hurried away to the far side of the cage, as if it didn't like what it saw.

"Pretty bird," Lucullus said in a whisper.

"Shhhh." The parrot edged away.

Lucullus picked up a chair and brought it over to the sideboard and then climbed on top of it. When he began to lift down the parrot's cage, he saw it was too heavy for him, heavy as a safe. Trembling under its weight, he managed to replace it on its hook, and then he climbed down from the chair and stood by the sideboard. Sweat had broken out along his hairline.

In the hall the crystal tears on the candelabra tinkled suddenly. Lucullus froze. Sunbeams advanced along the floor. But no shape of Miss Massie Rivers darkened the door. The sunlight lay there, quivering.

"Shhhh," warned the parrot again.

But Lucullus reached up and opened the trap door on the cage. When he extended his hand, the parrot looked at it disdainfully, as though the thing proceeding slowly toward it on its perch were something inferior. Lucullus rested his hand on the perch, hovering just beside the parrot's two mighty feet.

Finally the parrot bent down and tested Lucullus's thumbnail gently with its hooked beak. It looked up at Lucullus and cocked its head.

Lucullus held his breath.

The bird looked away when it stepped at last onto Lucullus's hand, as if disguising its capitulation with nonchalance. It would stand on Lucullus's hand because that was what a hand was for, but it would not acknowledge its captor. Lucullus was astonished at the creature's puny weight; somehow, the cage's heavy black bars had suggested that the bird might be capable of terrifying feats of strength. But it weighed nothing at all, not even as much as a cup of water.

Faker! he thought. *Pretender!*

Perhaps it would fly away now. The air would be cleared. The inn would be full of comforting silence, a promise of rest. It would have been an accident.

But the bird didn't move. It even bowed its head when he slipped the sack over it, as if it were used to clandestine journeys into a dark estate, as if it knew what waited there at the end and was not afraid.

It was not until he was almost home, the parrot stunned into silence in the sack he held carefully under his shirt, that he realized the other purpose of the heavy bars on the bird's cage, the iron cage that looked as if it could withstand fire and flood. The bars were not just for keeping the bird a prisoner, he thought, and felt ashamed.

In the jungle, there must have been many enemies.

THEY HAD NO ANIMALS, but his mother kept two peacocks that roamed the lawn in her absence like disappointed lovers. Lucullus chased the peacocks away, and now the parrot sat quietly in a squirrel trap in the gloomy shadows of an empty stall in the barn. Lucullus knelt before it, his fingers at the wire mesh. "Pretty bird," he said. "Pretty bird." The parrot had said nothing at all since they'd arrived at the barn an hour ago.

"Hello," Lucullus tried again. "Hello, bird." He wanted the bird to speak to him now, to tell him what came next. He realized that he had been counting on that in some way. He had not thought about what he would do.

And then he heard the clanging of fire bells.

The parrot let out a scream. Lucullus jumped up. "Don't," he said, frightened. "Don't make that noise." He knelt down again before it. "Pretty bird, pretty bird," he said desperately. "Nice bird." And then the parrot began to make a whimpering noise, the sound of a man weeping quietly, Charles the missionary brother alone in his mud hut at night, when he knew he was dying. Lucullus put his hands over his ears. But he could still hear the fire bells.

He peered in at the bird. It jerked its head in and out of its collar of emerald feathers as if it were strangling and struggling to breathe.

His fingers shook as he fumbled with the old latch. At last it gave way and opened. "Quick," Lucullus said. "Fly away. You're free." For if the bird flew away, everything would be as it had been. Miss Massie Rivers would not close the inn and go away. He would have his job. His mother would come home. The air would be clear, bright as the streambed of Father Judge Run. The cloud of the Tabernacle would remove itself from the trees.

But the bird didn't budge. Lucullus inched his hand into

the cage. The parrot came out of its neck-twisting trance and bit him, quick, on the knuckle.

Lucullus sat down, sucking his sore finger. He was so tired. He put his head down into a pillow of straw. Far away, the sound of the fire bells drained into the sky. The parrot made little clucking noises, fussing with itself, picking up its feet and nibbling at its toes. Above them, sunlight shone like stars through the chinks in the barn roof.

WHEN LUCULLUS WOKE, the parrot was gone. He jumped up, dazed, but it was shadowy in the barn; he must have slept away the whole afternoon.

"Bird? Bird?" He searched the rafters, but there was nothing. No cry of lamentation, no word of accusation.

The picnic would be over. The girls would be back at the inn, soiled and tired, wanting ice or coffee. Everyone would be looking for him.

And for the parrot.

Why had he done this? He felt his stomach curdle. His skin prickled, as if tiny, uncomfortable quills were sprouting from his chest and loins. He could not say, now or maybe ever, why he had stolen the bird, or whom he had wanted to hurt most. His father? His mother? No, certainly not his mother—though she had not even touched his hand when she left. Was it Miss Massie Rivers, for forgetting she owed him money? For being so unaware of them all? The air had grown thick and sour around them since she'd come back from Africa, the days full of the parrot's spells and portents. At night, Miss Massie Rivers would drape the cloth over the parrot's cage and whisper to it through the bars. Sitting in the kitchen, watching this ritual through the open door, Lucullus had thought of the icy, healing wind that blew along the halls of the sanatorium, of his mother standing at the open window, her nightdress billowing.

"Bird?" he called out again now. "Please."

But there was no reply.

BY THE TIME he got to the edge of the tobacco field, he could smell the fire. The twilit air was full of dark bits of bitter-tasting ash that fell on his lips. He came up into town; a crowd of noisy boys were up in the full, dark velvet of the oak trees by the post office, talking and leaning out along the branches, trying to get a better look.

Hurrying past the post office window, Lucullus thought of the posters of wanted men hanging inside on the white walls; he was always afraid to look at those men.

"Young Lucullus!" It was thin old Marcus, standing in the shadows of W. Ward Hill's Real Estate, resting like a dark grasshopper against the tall letters painted on the side of the building, which advertised BUGGIES, HARNESSES, AND WAGONS. He waved Lucullus over.

"Yes, it's terrible," Marcus said when Lucullus stood before him. Marcus nodded as if Lucullus had said so himself and Marcus was only agreeing with him. "Terrible."

Lucullus stared up at him. Marcus stepped away out of the shadows then and came close to him. He looked down into Lucullus's face. "Oh," he said. "You ain't seen it yet." There was a little hesitation. Marcus watched him. "Where you been?"

Lucullus glanced behind him at the boys massed in the

tree; their shapes seemed grotesque and threatening among the shiny leaves, their flapping white shirts ghostly like loose bandages. "I heard the fire bells," he whispered. "I fell asleep."

Marcus watched him. "Well, it's all gone," he said slowly. "And everything in it."

Lucullus felt himself begin to pant, as if he had run a long distance. He heard men shouting two streets away where the inn was. Had been.

"Hold on," said Marcus kindly, seeing this and putting out his hand. "Signora's safe. The missus is safe. She wasn't home, and Signora got out. But I'll tell what I heard," he said. "People don't waste time, do they?" He leaned close toward Lucullus. "They say she done it herself." He nodded sadly and then closed his eyes as if in prayer. When he opened them, Lucullus could see how the old man's eyes were reddened. "I'm going on now," Marcus said, nodding, "see about Signora."

Lucullus watched him go. He stood under the oak tree. Some of the boys called to him to come up, but he shook his head. After a time, he went away down the alley toward the inn.

Miss Massie Rivers was standing alone near the old well in a patch of trampled and blackened phlox and mignonette. Men milled around her in the early dark of evening, filling buckets and tossing them onto the heaving pile of ash and bright embers that groaned and creaked like something at sea. The inn's chimneys stood up, blackened, against a sky that had gone from dusk to night but was filled with an odd light, as though the floating ash in the air glowed with bright life. Sloping parts of the inn's shingled roof sagged from the brick.

Miss Massie Rivers did not seem to notice the people around her but stood quietly, her face expressionless.

Lucullus slid toward her and the remains of the fire like a ghost among the oak trees; their wide trunks were warm against his hands. Soon he was near enough to touch her if he'd wanted, and now he could see she was trembling. Someone came and tried to lead her away, but she shook her head, and he saw her lips move, saying something to the man who put a hand on her shoulder. Then she stood alone again.

She had wanted to go away, Lucullus thought. That was what Signora had said.

But would she have set her own place on fire? What was the need for it? he thought helplessly. What if the world turned out to be a place where what you loved had to burn to the ground, reduced to ash, before you could change? He stood behind her, trying to listen. Something had been happening to Miss Massie Rivers. If he could get close enough now, he would know what it was that happened to people when they were disappointed, when they were in grief, when they lost something.

She turned around quickly, as if she had known he was there.

"Oh, Lucullus," she said, and he saw that her face was composed, though her body quivered. "Your father's worried. You should go and find him."

But he didn't move; he wanted her to stop shaking. She seemed to understand that there was more to be said, that he was waiting. She turned away again to look at the ruins of the inn. A smear of dark ash was laid down over her bare arm as though she had been scored. Her dress smelled of smoke. She gave a long sigh, and her body quieted.

"I'm sorry about your job, Lucullus," she said softly. "I know how you worked so hard. I'll speak to someone on your behalf." She paused. Rivers of flame like serpents' tongues climbed the brick walls, fell away. "Don't believe what you hear, Lucullus," she said then. "I would never have laid such a fine old place to waste. They only say such things because —" She stopped. "Why do they say such things?" She looked at him as if genuinely puzzled. "Because I have no husband?" She licked her lips. "Well," she said, as if he had confirmed it. "That's a lesson."

She turned away, but he could see a strange, sad joy in her face. "Isn't it funny?" she asked him. "Do you know what I am sorriest for?" She didn't wait for him to answer. "I am sorry about Charles's parrot. He made me laugh." She smiled down at Lucullus, and he thought then that she had a kind of bright bravery to her face, like a head on a coin. The fire behind her seemed like something that had burned everything but her, that she had stood in its midst with the flames at her feet but would not turn to ash, would not be ruined. "He made us all laugh, didn't he? Charles had him for years and years. Listening to that funny bird, it was almost as if I had Charles back again." She sighed. "I might have moved on, you know, sold the inn or just closed it up for a time and traveled. But I would have taken that bird with me."

She pondered Lucullus for a moment, and then she put a cold, dirty hand briefly on his head. "I owe you money, I think," she said. "Don't worry. I have money." She looked away. "Go and see your father. He's worried to death."

• • •

HE RAN THROUGH the field and down the lane where the wagon had carried away his mother. He ran over Father Judge Run, the stream full of the rippling sound of conversation, the voices of his childhood murmuring in the dark, and then across the still warm grass of his lawn. The barn door was open. He slipped inside and stood in the darkness, breathing hard. *I am only eleven,* he thought, *but I have already committed a sin. Will my mother die now?*

He dropped to his knees and clasped his hands together. He looked up into the rafters. *Forgive me,* he prayed. *Come back.*

But there was no sound other than his own frantic whispering.

Behind him, the open barn door glowed with a pale gray light. He glanced over his shoulder. Did he see a shape move there against the light? Who was there? He stood up, for now he needed to be prepared.

"Charles?" The sound of his own voice fell away, a rock rolling downhill. "Hello! Charles!" he screamed. "Hello, hello, hello!"

But no one came forward.

When he quieted at last, when he stopped crying, he sat up stiffly. Now he was on the other side of the mountain, he thought; now he was someone who has crossed the river and passed through the darkest night and stands in a foreign place where nothing seems familiar. He stared around at the bales of hay, the wagon removed from its axles and laid to rest. Swallows gusted in and out of the barn door, their wings forked.

And then, as if the barn had no roof, as if the sound were traveling from the stars, he heard the voice.

"Pretty bird," it called lightly from the rafters, out of the gloom. "Hello."

Lucullus leaped to his feet, trying to see in the darkness, his legs trembling beneath him. "Hello!" he called back. "Oh, hello!"

And when the parrot flew down to land on his arm, it seemed to Lucullus like an angel of the tropics, a flash of emerald and sapphire and ruby, swooping through the soft, warm night air of his father's empty barn.

"LET'S HAVE A PICTURE, son," his father said, when Lucullus and Miss Massie Rivers were settled on a bench at the depot, waiting for the train that would take Lucullus to White Hall. His father liked to take pictures; he was the only father Lucullus knew who had a camera. He set up the tripod some distance away from them down the platform and then ducked under the cloth. "Hold still," he called out, his voice muffled. "Hold still."

Miss Massie Rivers had come to see Lucullus off; she herself would be going over to Europe and would be gone when he got back from his visit to White Hall. She was to sail on a big ship, she had told him, where she would sit on deck with the parrot and watch for whales.

Lucullus felt her beside him, her skirt brushing his thigh. "Miss Massie Rivers," he said urgently, quietly, so his father might not hear. He knew now, waiting for the train that would take him to White Hall, where he would see his mother at last, that he could not leave without telling the truth.

"You have your ticket?" she asked him. "Your father gave you the money?"

"Oh, yes," he said quickly. "Thank you."

She nodded. "It's your reward, Lucullus. I told your father so. Don't think of it as charity." She reached up a finger to the parrot, who sat hunched on her shoulder. It swiped amiably at her hand with its beak. She inclined her heavy cheek toward it.

Lucullus looked away. His father was still under the black cloth, his shoulders moving like thunderclouds massing on the horizon. Behind him ran the shining tracks, away, away, away into the future. The train would come soon. He wanted to stand up, but his legs would not hold him.

"Miss Massie Rivers—" he began. "The truth—"

But her body beside him shifted, grown alert. This stopped him. The truth might not always have been a kind thing for Miss Massie Rivers to have heard in her lifetime.

But she reached over to put her arm around his shoulder as he sat beside her. "Lucullus," she whispered, looking toward Lucullus's father. "Do you know what I found? In the ashes of the fire? I found the parrot's cage."

Lucullus held his breath.

"The door was open, you see," she said quietly. "Someone had carelessly left open the door on the cage. A small mistake, to be sure, but in fact a fortunate one, as we have now seen. I have come to think of that person, that person who left the door open, as my . . . friend."

"Just another minute," his father called to them.

Miss Massie Rivers squared her shoulders to face the camera. Her fingers felt light on his shoulder, and warm. "So it was a blessing." She shrugged. "He could just fly away."

Lucullus looked up. The train's whistle sounded, though they could not see it yet, not for another minute.

"I just found him," he had told her the night of the fire, coming back to the inn with the parrot under his shirt. "He was just up in an old tree around here."

But what was she doing now? Was she forgiving him? But she didn't understand. He hadn't just opened the cage and forgotten to close it. He had taken her bird, stolen it. He had wanted it to fly away.

He was so afraid of hurting her. But it had to be said.

"What if the bird didn't just . . . fly away?" he asked the air over their heads, the air now ticking with electricity, something approaching.

The train's whistle sounded again, nearer now. "What if someone . . . stole it?" he said.

Miss Massie Rivers was silent beside him, and in the silence Lucullus felt his soul leave his body for an instant, a sensation of utter weightlessness like a bird in flight, as if he had risen above the place he knew and could now see far, far beyond it, over the charred remains of the inn, over the town, the fields, his house, all the way to the bright, silver vein of Father Judge Run, which divided what he had known from all that would come next, whatever lay ahead in the future. What was it? Oh, what was it? What could he see?

"Ah," she said after a long moment.

The shape of Lucullus's father at the end of the platform, far, far away, surged once more under the black drape. One white arm emerged, a finger raised.

"Stole it. I see." She paused. "And you are wondering . . . if that makes a difference."

He turned, dared to look at her.

She squinted at the train, which had appeared now, a black thumb nosing around the corner of the hill. "No,

Lucullus," she said finally. "I think it makes no difference, in the end." She looked at him. Her face was grave at first, and then it gave in to gentleness.

Nothing could make her pretty, he thought. But a person could like her, he thought, very much.

"You have an absolutely clean heart now," she said. "Perfectly clean. You may go and see your mother with a clean heart."

She turned away from Lucullus to face the oncoming train and his father's shape, still bent over and struggling beneath the drape. She patted his shoulder. "Smile for your father, Lucullus," she said. "We'll always remember this day."

Postman

Late in the afternoon he followed her out behind the house to the grove of cedar trees where the old caravan had come to rest. The trees formed a dark, dripping tent over the caravan's peeling roof.

She hesitated as they reached the steps up to the door. "It looks a bit sorry, I'm afraid."

Henry took in the battered trailer, propped up at one end with a trestle of cinder blocks and listing slightly. It looked as if it had been abandoned long ago.

When she put her foot on the bottom step, the caravan tilted under her weight. "Mind yourself," she said, but Henry's hands had already flown up, ready to catch her. "A stone under the front would fix that," she said, turning the metal latch to the door.

Inside, she twitched aside the curtain at the little window

over the bed, allowing a spill of gray, dirty light to fall on the pillow. The faded material of the curtain was patterned with a dark green tracery of leaves, odd little silver capsules, and pink flower shapes like poppies seen through a watery eye. A red woolen blanket had been folded at the end of the narrow berth, over the tufted white spread, a towel and washrag on top of that.

"Will it do?" She turned to Henry. "You won't mind? I thought you might enjoy the privacy." She looked anxiously at him.

Henry put his suitcase on the floor, realized it blocked the way, and shoved it with his foot. Still, he'd have to step over it to get in or out of the caravan.

"It's fine, Aunt," he said, though what he felt was a small wave of panic, a repulsion for the narrow little space, its dank stench, its miserable little window and modest curtain. He realized he'd have to go indoors to use the lavatory, or step out beneath the trees with their percussion of dripping rain. Last summer he'd slept in the house, but this year there were two more girl boarders, and there was no room for him indoors.

His aunt cast a critical eye over the space, the little cabinets with their scarred doors, the brown skins of masking tape with faded writing on them over the drawers, the carpet with its rusty iodine stains like ginger-colored birthmarks, splotched and uneven.

"Hard to remember this was all spanking new once," she said. "It was such a smart little thing when your uncle brought it home. Cozy." She squinted.

Henry looked around blankly at the bed, the tiny folded-up table, the shelves on wire hinges, everything compartmentalized, sealed away, the walls close by. The cabinet door under the sink had a jagged dent down the center, as if someone with a heavy boot had kicked it.

"Well, come along then." His aunt shooed Henry back out the door with her red hands, calluses blooming at the knuckles, her cardigan rolled at the wrists, like a child's. "You can unpack later. Would you like a wash? And then it'll be time for dinner. You can meet all the girls. We've chops and potatoes and spinach and blackberry pie. And stuffed tomatoes. They've been lovely this year."

Henry backed carefully down the steps, then paused to wait for his aunt while she closed the door and stepped unsteadily to the ground.

"You'll have to watch that in the dark," she said.

Henry followed her to the house. Black streaks of damp ran down its pale stuccoed facade in a varnished trail, as if the tall windows had been weeping. The muddy path ran with rivulets of filthy water. Henry and his aunt stepped together into the cold brick passageway between the outdoor larder and the coal shed, sweet-smelling black dust spilling from the sill. His aunt hurried on ahead of him through the back door and down the long hallway lined with the girl boarders' coats and boots. Henry paused in the doorway and looked back. The latch on the caravan's door had failed, and the door had fallen open. It gave the little trailer under the trees the feel of a place in which something sad had happened, long ago.

Inside, in the large and untidy kitchen, the windows had clouded with steam rising from the pan of potatoes boiling to a scum on the Aga. A huge pile of chops lay on the table in a mangled heap. Over the old fireplace where the Aga had been installed, the mantelpiece was crowded with a collection of plates and mugs, as well as a radio, some rubber currycombs, a saucer holding a heap of syringes with a yellowish residue inside, a dirty jar of psyllium to control colic in the horses, a black tin of ichthammol dressing. Stuck in a vase was a snapped-off branch flowering with red blossoms like tiny waving fingers. A broken bridle and a rope halter hung over the back of a chair.

His aunt stood by the table, holding a candle flame-down to drip a seal of wax into a saucer. She fixed the candle in place as Henry stepped into the kitchen. "We'll see if we can't find you a torch," she apologized, handing the candle to him. "But this will do if you want to read before you go to sleep tonight. Your mother says you're quite the reader. You've brought a book, have you?"

Henry shook his head. He'd forgotten books. He wasn't all that much of a reader, really. He'd read more when he was younger.

She looked surprised. "Well, there's magazines and such in the drawing room. Choose anything you like, anything that catches your fancy, though I fear it's all horsey business. Supper in half an hour." She turned away.

In the drawing room, the last moments of afternoon light had been released from a sudden rent in the clouds and poured in through the windows in a dusty, golden blur, making Henry blink as he stood in the doorway. In a little while, the light would fade and then withdraw, and the sun would set fully behind the trees at the bottom of the meadow. Henry had a sudden premonition—or was it only a memory, from previous summers?—of the farm and all the surrounding fields sunk in the complete blackness of night, each of them, his aunt and uncle, the girl boarders, himself, lying awake in their beds in the dark, waiting for something.

He moved carefully into the room, went to the bookcase, and looked up at the titles there. Behind him, the girls attending the first weeklong session of his aunt and uncle's summer pony camp were displayed over the furniture like a lambent assembly of fallen leaves, their shining heads resting against the faded upholstery, their downy arms thrown over chair backs, their legs curled beneath them or outstretched along the tired sofa cushions. Four of the girls had draped themselves in postures of fatigue over the unsteady card table beneath the windows; their fingers held fans of worn, creased playing cards. Another sat curled in a chair, her chin in her hand, staring into the cold fireplace. Two girls sharing a sofa, one at either end, appeared to have fallen asleep, their legs entangled. A few held books or magazines up before their faces, the pages rustling.

In their socks and woolen jerseys, their hair brushed for the late afternoon supper, the girls seemed completely at ease in this new place. Henry stood there staring at the bookshelves, and behind him the windows dimmed suddenly, as if a hand training a flashlight beam had moved on outside, still searching for something else. The impression of gleaming surfaces was gone, and the long room, with its tall windows and faded gold drapes, became shadowy. Now it was illuminated only by the old yellow-shaded lamps with their snarled tassels and fraying brown cords trailing over the carpets. And yet to Henry, as he turned around, it seemed perfectly composed, lit gently and experimentally as a stage might be in the scene before the revelation, the figures at rest but expectant, waiting for an interruption that they knew would change everything.

A few heads turned toward him as he left the room, the girls' dark eyes reflecting light, and then turned away again.

AT DINNER HE SAT across from a bristle-haired girl—one of the younger ones, Henry thought; she looked to be eleven or so. Her hair was a strange color, so blond it was nearly white, and contained ineffectually in an elastic at the nape of her neck. She was crying, and remained crying throughout the meal.

His aunt, passing around plates, stopped at the girl's shaking shoulder. "Would you care to use the telephone, dear?" she asked quietly. "Call home? They'll tell you it will be all right. You'll have a lovely time." But the girl had shaken her head, miserable, and said nothing.

Henry, busy with his food and the platters that kept appearing at his elbow to be passed along the table, struggled to keep up. He felt as though he couldn't catch a mouthful before someone called for the salt, or the milk pitcher, or the bread and butter, the voices swelling around him like foreign music on a radio station not quite tuned in properly. He knocked his glass over and jabbed the girl to his left with his elbow trying to catch it. Between awkward bites, he watched the crying girl, her strangled noises, through his own averted eyes.

A girl in a handmade blue jumper leaned toward her. "Would you like me to help you tack up later, Nicola?" she asked, her fingers resting lightly on the girl's forearm. "You've such a pretty pony. I love the shape of her head— don't you? I think you've got one of the prettiest."

The girl Nicola didn't look up, but stopped crying for a moment. "Yes," she said quietly into her lap. But that was all.

The conversation among the twelve boarders at the table wore on with the steady patter of many drums, a syncopation halted now and then by the presence of the crying girl. Everyone's eyes would slide unavoidably toward her at the same moment, it seemed, as if they had all become simultaneously exhausted by the effort of pretending she was not among them, weeping as if her heart would break.

Outside, a light rain sloped down the windows. A sad pink light, boiled thin, filtered through the black trees at the end of the field. The tablecloth stretched away endlessly before Henry. He gazed out over the chipped pitchers, the platters with their few remaining sunken tomatoes or curling chops, the butter dish with its ruined lump, the wet stain spreading out from beneath his own glass, the tea mugs with their quarter inch of cold tea.

"Could have had better weather for the first day, couldn't we?" Henry's uncle nodded to Henry at the far end of the table. "But I think it'll be all right for the bonfire tonight. You lot still want to have the bonfire?"

The girls chorused their approval and all heads turned toward him, toward the tolerant wag of his jowls as he gazed round, his long cheeks wobbling as he feigned astonishment, gaped, stared from side to side. "Well, we *are* a daring crowd, aren't we?"

He needed a haircut, Henry realized as he watched him, trying to account for the change in his uncle since the previous summer—the way in which he seemed to have grown unkempt or seedy, as though he harbored a terrible secret about himself and was making only the barest effort to conceal it in public. *He's letting himself go,* Henry thought, and another wave of dread came over him.

Speaking over the girls' heads, his uncle addressed Henry's aunt. "Catch Ned, would you, Helen? Ask him to ferry some wood down to the pasture? Under the trees I think we'll be all right. Henry, you'll help the girls?"

Henry nodded.

"Time to digest then, and we'll set out at half past?" His uncle pushed back from the table, pulling the napkin free from his collar.

In the drawing room again, Henry moved past the boarders. Revived by the meal, they were chattering noisily. He stole a look at the stricken girl alone in a chair near the window, her face buried in her arms, but her back was quiet and she seemed to have stopped sobbing. He riffled through the selection of newspapers and magazines in the basket by the fire, chose a magazine, and then retreated with it under his arm down the hall, past the kitchen and the cozy Aga, where his uncle sat drawn up to the long table, his glasses on his nose, looking through some papers.

"Henry!" His uncle caught sight of him. "Go on down to the barn in just a bit, will you? They'll be hours tacking up otherwise. You can get them hopping, there's a good fellow." He looked up at Henry and took off his glasses. "He doesn't look a bit like Andy, does he? Or any of *us.*" He spoke to his wife as if Henry couldn't hear him. And then he addressed Henry himself, as if Henry had just come into proper focus before him. "I think you're going to look more like your mother's side of the family after all." He paused, still looking at Henry in that vague way, as if he were thinking of something else entirely. "And a good thing, *that!*" he said then suddenly, loudly, as if he'd made a joke. "A fine thing that! Yes? Ha ha!"

HE WAS COUNTING the days. "A month," his father had said. "You've nothing better to do with yourself, in any case, and we shan't need you here. Richard and Helen could use the help. Come on, Henry. It wasn't so bad last year, was it? All those girls? Should be lovely! Come on, be a sport."

But Henry had not wanted to go, though it was true he'd no other plans. His parents would take him along to Cornwall for a holiday at the end of the summer before school resumed, but his own ambition—to work for the mechanic in the village retooling motorcycles—had been dashed when the man had turned him down apologetically. "I can't really afford to have you, Henry," he'd said, wiping grimy hands on his overalls, "not so's it'd be worth your while. You're welcome to hang about, though, much as you like."

So Henry had gone to Stoke Charity after all. At fourteen, he didn't have many choices in his life. But heading out toward the barn that evening, he thought he should have tried harder with the garage, wondered why he'd given up so easily.

He shied away from his aunt and uncle's poverty-stricken life, their farm fallen on such hard times that the pony camps in the summer had been mounted to help meet expenses. He did not like the girls—their appetites, the way their mouths worked as they ate, thoughtlessly taking in the food his aunt prepared, sometimes complaining about how rotten it all was. He begrudged them every mouthful. They did not realize how their presence degraded him, degraded them all.

His aunt and uncle had undertaken the camp venture with a dignity that made Henry burn with embarrassment. Their detailed arrangements, their colossal energy for entertaining their girl boarders—the work of it all exhausted him unnaturally: clean sheets twice a week, and three meals a day, plus high tea at four; the bane of a dozen unreliable ponies with chopped manes and, in a few, an evil eye. He had spent a month of the previous summer there as well and knew the labor of having so many girls about the place, especially with the farm itself still requiring much of his uncle's attention; some of the cows had gotten into something poisonous the previous summer, falling painfully to their knees at the heavy bank of yews that divided the house from the fields, and dying a slow and cumbersome death. They'd had to be burned.

His uncle hired a neighbor to run the riding lessons in the ring in the morning. She was a bustling woman with a bright, energetic manner and sharp breath, Henry noticed, as though she held a eucalyptus lozenge in her cheek. His uncle led half the group on an afternoon trail ride, and Henry took the slow ponies and their tentative beginning riders for a rambling hour's walk to the quarry and back, finishing with a trot, the girls jouncing along behind him, through the woods and across the fields closest to home. His aunt, with her chapped hands and distracted manner, ruled over the mess of the kitchen with its noisy plumbing and windowsills of crumbling plaster, preparing the enormous meals for the boarders, the small radio between the china nightingales on the mantel playing classical music.

"You'll have a host of pretty young ladies on your arm again this summer," his aunt had said to Henry when she'd fetched him at the bus that left him off at the post office in the village earlier that afternoon. "Haven't you grown tall and handsome!" She'd waited while he climbed into the car beside her, and then she'd leaned over and kissed his cheek quickly. "Thank you for coming, Henry," she murmured. "Richard's so appreciative."

But Henry did not expect to have any of these girls—this week the youngest was ten, the eldest thirteen—on his arm, or taking note of him in any way. Last summer the girls had treated him as a servant, someone to help them wrestle with tack or muck out stalls or bridle an ill-tempered pony. His own sullenness had caused him to distance them; he understood that, and the girls had kept away in turn, sensing his hostility. As a child he had measured big things by throwing his arms wide open to suggest their enormity. But no gesture could begin to express how much he hated being there, being put to work in this way. The girls made him feel as though nothing better would ever come his way, that he and his family—his own parents struggling with a small grocery, his aunt and uncle with their farm—were losing their foothold in a terrifying slide toward a dimly understood ruin, while the girl boarders went on placing their filthy boots into his cupped hands to mount their ponies, one after another.

When he saw himself in a mirror—there was one in his parents' bedroom, on the back of the door— Henry tried to assess himself realistically. He was tall for his age, almost six feet, with long, thin arms and legs, and a soft brown mustache starting at his upper lip. He supposed he was not a bad-looking boy—he could identify ugliness and counted himself lucky that he was not among the boys his age who were shamed by pimples or rolls of fat at their waists—but he did not like something about his own posture, the apology contained in the slope of his shoulders, or the extreme thinness of his neck, which made him look overeager.

Sometimes last summer he had watched the girl boarders—their seductive ease, the shape of their teeth, the moles on their necks or cheeks. They had a special smell, the scent of girls' deodorant, glazed with the salty odor of the ponies and with their own, particular, unidentifiable fragrances. As they filed past him into the ring for lessons in the morning, he'd watched their backsides straddling the ponies, their handfuls of buttocks and their winged hipbones, their digging ankles flailing the stubborn ponies' flanks. The sight of them gave him a wrenching feeling in his stomach, shamed him.

IN THE BARN he grabbed bridles, fit bits between the ponies' protesting, slavering jaws, led them to the rail outside. The tradition of a bareback ride to the end of the field, to the copse of oak trees, with its vault of high branches and crumbling hearth for a fire, was part of the summer's pattern of entertainments. The first night always began with this ride, but Henry wished fervently for the rain to begin again and drown the adventure.

At last, the clouds hurrying away toward the horizon, they turned the ponies and their riders out, just before sunset. Ned, the hired man who had been with Henry's aunt and uncle for as long as Henry could remember, had stirred up a presentable bonfire at the end of the field by the stream. Henry helped the girls mount, throwing them high over the ponies' shoulders, letting them go roughly as if they were hot to the touch. A few glanced at him, surprised. Most did not seem to notice his handling, placed their muddy boots into his palm, shoved off.

The younger ones kept to the high shoulder of the lane, away from the muddy ruts, though a pony slipped from time to time, stumbling in the wet and matted grass. The girls laughed, called to one another, the sound fading away. The little band spread out.

But there was, as always, one girl falling behind the others.

There was always one, struggling with her reluctant pony in the gathering darkness, the rising mist now lit sideways by the long, low rays of the descending sun. Henry leaned on a post, watching; the yews bordering the lane dripped, stones clattered under the ponies' hooves. The straggling girl and her pony fell farther and farther behind; the dark shapes of the others wavered ahead of her, single file. When they reached the distant grove of oaks, the girls dismounted, sliding off the ponies' backs, their riotous voices sounding from afar like music playing inside a box whose lid is lifted briefly and then replaced, lifted and replaced. In their rain ponchos they darted around the distant fire like small, dark birds testing their wings, jumping on mincing feet.

The last girl—it was the bristle-haired one, of *course*, Henry thought—and her pony had now left the lane entirely and stood some distance into the field, the pony grazing determinedly, shaking its head angrily from time to time. The girl on its back had given up and lain down on the pony's neck. The pair were slowly vanishing in the growing dark.

His uncle stepped up beside Henry. "Go and fetch her, will you?" he asked, nodding his head toward the bristle-haired girl in the field. And then he strode on, a hamper in his arms containing the instant coffee and tea things, a tray of iced buns covered with a tea towel balanced on top.

Henry looked down into the field, the obscuring dark, and as he did, all things seemed suddenly to separate before his eyes, the world pulled apart at its invisible seams like the mesh of a fine cloth melting. Voice and tree, the lumped, uneven line of the horizon, the eggs boiling to a dark scum in the kitchen, the distant flame of the bonfire under the black trees, the big house sinking slowly behind him, the tilting caravan—all these seemed not to belong together anymore, as though the essential mathematics that held them in gravity's matrix had collapsed, each sensation un-loosed, beyond his reach, uncontainable. He started, registered the far-off child supine on the pony's back, her head buried. He willed his feet to move.

"Come along, then," he said, breathless, arriving at her side, his feet soaked. He jerked the pony's mouth up from the turf. The girl lay with her face averted, her arms drawn up against her sides.

She did not raise her head. "Are you ill?" he said.

Still she did not answer, and Henry waited, unsure. "She's only stubborn," he said then, tiredly. "You've just got to keep her away from the grass. Come *on*, Rosie." He cinched the reins under the pony's bristled lower lip. "Sit *up*, will you?" he said to the girl. "You might *help*."

The girl pulled herself up, turned her face away, a sob loosening from her throat.

"You're not *still* crying?" He was mostly amazed. How could anyone cry for that long? Did things matter so very much? Yet in a moment his amazement became frustration —he was furious suddenly to be out there in the middle of the field alone with her. He was horrified by her absolute lack of dignity.

"I want to go home," the girl said quietly, stiff at his tone.

"Well, no one's going to come and fetch you tonight," Henry said roughly. "You can go in the morning if you want. No one will stop you."

But he was immediately ashamed. "Come on. Let's join the others," he said. "Don't mind Rosie. She's only a pig." He took the reins from the girl and led the pony forward— the girl still as a stone on the animal's back, her face turned aside, her hands winding in the pony's mane—across the long meadow with its recumbent shadows and the sharp, beery smell of wet grass.

"It would be my dad," the girl said then.

"What?"

"It would be my dad who would come and fetch me."

Henry said nothing. He was watching where his feet went; the ground here was full of holes, dangerous pits where one could turn an ankle and go down.

"My name's Nicola," the girl said quietly. "And you're Henry."

"That's right," said Henry, who had been introduced to them all at the table. "That's the both of us, then."

Henry's aunt came to meet them as Henry advanced into the clearing beneath the trees with the pony and Nicola, un-smiling, on its back. "*Here's* Rosie. Never one to miss an extra bite now, are you?" She addressed the pony fondly, then took the reins from Henry and rested her hand on the girl's narrow thigh. "Come along, Nicola." She smiled up at the girl. "Have a cup of tea."

The child dropped from the pony's back, her face set. Henry's aunt bent to tie the reins to the ground tether and then steered Nicola gently toward the fire and the tumbled logs with their mossy backs, set a few yards away from the flames. A few of the other girls sat there already, their hands wrapped around the brown enamel mugs, their expressions dazed in the light, their eyes fixed upon the flames. Henry lifted the lid of the hamper, took in the sweet dairy smell of condensed milk.

"Henry, fix a mug for Nicola, won't you?" his aunt said, taking a seat on a log, reaching into the fire with a stick to collapse the fragile framework of burning twigs and raise the flame. Henry lifted the kettle from its tripod over the fire, poured two cups, the rising steam traveling up his arm like a damp sleeve. Water from the trees dripped into the fire, issuing a crack and a hiss. He passed a cup to Nicola, who was seated beside his aunt, and she raised her two hands oddly as if to receive a chalice, an item of religious significance, as if this were something more than tea he passed to her, as if it were some secret between them. Henry saw how small her hands were around the mug, how when she raised it to her mouth, her lips parted like a bird's beak against the hot liquid, her eyes squinting shut. Her hair, her strange silvery hair, flowered around her head in the dusk; for a second Henry thought to touch it, to push his palm flat against it, disturb its glittering, delicate surface, so light and fragile.

Other girls ran beneath the trees by the dark stream, sugar from the buns on their chins and cheeks, galloping like the ponies, knees high. "Tetch, tetch, go along," they cried, their hands flailing imaginary crops, making a circuit among the dark tree trunks, jumping the fallen branches. Henry felt them through his feet, felt their thudding on the soft, wet ground.

"A lot of galloping guineas," Aunt Helen said, putting her arm around Nicola's shoulder, pulling her close. And Nicola, her cup before her face, searched Henry with her eyes from her vantage point in his aunt's embrace.

"I've my own pony, at home," she said then, almost too quietly to be heard.

"Have you?" Helen said, when no one else spoke.

"Yes. But she's ill," Nicola said. "That's why I'm here."

Across from Nicola and his aunt, on the other side of the fire, Henry looked at the child, at her small white face, her corona of strange hair, her body pulled aside into his aunt's bosom, and in her eyes, fixed upon him, he saw the lie, the fiction of this pony of Nicola's; startled that he knew it as surely as if she had confessed it to him, a voice in his ear like a reed's whisper, thin and confiding, he turned away quickly. He brought his own cup to his mouth. When he drank, too fast, the hot tea burned his throat and he coughed, sputtering, wiping a sleeve over his mouth.

"All right, Henry?" his aunt asked. "Come in now, girls!"

One by one the girls advanced to the fire from the ring of trees, received a cup of tea or coffee, grew still. The sky dropped above them, black at its domed crown, a thin, wet-looking line of purple at the western horizon. The fire shook and settled, releasing plumes of orange sparks into the smoky air. Henry thought of Guy Fawkes Day in his own village, the massive bonfire mounted each November to burn the effigy of the Catholic traitor to the king, the shirtsleeves of the crude likeness stuffed with hay, the blaze licking at the grostesquerie's cast-off coat and trousers, potatoes roasting in the embers at his bound feet. Each year, Henry and his parents and their neighbors stood by, dumbly watching as the figure was consumed by flame, though Henry never really wanted to stay for that part. When he was a small child, it had frightened him.

He looked up when his aunt began a round, singing in a wobbling tenor, "White coral bells, upon a slender stalk; lilies of the valley deck my garden walk," and the girls' high, pretty voices took up behind her in the song, exactly like church bells yielding one falling tone to the next, music raining down from a steeple.

When they had finished, Henry and Ned, a perpetual cigarette in his hand, packed away the tea things in the hamper, helped the girls shinny onto the ponies' backs, saw them back to the stable, where they rubbed down the long hairs on the ponies' bellies, fed them apples from the wormy tree, kissed their deep necks. Nicola, lifted like air to Rosie's back in Ned's pincerlike arms, steered home without trouble, Rosie eagerly inclined toward the stable. There, the child was oddly high-spirited, Henry saw, as if she was relieved to be back, this first night almost done, vanquished. She behaved affectionately with Rosie, elaborately nuzzling the pony's warm shoulder, trotting off toward the house at last in a group of other girls.

There they mounted the stairs, where Henry imagined they each took a washrag to their dirty faces one after the next in the cold lavatory, rinsed their teeth, and raising their arms, slipped into flowered nightdresses and then between the sheets.

By the time Henry reached the caravan with its guttering candle, the only light left on in the house was in the kitchen, where his aunt Helen would be laying out dishes for breakfast, working late into the night, stars fading in the sky, sometimes a tear in her eye from tiredness.

IT WAS THE SOUND of the church bell in Stoke Charity—its iron clapper striking within its heavy cup, a deep, solemn note that rang from the center of the earth— that woke Henry each morning that first week, sweating inside the rough sheets. His eyelids flickered against the seeping light. He turned, rubbed his face into the thin pillow, felt its slippery feathers part and gather like wet mud. He was too tall for the caravan's bed; his feet hung off the end. This morning, the next-to-last day of the first week, he listened to the metallic drip of water on the roof. The sound was so casual and irregular that he could not tell if it was raining, or if water was simply trailing slowly down the fingers of the cedars in the aftermath of a rain. His candle had burned down to the saucer, the wick drowned in its own pool of greasy wax.

Henry got out of bed, stepped around the back of the caravan, and released a stream of urine into the mist. *Only three weeks left,* he thought.

"YOU SHOULDN'T BE MEAN, Sybil," Henry heard one of the girls saying outside the tack room. It was the fattish one, her face bunched like a pig's; Dierdre, Henry thought her name was.

Henry was filling feed buckets in the annex off the tack room, turning aside, hunched and secretive, to put a handful of the molasses-threaded grain into his own mouth from time to time. The accused Sybil sat cross-legged on the floor of the tack room, cleaning a pony's bridle, her legs with their long blond hairs folded beneath her.

Henry turned. Dierdre stood at the doorway, holding a saddle in her arms over her round belly, which was cinched tight with a beaded belt; her face was flushed, prickled with heat. It was almost noon. Half the class of riders was finishing their lesson in the ring. The others, done for the morning, were cleaning up, trailing down the lane to the house to wash up before the last midday meal. By this time tomorrow, Henry had thought a little earlier, they would all be gone, and there would be a day to clean up again before the next lot came Sunday afternoon.

"It's all a lie. She hasn't got any pony at all," replied Sybil carelessly, not looking up. "She shouldn't lie. It's a sin."

"But it doesn't matter, does it?" Dierdre persisted.

Henry heard the effort in her voice, the bravery of it, to stand up to this older girl, pretty and blond.

"She's crying now, anyway," Dierdre insisted. "You've made her cry."

"Well, that's nothing new," Sybil retorted.

"And her mum is ill, as well," Dierdre continued. And stoutly, repeating herself, she added, "You shouldn't be so nasty."

Sybil shrugged. "She's a little twit," she said. And then, quick and sharp, "And *you're* a fatty. Mind your own business, why don't you?"

Henry saw Dierdre stiffen, her buttocks clench. "I've a

thyroid," she said after a second, very loudly. "I've a *medical* condition. And *you're* a very mean girl." She dumped the saddle on its peg and turned away, angry and embarrassed in front of Henry, who was watching from the annex. But Henry gave a silent cheer for Dierdre. Sybil did not look up.

Henry hoisted the feed buckets, wandered down the aisle between the stalls. He realized as he went that he was listening anxiously for Nicola, for the familiar sound of her crying, but he could not find her. He didn't know what he would do if he came upon her, prostrate on the floor of the barn, or huddled in the corner of a stall; she was always in postures of such extreme despair. He would like to pat the fat Dierdre on the back, clap her shoulder with congratulations for her stout heart, though.

He knew Nicola lied; she lied egregiously, and with no apparent provocation. She did it particularly in front of him, he had noticed, within his earshot, as though wishing him not only to believe her and be impressed, but also to rescue her from her fibbing, both in equal measure, equally painful to confront. He had been careful to ignore her over the past week, even more so than he ignored the other girls, his unconcern held up before him like his hands over his ears or a braid of garlic over his heart; but still he sought her out, he knew he did, catching sight of her and her wild hair like a freakish white crown and waiting to see what she would do next.

He had never in his life been around anyone like her. He could feel the heat and the cold running through her when he passed her in the barns, as though she emanated such ferocious extremes of emotion that her own body could not contain them, but instead threw them his way as though giving off excess bursts of electricity. He was aghast at her, at her lack of caution, her stupid stories, at the way she threw herself to the brink time and time again. And yet, she made him think of the movies—he'd seen everything in the damp and smelly cinema at home, with its creaking armchairs and mossy headrests. And when he saw Nicola, or thought of her, he imagined lifting her in his arms and bearing her swiftly away from some mortal danger, her head lolling upon his shoulder, her eyes opening and meeting his with an expression of joy and triumph as he set her down safely.

But Nicola was nowhere to be found. If she had cried because Sybil had been mean to her, she had stopped by now, or had taken herself off somewhere alone. She did that sometimes. Henry felt contrite, thinking that Nicola's mother really *was* ill, as Dierdre had said. He'd heard Nicola say this but hadn't known whether to believe her or not.

But maybe her mother was dying, he thought. Maybe that explained everything.

HENRY STOPPED AT the ring to watch the last of the lesson. For a week now he had watched the shifting alliances among the girls, their affections for one another so fierce and provocative one moment, so easily changed to scorn at the next. He was horrified and fascinated at the risks they took with one another, their swift recoveries, pairs forming and parting company as though they had no memory, no conscience, as though each moment was freshly invented. In the ring, though, at their lessons, they behaved with gracious democracy, each girl doing her part to keep the circle even, to take her turn in time, each silently assessing the group's collective pace, working to keep it steady, like a wheel. He admired the common order of it, so unlike the business of boys at play, where each took his place and tolerated no encroachment there. Boys worked to widen their own circles by brute force, by the feral warning implied in a facial expression, by the circumference made with their own outstretched arms. And yet it all dissolved so quickly, he thought, this harmony among the girls; released from the group lesson with its charmed ability to produce fair play, they became dangerous and elliptical. It only looked as though you had a friend, if you were a girl, he thought. But really there was no one to help you but yourself. And if you could not help yourself, eventually you would be torn to bits.

AT THE TABLE at noon he took his place by his aunt.

"Tonight's the party, Henry." She ladled soup into his bowl, a vinegary beef broth, rich with potato and turnip. Surreptitiously he watched the girls exchanging dark looks as bowls were placed before them and they smelled the soup. "You remember the McIntyre boys?" she went on. "Loren, Kyle . . . Tony's the youngest? I've asked them for after supper, for cakes and coffee. They'll be a bit of a hurrah for the girls on their last night. And some company for you. I'm sorry we haven't had them here before now. What a busy time it's been." She sighed, sniffed, recollected. "I think Kyle is your age exactly. Do you remember?"

"They're the rugby players." Henry tore at his bread, sopped it in his soup. "The redheaded ones."

"Like their father." His aunt nodded.

Henry's uncle looked up from his soup. "Will you take the group round to the quarry and back this afternoon, Henry?" he asked. "I'll take the other lot over the downs."

"All right," Henry replied, but he was thinking of the party, of the McIntyre boys with their high spirits and cigarettes stolen outside the larder, their insinuations and dirty mouths. He resented their interruption. Though he held himself aloof from the girls, this week he had felt himself exploiting their dependence on him, especially the younger ones, like Nicola. He had a feeling of tilting power when he reached down from his own horse to catch the reins of a misbehaving pony, its rider wide-eyed on its back. He had almost enjoyed rescuing them, his thigh brushing a girl's as he pulled her pony in close to him, roughly. He had heard himself giving gruff instructions, like a much older man.

NICOLA WAS AMONG the small group of six that he took out that afternoon, a lead line coiled on his saddle, his head bare; he disdained a hard hat.

The sky threatened, gray and withdrawn, but Henry calculated that they could still ride to the quarry and back before the rain, which had arrived almost every day dependably at five, just as the girls returned from their afternoon ride. They always rushed through the downpour into the house after rubbing down the soaked ponies, the hard water slapping their shirts against their backs, drenching their hair.

He leaned from the saddle now to hold the gate ajar for the girls, who ambled past him, dreamy-eyed the way they often became in the afternoon, hardly working at all, just letting the ponies carry them, one behind the next like an obedient camel train. Nicola was last. Henry waited until she was almost beside him before looking up directly into her eyes. For a second they held each other's gaze. And then it was too much for Henry. It was as if things he did not intend to say were pouring out of him, and he was holding them out helplessly in his hands, overwhelmed.

He turned his burning face away, swatted Rosie hard on the rear so that Nicola lurched backward in the saddle. He twisted hurriedly to latch the gate and then spurred past her to the head of the line. Nicola had recovered, he saw as he rode past her; she looked after him eagerly, nearly rising off the saddle with a queer excitement.

They meandered slowly through the fields, the ponies picking their way, heads down, trying their teeth on the grass from time to time. Henry, sleepy himself under the quiet, widening sky with its white eye, almost forgot the girls were behind him. He started when one of them called out, "Henry, you've a butterfly on your back."

The girls giggled as Henry wrenched around to see the monarch flutter off over the tall grass.

He thought he could feel Nicola's eyes boring into his back at the place where the butterfly had alighted.

By the time they had circled the quarry, with its empty green pool of limy water at the bottom of the white basin, the sky had darkened considerably, going from ash to a deep purple, like a bruise. A wind picked up, restlessly furrowing the hay in the fields. Henry looked at the sky, felt the rain gathering. He stopped, trying to recall the path through the woods, a shortcut back to the farm.

"Do you mind?" He reined in. "I used to know a path back through the woods. It think it's a bit quicker. Let's go that way."

He turned his pony. The others, straggling, fell in behind him, back around the thin, crumbling path at the edge of the quarry. By a monkey puzzle tree, set like a marker at the periphery, the woods parted to form a cavelike entrance into the dark. Henry dipped his head to nose the pony into the gloom, then heard thunder rumble high above the trees. The pony behind him skittered to the side. He felt his pulse quicken unpleasantly.

The narrow path, notched by tree roots, climbed a hill. Henry moved his pony forward; the other ponies' hooves clattered behind him, and saddles creaked. And then the sound of the rain, released like birdshot, suddenly smacked the high branches overhead. Henry felt the urgency in his own pony as it stumbled forward, straining at the reins. He wished they were all safe inside the stable.

When a flash of lightning illuminated the woods with an explosive green glow, an instant of rapturous light, he heard a quick sliding sound behind him, the alarmed combustion of cracking branches, and Nicola's cry. He turned sharp to see Rosie driving off into the thicket of trees, galloping wildly ahead, Nicola clinging to the reins.

"Turn her, turn her head!" Henry shouted, but Rosie thrashed on, breaking branches, forcing herself through the trees, disappearing into the terrible light. The girls behind him were struck silent, though one began to cry after a minute, frightened, her own pony sidestepping quickly in alarm off the path into the slippery leaves, wide-eyed. They jostled one another, collided behind him. Henry raked up the reins, spun in the saddle, turned to the girls behind him, furious; but they presented him only with the white of their faces, their utter dependence on him. He turned back, peered ahead, hauling on his frantic pony's mouth. He could not think what to do—follow Nicola or stay with the others. The rain began to reach them now through the leaves, and his pony decided things by jumping forward as if bitten; the others came behind quickly, the rain falling fast now. At first Henry could hear only the sound of the ponies panting behind him, and Rosie crashing through the branches somewhere ahead in the distance. And then they all heard Nicola's high, wide scream and the sound of a large branch tearing free, the sound of the world rent at a weak seam.

Breaking free from the woods at last and into the full force of the wide-open downpour, Henry saw the racing pony up ahead across the field, running wildly toward home, and he spurred his own pony forward, its feet hard against the ground. As he drew even with the runaway, his hands bunching the reins far forward along his pony's neck, he leaned over, nearly losing his seat, to grab Rosie's dangling reins and try to drag her to a trembling stop. He was breathing so hard he could feel his ribs sawing in and out.

The other girls emerged from the trees behind him, riding sloppily, bouncing loosely in their saddles, all pretense of control gone. Several were in tears. The rain, so fierce for those few moments, slackened suddenly and adjusted itself to a thick, steady mist. Henry hauled hard on Rosie, at last halting the trembling pony, who was frothing white at the mouth. Foam was splattered all along her heaving neck and shoulders.

Henry wiped his eye with his elbow, secured Rosie's reins

in his hand, looked up into Nicola's face. "Nicola," he said, panting, and his whole body shuddered with relief to have her within his grasp. It was like having thrown something overboard, something you did not mean to toss away so easily, and then snatching it back in an instant of the world's amazing forgiveness, just when you thought it was lost forever.

But his relief died in his throat. Nicola was staring straight ahead, her face awash with red, a curtain of slippery blood pulsing from a long gash above her temple.

"Oh my God." How had she kept her seat? he thought wildly. How had she kept her seat?

Another girl came up past them, going fast; she turned her head to see Nicola, screamed.

"Go," Henry shouted at her as her pony hurried on. "You can see the house."

He leaned in toward Nicola. The other girls came crashing past them and took in, appalled, Nicola's bloody face, then disappeared into the mist toward the farm.

Henry reached and touched Nicola's arm. He turned her head to look at him. Blood fell from her cheek onto his hand.

Nicola put her hand to her head, touched the place above her eye, grimaced. Her hand came away drenched with blood. She gagged, turned aside.

"OK," Henry whispered. "You're going to be OK."

Nicola nodded, her hand roving experimentally, lightly, over her face; blood fell down her shirt, dripped onto the saddle horn.

Henry swallowed hard; he had to close his eyes for a moment. When he opened them, raised his chin, the world

reeled for an instant, land and sky jostling in the picture, set-
tling, everything ringed with stars, electric points of light.

He kicked his pony, pulled Rosie in close, led them home,
Nicola behind him, staring ahead through her bloody hair.

"YOU'LL HAVE QUITE the shiner, as well." His aunt
leaned toward Nicola in a chair in the kitchen, pressing ice
wrapped in a cloth over the girl's temple. Nicola, stripped
of her wet and bloody clothes, sat wrapped in a blanket,
her stained camisole hiding her thin chest, the knots of her
nipples like tiny swelling corms. Her hair, unloosed, was
matted with blood. Dierdre patted at it ineffectually with
a soaked washrag.

A few of the other girls crowded at the kitchen door.
"She'll be all right?" one asked quietly.

Henry's aunt dabbed at Nicola's face. "Dr. Warren's given
her five lovely, neat stitches, right in the eyebrow, so there
won't be any scar to be seen. She's got quite a headache,
haven't you, Nicola? But I think she's earned her medal today! Been through the Wars of the Roses, haven't you?"

She glanced up at the girls in the doorway. "One of you
be a love and run up and fetch her a blouse, would you?"

Henry came in through the back larder passage, shoulders
low, sopping footprints trailing behind on the floor. He'd
seen Dr. Warren's car leaving at the gate.

He stopped at the sight of Nicola on the chair, the white
points of her shoulders, the brilliant hair, the ruined face. He
swallowed hard against the queasiness rising in his stomach
at the sight of her. The girls in the doorway watched him.

"I've come to say I'm sorry," he said.

His aunt turned to him briefly, smiled, turned back to Nicola, to her ministrations. "There you are. Oh, it was an accident, Henry. It wasn't your fault. Such things *will* happen. There's always one runaway pony in the lot. Go on," she said, tapping Nicola's knee. "Tell him you're all right. Relieve the lad of his guilt."

Nicola looked up at him. Her face was white as chalk. But she smiled. "She says I won't have any scar."

A sudden laugh, relief, broke free from Henry. He stepped forward, the child's eyes swallowing him, the gash through her eyebrow sewn shut with black thread. Reaching his hand forward, he touched her forehead, felt her flesh dimple under his finger; he was astonished at the softness of it, the way her skin gave slightly beneath his hand, the delicious delicacy of it.

I'm older now, he thought. *I'm years older than I was earlier.*

He looked up to see the girls in the door, gave a mock growl. "What are you lot staring at?" he said, pretending to lunge at them. They giggled, scattered down the hall.

When he looked down at Nicola again, her eyes were closed as if she had fallen asleep. She looked magical, like something drowned and raised from the troughs in the fields, the breath of life suppressed in her narrow chest, waiting. His aunt smoothed the child's tangled hair, helped her to stand, wrapping the blanket over her shoulders. "Let's put your head under the tap and then have you a bit of rest," she said. "You'll want to be right for the party tonight. I suspect you'll make quite an impression."

• • •

LATER, WHEN HIS AUNT rang the bell for dinner, the girls flowed into the dining room, scraping their chairs back from the table, but Nicola did not appear with them. Henry stood beside his aunt in the kitchen, helping her carry platters of sausages to the table. The girls were dressed up for the occasion, some of them in skirts. Several of the older ones had painted their lips, touched rouge to their cheeks, darkened their lashes with mascara.

"Isn't she coming down?" he asked his aunt.

"Who? Nicola?" She handed him a platter of peas and carrots, gave him an inquisitive look. "No, I've taken her up a cup of soup."

Henry took his seat. The McIntyre boys and also the Hughes-Onslow twins, Lawrence and Martin, arrived at the door. Chairs were found for them; they fitted themselves in among the girls, who, once breathless with excitement, were suddenly polite as could be, their usual riotousness draining away in the presence of the new arrivals and replaced with a primness, calculated and stiff.

"We're a bit late with the meal," his aunt apologized. "We had quite an adventure this afternoon."

After dinner the group withdrew to the sitting room. The girls, princesses, led the way carefully. The boys stood awkwardly by the bookshelves, scanning the spines of the books; the girls took seats before the fire, two or more to a chair, nestling. Henry lurked in the doorway. His aunt called to him: "Henry, come fetch this tray?"

He walked back to the kitchen, where his aunt was stacking plates on a tray beside a cake iced with powdered sugar, jam between its layers, and a plate of graham biscuits, frosted with bitter chocolate. "Come back for the coffee, would you?" she asked.

Henry set the tray down on a table by the fire in the sitting room. One of the girls sat up, looking over the sweets. "Shall I slice it?" she asked him, suddenly subservient, indicating the cake. Henry shrugged. He had no interest in this affair.

When he came back, the boys had moved over to the fire and were accepting plates of cake from the hands of the girls. Talk had sprung up among them. Henry watched the girls toss their heads, run their hands to the back of their necks to lift their hair, arch their bodies.

He wondered what Nicola was doing upstairs. He had an image of her, laid out on the bed, still as a corpse, her face white, her hair with its elaborate crimps and folds and curls flowing away over the pillow, her hands folded. He was so involved with this picture that he did not recognize her for a second when she appeared in the door of the sitting room, the fat Dierdre behind her, smiling.

The girl looked absurd, medieval, swathed in a too-large dress that Henry took to be Dierdre's, a white, shirred cotton affair with laces on the bodice crosshatched over Nicola's narrow chest. Her hair had been fixed into a bun bursting at her neck, its coils springing loose. Her face, with its purpling wound and clenched eye, looked macabre. Dierdre stood behind her, protective, maternal.

"Good lord. What happened to *you?*" Martin Hughes-Onslow set his fork down slowly on his plate.

"A tree hit me," said Nicola, in a new voice, smooth. She advanced across the room.

"I should say it did," Martin said, laughing. "Well, I hope you hit it back."

"Oh, I did," Nicola said, reaching to her head. "With this."

The boys laughed, the girls joining them. "Have some cake, Nicola," said one.

"Let's have a game," proposed one of the girls. And, bold, she suggested, "Let's play postman."

The boys chuckled, shuffled. The girls darted their heads toward one another, giggling, conspiratorial. They rose to fetch paper to tear into strips, into the letters each would blindly draw, sending couples, each party unknown to the other, to the dark hallway to complete the instructions on the letter: a handshake, a bow, a curtsy; a confession; most daring, a kiss. One girl jumped for the lights, extinguished all but two, the pair by the fire, so that the children, close under the lamplight, appeared to a far eye utterly innocent, magical, so absorbed in their game that they were unaware of the darkness encroaching on their circle, the menacing outdoors, where the dark shapes of tree and shrub, low-lying stable and whinnying pony, rocked loose from their foundations, wavered, petals of black falling open.

Two by two, the children disappeared, returned to the circle, giggling and blushing. Kyle McIntyre had gotten his arm about a girl's waist. The Hughes-Onslow boys were cornered by a triangle of girls, three seated on their knees, cozy, laughing. They waited, breathed in, for the next to draw her marked slip of paper.

Nicola, hesitating, took one as the hat was passed, rose quickly to her feet and stood still, staring at it. The girls giggled wildly. "Go on!" they said. "Nicola's got it! Go on, Nicola." And they pushed her from the room.

The hat was passed round. Henry reached in, took his slip, saw the mark on its reverse. He rose on unsteady legs.

"Oooh, it's *Henry*," squealed the girls as if he were their best friend, as if they had adored him all week long and were now championing him as the best and brightest among them.

"Shhh!" exhorted the others. "She'll hear who it *is!*"

"Now there's a face to launch a thousand ships." One of the boys laughed, low.

But advancing into the dark hall, Henry could think of nothing but Nicola's face, its elliptical shape, its tender flesh, its flash of brilliance.

She was there in the dark, waiting by the stair, resting her head, averted, against the carved newel post. Henry's heart fluttered, leaped. He crushed the paper in his hand, did not look at its instruction. He came to stand before her. Her head turned and their eyes met in the dark. And then he reached for her, cupped his hands beneath her arms to raise her up two steps on the stair, until her face was even with his own, and inclining his lips, he brushed them first to her eye, its swollen bud, and then to her mouth, where he lingered in their conjoined breath, the little gate of her jaws parting beneath his own, the world rushing, rushing in.

The House on Belle Isle

My granddaughter Ann is upstairs in the spare bedroom, the curtains drawn against the noonday sun and the crackling light of the sea, thrown up against this house like fat from a fire. How the young can sleep.

Eventually she will edge downstairs, still wearing her sleep like a mask, and come and sit beside me here, where there is the best view of the water. I'll make her some coffee and wait while she drinks it, and when she turns to me at last and says, "So. Daddy Louis. My last day," I will have to tell her this story. I have been dying to tell her this story.

But how does one begin? Surely not with the shocking thing itself, the severed hand that forms just one piece of my grandmother's bizarre collection of curiosities. I almost wish it had a life of its own, could speak its own version of the events that seem to me now not less real in time's long wake, but more so. Sometimes, gazing at it within its bell jar, I almost expect it to rise crablike on its stiff fingers and scuttle forward, tipping the glass ceiling to sally forth in search of its lost arm, a floating island seeking the jagged shore of land from which it was torn.

The hand itself is an awful thing, to be sure, bound at the wrist with a thong of deer sinew, a cord untwined from the tendon of a beast native to this outpost of white pine and black basalt. Cinched tight at its root like a balloon, the five small digits curling gently, the hand is miraculously preserved. God knows what my grandmother did to assure it such life after death.

Gruesome appendage, it is the strangest of my grandmother's strange possessions, which include a host of ghastly but marvelous contrivances; one wishes to look away, almost, but is drawn back to discover the secret of the materials applied so cleverly: the slender bracelet of human hair, a child's teeth pinched in its braid like semiprecious stones; the landscape painting fashioned from the wings of butterflies; a tiny Chinese cage of carved ivory whittled to bars the size of stickpins; the musical bird built of feathers rising from a silver box at the turn of a key to issue a string of haunting notes, its beak snapping, its head pivoting.

In my grandmother's life—Ann's great-great-grandmother —the hand signifies a moment when it might be said that my grandmother's past divided from her future, and the shape of her life changed unalterably. Lately I have begun to ask myself whether the moment of the hand's parting from its owner—I can find no other way to put it—could have been prevented. I am preoccupied with these things, I know, these matters that took place so many years ago. Some might say that mine is a morbid curiosity, as the story is not a happy one, and I might even agree with them. My former wife, Ann's grandmother, would say so, certainly, and I can think of no way to explain myself that would put me in a better light in this regard. In a life of few enthusiasms—indeed a life in which enthusiasm has been a stranger—I cannot account for how the things of the past, indeed the dead themselves, have come to exert such influence over me.

I think about this house and everything that took place here, and I know at least that I am not mistaking the urgent need I feel to tell the story of what happened. Here, where there was so much death, there was also life.

That is what interests me.

LET ME BEGIN by saying that this house is the perfect museum for its collection. It is a folly, as such things are called, a house built not of a single, sane, unifying vision but like a dream that escalates in absurdity; there are turrets and porticoes and towers, widow's walks, flying buttresses, and cantilevered wings, all stapled together, one woman's ambition run amok with architectural hysteria. And the house is a folly, too, in the way in which it killed her at last, though not with cost or pride, as some said; it was less complicated than that, really. Or maybe more complicated.

One afternoon, my grandmother slipped from the roof of her house and fell to her death on the pebbled drive below.

I have often imagined her up there, the gray Maine sky behind her like a fish belly wallowing in air, bursting with scales of light, rose and green and gold and sapphire blue. I can imagine her hammer raised, the roof tiles strapped in a sack on her back like a giant pack of playing cards into which she reached, withdrawing one shingle after the other, driving them home with a ring of her tool. Sometimes when I am outside trying to address the thousand and one ways in which the wind and sea take their toll on the house, I imagine that I hear the sound of her hammer echoing across time, each note closing with the final sound of condolence.

The explanation—the explanation that exists but does not satisfy exactly—is that the fall was an accident. But I wonder if anyone really believed that my grandmother, the woman who never took a false step, lost her footing that day. No one saw what happened, so we have all had to imagine it for ourselves, her feet pedaling backward across the slippery shoals of her new roof. She must have gone headfirst, they said.

Her hammer, sailing forth from her outflung hand, was never recovered.

There was no one equipped to lay her out properly after she died. My grandmother was Belle Isle's only undertaker. There wasn't business enough to sustain more than one. In a lonely place like this, threaded to an equally remote mainland by an elbow of jutting rock, there are only a limited number of clients, even if they are all sure to need your services one day. And who would have dared encroach upon her territory, in any case, this woman with slightly bulging eyes and hair like a goddess's, wound around her head and pinned firmly to her white scalp?

But in fact there was someone. Not one of her four children, whom she had banished from Belle Isle as quickly as

possible, hurrying them off to universities for exactly the education, classical and powerful, she herself had never had
and that was rightfully theirs. Each child was to reward her
in time with service in fine careers: the banker, the jurist, the
physician, and my father, a cellist with the symphony or-
chestra in Boston. No, my grandmother did not want a life
on Belle Isle for her children. She even discouraged their visits home after they left, preferring instead to arrive unan-
nounced at their doorsteps, stopping over on one of her
missions forth into the world of civilization.

Still, someone had to lay her out, and as it happened, the
hands that performed the final ministrations belonged to
someone deeply familiar with my grandmother's industry,
her terrible genius for invention, the proof of it now rust-
ing in the basement here: a sunken galleon of ropes and
pulleys and chains for lifting the dead weight of her neighbors to and fro upon the table, a set of webs and weights
that looked more like an instrument of torture than what it
was—a practical woman's solution to the limits of her
strength.

Jack Benoit, the wandering French Canadian with his
wings of shiny black hair and his blue eyes: *he* was the man
who, when push came to shove, bore the body away to the
basement laboratory and later arranged for the photograph
to be taken. Harry Chan—that's the photographer's signa-
ture affixed to the back of the photograph, and I can imagine the little man with his camera, disembarking unsteadily
at the port on Belle Isle, his equipment carried on his back
like a folded black grasshopper, the ship still pitching in his
lens. I have the receipt for it, as well as the photograph itself,
the sad, strange picture of my grandmother laid out, her hair

cascading around her, dripping off the edges of the table, unleashed for posterity, for Jack Benoit.

I have stared at that photograph, wondered at the feelings of the man who arranged for it to be taken—for it is his hand on the receipt, "J. Benoit," with a downward flourish. Where did he stand as Mr. Chan raised his black apron to fix my grandmother in his eye? I have wondered what expression crossed the face of Jack Benoit as the light flashed and the clattering shutter ground my grandmother, square inch by square inch, light into dark, into the improbable pose of death.

I make no accusations, you understand. I only wonder. I only speculate.

Ann knows that I could stare at the sea for hours. The gray-green waves below the cliffs on which this house is built appear empty; one could be deceived into thinking that the sea itself is nothing but a vast emptiness. But I know that if I could dive down deep into the interior of the ocean, I would find the waves bubbling with ampules of air, crossed by transparent fish with their silvery, threadlike intestines, and navigated by creatures of the deep with their glossy black fins and feathered tentacles. And down at the very bottom, in the shifting sands of the ocean floor, would be the rotting hulls of shipwrecks and the separating bones of sailors. I tell myself that nothing is ever really lost at sea.

MY GRANDMOTHER, Louise Jacoby Tate, was Belle Isle's least likely candidate for marriage to the man who became, briefly, her husband, Arthur Leonard Tate. Young Arthur was the son of a captain of the earliest timber in-

dustry here, and heir to hundreds of acres of straight pine
—a fortune in domestic lumber, and a magical and dangerous kingdom of deep snows and darting birds and searching rays of sunlight that scored the deep forest with a
quivering lattice of light. Arthur's family was educated and
wealthy; their home here was stocked with fine china and
exquisite glass, a library of leather-bound volumes, dressers
full of beautiful linen.

Louise was the daughter of the town's widowed barkeep,
a man who maintained, despite state laws forbidding the
sale of alcohol, an infernal supply of spirits served up in a secret shanty closely guarded by the foes of Prohibition and
the hard-living men of Belle Isle. Louise went to school until she was twelve and then educated herself as best she could
with whatever books happened to fall into her hands; she
could hardly have been expected to eat at the Tates' long,
baronial table with anything approximating their cultured
conversation or practiced manners. I remember the dining
room of that great house, for I saw it once a few years ago
when the house was put up for sale—its painted walls
showed Niagara Falls and a minutely rendered tableau of
Indians and British settlers busy at Port Colborne. I can
imagine my grandmother in that room—that lovely profile,
her head held high over the heavy silver, the awful silence.
There could not have been more than one such dinner at the
Tates', I am sure, if there was even one. The family's oppro-
brium would have been too great.

But Arthur and Louise were married anyway, under circumstances I can only speculate about, for there is no record
of the ceremony beyond the certificate that proves that it
took place here on Belle Isle, at the Presbyterian church.

But why did Arthur, who by all rights should have had a bride his equal in wealth and breeding, choose my grandmother Louise?

Well, she was beautiful, a fact that no doubt goes a long way toward explaining many unlikely and inauspicious matches in this world. And Arthur himself was said to be on the wild side. Certainly he offered her, with his wealth and learning, a passage into a world that would have been, had the circumstances of her own birth been different, the perfect bath for a woman of such lively and enterprising intelligence. Yet it would not have been social stature she sought, nor money; I think it was those books in the Tate library that she wanted. They filled her with longing, perhaps even with greed. And she offered him—what? A romantic companion? Someone unafraid to accompany him into the deep and beckoning spaces of the pine woods? Someone whose powerful nature matched his own with an exciting strength? Arthur had found his true home in the Maine wilderness, by all reports. He never expected to return to society, with its rewards too pale for a man intoxicated by the forces of nature itself. Perhaps Louise was the perfect partner for this man who disdained formality, who loved the wild frontier, and whose own social circle would have been unlikely to produce a wife content to live in a place as remote and wild as Belle Isle.

So their union took place, but certainly despite the furious misgivings of his family, despite a hailstorm of threats and promises. And theirs was a fruitful marriage; she bore Arthur four children—my own father, whose name was Henry, and Matthias, Timothy, and James—in five short years, during which I imagine childbirth made her even stronger, spreading her hips and adding heft to her bosom.

Their happiness, however—what happiness they must have had, what promise—ended in the sixth year, when Arthur Tate, speculating over his holdings in the deep white-pine woods near Calais, a shimmering chimera of ice and needle, became lost and disoriented, and died in a sudden snowstorm.

It was the snow, I believe, that gave my grandmother her accidental career as an undertaker. When her husband was carried home at last, recovered by a search party of men, his body would have been perfectly preserved, frozen solid and frosted white with a beard of dusty crystals, his skin cold as ice. Louise would have appreciated the permanence of the snow, saw what it bequeathed her.

AFTER ARTHUR'S DEATH, Louise did not, nor did her sons—or their sons, for that matter—inherit their fair share of the vast wealth from the Tate family holdings. The family used the excuse of Arthur's death to sever Louise and her four children from the fortune, carving off a distant tract calculated to supply her with only a remedial income. It is hard now to imagine their cruelty, the short shrift they made of their obligation. But their sorrow over their son's death must at least have been genuine. Undone by the tragedy, they fled the area altogether after his death, back to Boston's muddy byways and lifted hems and burgeoning mannered class, leaving the dirty, dangerous business of the timber company in the hands of an overseer, and leaving their young daughter-in-law and four grandsons to fend for themselves.

Louise, newly widowed and encumbered with four children, was without many resources. And yet she had wit and
strength and the unwelcome goad of what I imagine must
have been a furious anger to spur her along. And when the
search party left Arthur's body on the trestle table in the
large room of the cabin the young family had shared—none
of them was ever welcome in the Tate mansion after the
wedding—Louise bowed over the body late into the night,
considering what was left, considering what she would
make of it all.

Arthur was buried two days later, his body at rest upon
a fragrant bed of pine boughs. I am told that the funeral was
a chilling affair. Louise and her four young children—one,
my uncle James, still in arms—stood to one side of the coffin and the mouth of the grave. The Tates stood opposite,
and no one dared to bridge the terrible gulf that separated
them, separates them still. When it was over, each side withdrew without a word, the little boys following the sweep of
Louise's skirts as she turned away. Arthur's mother, re-
morseful perhaps, might have raised a hand to stay them, to
lift the boys' chins in her gloved palm and gaze into their
faces, already long like Arthur's, with his high, narrow brow
and green eyes. She might have reconsidered. But such a gesture would have come too late for Louise.

The day was cold. A stinging wind swept across the cemetery, scattering the mourners so divided by their loyalties
that none dared approach Louise that afternoon to offer
condolence. The Tates held most of the families of Belle Isle
in their sway; all but a few of the town's inhabitants depended upon the fortunes of the timber company for their
livelihoods, though there were a few independents—two

physicians, an attorney, a banker, and a handful of mer-
chants who helped balance the heavy hand the Tates held
over Belle Isle. Still, no one would have wished to risk
the powerful family's censure by showing Louise excessive
tenderness.

Only one man strode out from the cowering assembly to
catch the reins of Louise's team and steady the pair for her
as she lifted the boys into the wagon. She turned to him
then; she must have turned to him, her black hood billowing around her white face. What did he say to her? We cannot know, for his words were delivered in a whisper. But we
know he returned, stiff in Louise's answering silence, to his
own wife, who quivered with shame at the boldness of
Jack's indiscretion, at the way he showed the whole town
where his heart still lay.

So MUCH OF THIS story must be imagined, I confess. All the witnesses who were old enough to understand
what they saw have died by now, their own heirs the recip-
ients, like me, of handed-down tales or evidence of one sort
or another. I have my own father's speculations, and those
of my uncles, although they always talked about my grandmother with reluctance, as if they were ashamed of her ec-
centricities. I am the only one, it seems, who saw her in a
different light. Still, piecing together their recollections and
my own, I think I have fashioned a probable version of
events. And I have my old friend Albert Benoit, Jack's
grandson and my peer, who sits idly at the rest home, an
afghan drawn up over his knees. His mind is mostly unknown to me now, and to himself, too, but once we liked to

talk together about our grandparents, about what lay between them.

And I know—still know, thank God; *these* faculties are mercifully intact—what I saw as a boy in my summers here on Belle Isle, when the snows had melted away, when the waves fell on the shore with the sound of temptation, when the hills were covered with blueberries and the gilded tassel, when the black-capped chickadee with its piping remonstrance accompanied a boy everywhere, reminding him of supper, of home, of his bed. I remember just enough, I think, of Jack Benoit and my remarkable grandmother to imagine what must have happened.

It would have been like my grandmother to size up her options after Arthur's death and resist flinching from the most obvious one that presented itself to her, even if it seems, now, ghastly in the extreme. In those days the dead of Belle Isle were carried in rough coffins by train to Calais (those that weren't simply dropped into a rude hole in the ground), to be dressed and prepared by the undertakers there and then returned home for burial. But Belle Isle had pieties and aspirations, and after a while, I suppose, people felt that they ought to be able to look after their own dead properly. The Tates had given the town airs, and the fitting place for a proper funeral with all the trimmings was among them.

I am told that my grandmother's first funeral client was a child, and that she took such care, arranged the casket so lovingly, the fine hair of the little girl so delightfully, her own ruby brooch pinned to the child's slender throat, that the grieving parents wept with gratitude, and business fell her way speedily enough after that. Until she ran out, she is said to have bequeathed to each poor soul some treasure of her own from the limited supply Arthur had given her, a handful of rings and necklaces, a fistful of pearls, a scattering of pins. I do not know how she contrived to persuade that first child's parents to hand over their daughter. But I do know that for all her wild ways, all her seemingly cold independence, my grandmother had the gift of a perfect sympathy, of genuine tact. Her manner was perfectly trustworthy, and in her presence one did feel impelled—I felt it myself—to reveal one's sorrow.

I imagine she took the body of that first child in her arms as tenderly as if the child had been her own, and bore it carefully away, leaving the parents with that welcome hiatus that sometimes visits us in the moment of grief when we feel we have done all we can, that what we have done is our best, and pray that the hands that spare us the final preparations for death are as gentle and knowing as God's own embrace.

I WAS SEVEN years old the first summer I spent with my grandmother on Belle Isle. Parted from my parents— who no doubt worried a little about my grandmother's unorthodox life but sensed, too, what leaps forward in maturity and temperament I might make under her care along that rocky coast for a few weeks—I discovered an odd fact about my grandmother's effect on me: she could frighten me and yet offer the perfect protection from that fear, all at once. As her collection of strange artifacts proved, she herself appeared to have very little fear of anything that walked or crawled or flew. Perhaps she was not afraid of anything at all.

She had no hesitation about looking straight into the contrivances of the body—man's or beast's—and absorbing, by calm study, nature's great gifts of form and function: the way muscle clasps a ball joint, the way a snake's reedy intestines work upon its prey, how the liver absorbs and neutralizes bile. My grandmother saw beauty in utility, in the miracle of life itself and its amazing mechanical vehicle.

I will never forget how, once, when a bird was struck lifeless after colliding with a window at the house, she carried it inside to the kitchen table and unfolded its wings for me so that I might imagine the magic of flight, how the wing bore within its powerful and flowing field the mystery of aerodynamics. As she parted the feathers with her fingers, testing the extent of the wings and the strength of the skin, hefting the slight body to convey its buoyancy, I overcame, for the moment, my childish squeamishness; all I saw was the pillow of air, the impossible action of flight made possible; and all I felt, then, was a pure sorrow for the bird and an admiration for the still-warm body's ability to rise on nothing but a breeze.

"This, Louis," my grandmother said, "is a miracle."

I knew what she did for a living, and of course it scared me half to death at first. The day she picked me up from the train on my first summer visit, I could scarcely look at her. Somehow, seeing her on those few occasions in our home in Boston, I hadn't thought much about those dead bodies in her basement. But once on Belle Isle, where there was no escaping the fact of her livelihood through the distractions of my own household, I couldn't seem to think of anything else. I watched her hands, held together at the top of the steering wheel, that first afternoon as we drove the rough roads to her house, and thought I saw, with a boy's frightful imagination, gore dripping from those strong fingers.

But I believe she understood my terror. After we'd arrived and she'd shown me my room, she flung open the windows for a taste of the bracing sea breeze, which entered on a wild exhalation as if it had been holding its breath outside, just waiting to lift papers from the desk and billow the canopy over the bed. Then she turned to me and said, "Now, Louis. You've the run of the whole house. And first off I'm going to show you the basement, where I do my work, so you won't be ghosting around the door imagining the worst. Come along."

Well, I had my heart in my throat. But I followed her down from the second floor and down the planked staircase to the basement, where, in a moment of panic, I stopped at the threshold of the door to her workroom.

"Is anyone in there?" I imagined a bloated man, eyes rolled back in his head, blue and naked on a trestle table.

"Not a soul," she replied, and turned on the lights.

It was a commodious room, with stone walls and a high ceiling and a set of double doors at one end open to a second room stacked with lumber and unfinished coffins. One could enter the basement from outside through that workshop, with its spill of sweet-smelling sawdust and bunched herbs hung to dry from the roof. I learned, later, that for each fallen head my grandmother stuffed a pillow with pine needles or herbs from her own garden, lavender and lovage, lemon balm and mint and rosemary.

At the doorway that led from the basement into the garden, the tendrils of a blossoming trumpet vine crept around the door frame. A bright light fell across the floor, and just visible on the grass beyond a white curtain that hung in the doorway, two chairs were set at angles on the turf, facing the ocean. The interior room, with its high, wide wooden table in the center and shelves of buckets and implements, was tiled and swept clean. A rigging of pulleys and ropes with a sailcloth sling hung from the ceiling above the table.

I could hear the sound of the sea washing up the cliff.

My grandmother spoke. "I like a pleasant place in which to work."

And it was true: it was a pleasant pair of rooms, airy and clean, if infused with a terrible sadness. I felt not what I expected to feel—a horror at it all—but a sudden, profound sympathy for my grandmother, her hands dressing the bodies carefully, methodically, gently, adjusting the limbs into a pose of rest, the sounds of the sea and birdsong at her door.

And then she led me through the rooms out to the garden beyond, and as I stood on the bowl of the hill, with its view out across the sparkling black Atlantic, the dancing whitecaps and churning froth at the rocks, the sky an inverted shell of porcelain blue above, I felt a wondrous release at the thought that this place was to be mine for a few weeks. It's a feeling I have every day, still, when I step outside to take in the view, examine the sea for its inclination that day. And in that moment I felt, still feel, the overwhelming collision of it all—the great force of the sea, with its distant schools of diving whales and arcing fish, the solid foundation of towering rock beneath my feet, my grandmother's tender ministry, so small and domestic, at the lip of nature's vast industry.

That summer I ate and slept and wandered the hills and coastline, growing strong. My grandmother had purchased a piano so I could continue my instruction during the weeks that I was away from home; I practiced scales and simple sonatas to the accompaniment of the crashing surf. In the evenings my grandmother and I took our supper on the porch in sight of the wheeling swallows and distant terns drawing black, fantastic tracings in the air. And after supper I was sent to bed to read, often falling asleep with the light still burning, the book fallen open on my pillow.

It was the night I woke with a fever that I first saw Jack Benoit. The thudding ache of the illness had woken me, and I lay still awhile in bed, feeling gloomy and uncomfortable, uncertain exactly of why I felt so indisposed and strange. Finally I rose on wobbly legs to search out my grandmother.

The house was an oddity even then, though my grandmother had another five years to go before the labor of it would finish her. She had made enough money through her own employment as an undertaker, and with the steady trickle of funds from her share of the timber business, to invest in her house, sited so perfectly with the sea ahead and the hills behind. She needed neither architect nor engineer; everything she wanted, she found in the books Arthur had brought with him to the marriage, and later, as her aspirations grew, in those she found in Boston's public library. A pair of loyal carpenters, who surely knew a good thing when they saw it, turned at her summons from boatbuilding to house building; I remain convinced that everything one needs to know about engineering can be learned in building a boat, whose design must reckon with the quixotic and unreliable sea. Between them, those carpenters built for my grandmother, under her tutelage, a fine house, with the light air of something that, unmoored from the rock, might indeed have sailed capably on the waves. It is not exactly a harmonious construction, added to, as it was, each time something struck my grandmother's fancy. Still, no one can say it isn't an achievement.

Initially just a small number of white rooms circling a central hall flooded with light from a cupola set high on the roof, each summer the house acquired another appendage or appurtenance: a glassed-in, tiled orangery; a library with doors concealed among the bookcases, its reaches lit by green-shaded lamps stationed high on the shelves; an octagonal music chamber, where my piano rests, untouched now. That summer she had begun construction on the orangery, and the vaulted framing of it stood to one side of the finished portion of the house, looking, at night, like the shimmering construction of a spiderweb, ephemeral and delicate.

I descended the stairs uncertainly, a thin wraith of a boy, advancing through the sighing rooms. The kitchen and parlor were empty, though lights burned in the dining room, which opened to the porch with its ship's rail and wicker furnishings. I passed through the dining room to the porch, stood a moment on the cool floorboards. And then I heard voices.

Had I been a year or two older, I might have stopped to listen, aware, as one unfortunately becomes, of the terrible but priceless value of listening to conversations one isn't intended to hear. But no such motivation occurred to me that night. I was just a boy, after all. And that night, too, I was encumbered by a fever, which would have been gone by morning, as childhood fevers often are, leaving me weak and unsteady but perfectly well. All I wanted at that moment was my grandmother's attention. I did not know I might have heard something, seen something, to give all this pondering the certain weight of truth.

"Louise?" That was how I addressed her; she never cared for "Grandmother" or any other familiarity. I called to her and then stood rooted, the fever weighing on my head.

From the far end of the wide porch, two figures rose suddenly in the dark from the swinging settee, which hung on chains and formed a wonderful berth for reading through the late afternoons.

My grandmother stepped forward. "What is it, Louis?" She moved into the light that fell from the dining room door. The other figure hung back, wavered in the dark. I tried to see around her, discomfited by the unfamiliar presence, but my grandmother's hands on my shoulders stopped me. "You're burning up!" She turned me around and began steering me inside.

"Who was that?" I asked as she led me inside and back upstairs.

Remember now, I was only a boy, and probably a little delirious. Children can have even slight fevers and imagine all sorts of nonsense they won't remember come morning. I wasn't sure what I had really seen, and it was only later that I recognized the man who had risen in the dark beside my grandmother that night. She could have lied to me, and I would have been satisfied that she had told me the truth. But she didn't lie.

"Our friend Jack," she said. *Our friend Jack.* And I have thought about that, about the way she phrased it. Not just *a* friend, or *my* friend, but *our* friend, as if she wanted me to understand that his interest in her wasn't just personal but extended to her whole family, or, more specifically, especially to me.

I looked up at her as we stepped into the cool bathroom, with its film of salt and scented soap, and when she turned briefly into the light of the medicine cabinet, there was absolutely no expression on her face at all. Embarrassment or anger or impatience, I would have understood, even if I hadn't liked them. But there was nothing there, and in the end that was more troubling than anything else.

Back in my bedroom she fed me aspirin and a glass of water, sitting beside me, applying a cool compress to my forehead, rivulets of water trickling like mercury over my boiling skin. My limbs felt like stone on the cool sheets.

As I lay there, and in the moments before I slept again, I looked at her hard profile, the hooded eye and heavy knot of hair on her head, and thought fearfully, for the first time since my introduction to her basement, of the dead bodies sleeping beneath her hands.

WHAT ALBERT BENOIT, Jack's grandson and my now wandering, senile friend, told me in the days before he became so utterly unreliable, his memory full of unexplainable references and fragmented anecdotes, was that Jack Benoit's own fever for my grandmother hung over them all like a pall.

After Arthur's death, my grandmother discovered the extent to which her marriage had divorced her from the town's sympathies. In one way, she had thrown them over by marrying into such wealth — even if so little of it was to become hers. And though in fact her step up in the world was shallow indeed, her new name gave her a certain damning power over her neighbors. They accorded her the great intimacy and trust of laying out their dead partly because she had seemed to acquire, with her marriage, license to do so, the powerful knowledge of the rich. And yet they resented her for it as well, I imagine, for the way in which she refused to slip back into her old life but took the manners and customs and aspirations imparted to her through marriage as her own.

And no one might have resented her more, perhaps, than Jack Benoit.

Before Arthur's interest in Louise, a pattern of rough courtship had developed between the drifter who had settled on Belle Isle with his multifarious skills—sometime lumberjack, fisherman, trapper, blacksmith—and the daughter of the tavern owner. On several occasions, Jack and my grandmother were seen together heading for the hills, packing a picnic on a Saturday afternoon, or down at the rocky beach, tiny figures carving a slow, close walk by the swelling waves. People saw Jack Benoit with flowers in his hands, heading for Louise's father's house; they returned his smile, perhaps. It would have been difficult to resist the way his growing certainty over Louise made him sociable and charming.

I don't know how they first met. Maybe at Louise's father's bar, if you could call it that. It was a rough place, now gone, framed with a sneering tilt of boards and lit from within by a woodstove that burned red-hot on a weekend night. But I cannot imagine that Louise ventured inside the place much; one can surmise that she might not have approved or, at the very least, that it did not interest her to be there. But I do know that one night she agreed to go for a midnight sail with Jack.

She met him at the dock where his boat was moored. The town's business had long since concluded for the day; its shutters were drawn. Louise was accountable to no one save herself.

Whether there was a full moon that night or not, we cannot tell. I know from my own experience of taking a boat out at night, a foolhardy venture at best, suicidal at the worst, that a young man might feel there is something significant about his encounter with the world under those circumstances. It is hard, I admit, not to feel temporarily aggrandized when you consider your own minor weight against that of the sea and yet imagine it a contest between equals, a test of bravery. It is only later, if you are lucky enough to come home safely, that you recognize your foolishness, feel ashamed of having taken such a risk.

So I can imagine why Jack, no matter what my grandmother said or did that night, considered it an event of significance. Something must have passed between the two young people, awash in the dark, tempting fate. We know at least that the night meant something powerful to Jack Benoit, for he carried the memory of it with him. He remembered it so well, in fact, that he described it many times to his grandson Albert. By then, perhaps, Jack's memory was improved by the grandeur that sometimes characterizes our failed attempts at greatness in life, which allows us to live with what we have lost, or what we were never capable of in the first place.

It was a night that must have held, for Jack, a promise. Because when my grandmother abandoned him and the memory of that night, and perhaps others as well, for Arthur's certain advantages, Jack was deeply injured.

I HAVE STOOD on that same dock at night myself, inspecting the surface of the sea, weighing my own slight presence there, exploring the rail with my hands, raising my palm to the wind for the music it makes as I cup my hand and deflect it.

I do not play the piano anymore, though I harken almost instinctively to the tones of the wind off the Atlantic and can imitate their pitch. My own career as a pianist expired, while I was still young, in the bald light of competition, when just the sight of other young men taking their places before the instrument was enough to shake from me whatever confidence and talent I had. It was the one way my grandmother failed me—or I her—that though she gave me freedom here on Belle Isle, gave me all the resources to learn a strength of purpose, gave me her example, she could not make me strong enough or talented enough, could not convey to me how one makes a success of oneself.

Yet my grandmother was a success against all odds, and with so few resources. She took nothing that was not hers, took only, in fact, the discarded remains of life, as if in the wake of Arthur's death she had concluded that was to be her fate: to dress the dead, to admire how the detritus of life— what was left—might be rearranged in some new and beautiful form: the bracelet of human hair, the windup bird, the cage of bone. Like the long-ago children of Belle Isle who are reported to have found, each summer, the washed-up bones of a stranger buried in the sands on the beach of Corea's

Outer Bar and to have fitted him back together before the high tide scattered him again, my grandmother was given the leavings of life, what she might make of them. Her whole life was, in some ways, an example of how, denied everything, one might still discover a rich universe. That was her genius.

I was lucky that when it came time for me to retire from the store in Boston, the music business to which I turned when my own talents failed me, no one else in my family wanted this old house or the prospect of living out their days on Belle Isle. My wife, certain soul that she is, took the opportunity to leave me then, though I suspect she regretted not having done so before. My stated hopes to move to Belle Isle gave her a reasonable excuse to catch up what was still left of her own life and make something fresh of it. My daughter and Ann, on their anxious phone calls here, tell me that she has a pleasant time of it now, a gentleman caller who accompanies her to the symphony and to restaurants, a busy volunteer post at Massachusetts General, greeting new patients. I do not blame her. I think I knew, in fact, that my expressed desire to return here would amount to a tacit acquiescence to the conclusion of our marriage. And I have found, oh, something—what might I call it?—here on Belle Isle, threading my way through my grandmother's past, recalling my summers spent here as a boy, summers that ended when my parents stepped up the pace of my musical instruction and kept me home instead.

Each summer I play host here to Ann. Of all my grandchildren, and there are six of them, Ann is the only one who wants to come to Belle Isle every year. She is an elementary-school teacher, and I imagine she is beloved by her young students, that they crowd her knees and reach up to her with their arms. But she has begun to worry, she says, that she is too old now to take the whole summer off to be here with me on Belle Isle, doing nothing. "I'm grown up, Daddy Louis," she told me last night at dinner. "I need to find something else to do." She has decided already to go to Italy next summer, where she has applied to a program to study painting restoration. Ann is a talented painter herself, and I feel sure she will make a success of herself. But I could see the worry on her face when she told me of her plans. She did not have to say that she worries what will become of me.

After dinner, I went outside and stood on the grass and looked at Passamaquoddy Bay, with its faraway whales and riveting thunder holes, its gulls balancing in the geysers. It fell out at my feet like a heaving, expectant desert of gray.

LOUISE AND ARTHUR were explorers, in the true sense. It was the quality Louise admired in Arthur, I suspect, and he in her. To be the first to do something, the first to walk the hushed aisles of the pine forest's virgin timbers, the first to shake away the conventions of one's time and invent oneself as something wholly original—that was what they wanted for themselves, I imagine. And yet it is a lonely life, is it not, that of the explorer? So many retreat from the unraveling edge of civilization, return to its cozy, domesticated heart.

That is why, I believe, in the wake of Louise's marriage to Arthur, Jack Benoit took himself a wife. It was revenge perhaps, but not purely a strike at Louise. Just as the bold Arthur wanted a woman to return to at night, a meal prepared, a warm body in the bed, Jack Benoit must have believed he deserved the same, that Louise's brutal defection from his heart shouldn't stop him from taking what he wanted from a woman's presence in his life. And, in the end, from taking from her the only thing he ever gave her.

Well, perhaps that's not quite true. For though his marriage to Ellsbeth Ames, the young woman who became Jack Benoit's unfortunate wife, took place in a spirit of angry capitulation, they lived together for some forty years until her death. Unlike my grandmother, though, Jack Benoit was not a man to take stock of life's leavings and fashion a full plate from them. He was a man of the half-empty glass. Why else, despite so many years in marriage to this woman—who bore him a son, Luke, whose wife bore in turn the babe that became my friend, now the old man Albert Benoit—why else would my grandmother's continued presence on Belle Isle have served to sever Jack Benoit so thoroughly from the very thing he wanted, the thing we all want: a full vault of love. But Jack Benoit couldn't leave my grandmother alone, couldn't stop trying to get hold of what might have been, casting his line again and again into a sea that forever refused his hook.

He might have made something better than he did of his union with Ellsbeth Ames; certainly she stood by his side faithfully enough, despite what she must have known about his passion for my grandmother. Everyone on Belle Isle knew about it, after all. Albert, once my medium into his family's past, didn't remember her well. All he seemed to recall about her was that she was a tiny woman, dainty and gentle, and that she possessed a lovely singing voice. She sang hymns as she went about her day, he told me, in one of those sopranos that seems to belong to the rafters of church or sky, an effortless ascent of perfect clarity. It seems a shame that her God-given voice should have fallen on Jack Benoit's deaf ears, that its subject was so often the comfort of the hereafter.

And perhaps it was Ellsbeth Ames's plaintive voice that followed the wind of Jack Benoit's sails as he ventured to my grandmother's house on those evenings when he could not resist. Perhaps both he and Louise heard it, a keening on the wind, as they stood before each other under cover of darkness. I know such evenings occurred, though how often, I cannot say, for more than once I heard voices from my window, rose to look down on the figures of Jack Benoit and my grandmother, seated in the dark in those same two chairs we had occupied at sunset, the sound of the surf roaring in all our ears. Above my head, my ship models and balsa airplanes, built on rainy days at the dining room table, would heave slightly in the wind on their invisible threads, distracting me. And when I looked again, my grandmother and Jack would be gone.

The night of my grandmother's wedding to Arthur, Jack Benoit went on a rampage through town. He shouted in the streets, cut loose a score of boats from their moorings, was wrestled down at last and locked up for two nights to sleep off his drink and his grief and his fury. Albert Benoit told me that the occasion, one man doing so much damage in a single night, had made his grandfather a legend. And the town knew, as well, that after Arthur's death Jack Benoit found his audience before my grandmother again, was seen turning up the long drive to her house, though how often and to what end, no one could say. No reckless moment ever gave the couple away to make possible the outright censure of the town.

It is my own theory that, on one level, *nothing ever happened* between my grandmother and Jack Benoit.

Is this foolish, to believe something so romantic, so sentimental, so contrary to human nature as this?

Certainly my grandmother was lonely. I don't ever remember her enjoying herself with someone who might be described as a friend. The summers I spent with her—and there were only three, between my seventh and ninth years—went largely uninterrupted by the kind of casual traffic of neighbors and colleagues that characterized my own home in Boston. There, from the upper rail of the banister, we children would watch the arrival of dinner guests, shaking snow from their coats and wraps, the crowns of their heads glinting under the shivering arms of the hall chandelier, its crystals stirring in the currents of cold air that arrived through the door opened to admit one party after another. In my own home, my place as a child was strictly prescribed—I was fed and bathed upstairs before my parents' dinner parties and watched the proceedings of the adult world, with its infernal, murmurous conversation punctuated by peals of hilarity, from the shadowy confines of the upstairs hall.

But at my grandmother's, though I went to bed at the same hour each night—and went gladly enough, in fact, weary to my core from the fresh air and the exertions of my growing boy's body—I seemed less of a child. I was aware that my grandmother had few callers apart from the grieving families whose dead were borne to the basement, and the two carpenters who scaled over the walls of her house, which expanded and divided over the years like some many-celled creature under the microscope of the gray Maine sky. Even during her weekly shopping trips, my grandmother's small conversations in the town of Belle Isle felt, to my child's wary intelligence, without ease or joy, though the shopkeepers and women passing in the streets greeted her respectfully.

Still, she was a wonderful companion to me, exclaiming over my daily treasures—a stone or shell, a feather or some tiny subarctic flower—with genuine enthusiasm. At night, before our dinner on the porch, we would sit on the two chairs out on the lawn, absorbed in the sweetly descending light of the day, the brushstrokes of shadows that lengthened like lacy shawls drawn up over our shoulders, and speak of small things. I know that I was a good companion to her, that my antics to please her amused and charmed her. Those were, in so many ways, the happiest days of my life.

I like to think that the notion of taking what belonged, in title, to another woman, would have been beneath my grandmother. Remaining untouched by Jack Benoit would have allowed my grandmother dignity, made certain her independence. But of course I could be wrong. Something satisfying, or at least satisfying enough, must have happened between my grandmother and Jack Benoit in the decades after Arthur's death to keep Jack returning to her door. Something kept them there in the dark, sitting side by side, talking late into the night.

Sometimes I stand on the porch in the darkness and listen, straining to hear voices, asking to be let in. But all I ever hear is silence, and the crashing of the waves.

• • •

THERE IS AMONG my grandmother's papers a complete account of her career as Belle Isle's undertaker. Beside each name and date are listed the cause of death, the price of her services, notes on any special attentions she gave. That is how I know that it was my grandmother who prepared Ellsbeth Ames Benoit's body after her death, for it is there, plain as day, written in her firm hand for all the world to see. Albert Benoit told me that no one said a word when his grandfather Jack arranged for Ellsbeth to be carried to Louise's house; they simply turned away from what they could not speak aloud—the sacrilege of Jack Benoit, to offer up his wife's body in the end to the woman he had always longed for. But no one had proof of anything. Moreover, to protest Jack's wishes at that point would have been an announcement that Ellsbeth's long loyalty to Jack had been spoiled, had been worthless. So they let him go, let him have his way.

Now imagine, if you can—for that is what I have had to do—the scene in my grandmother's basement that night. What must my grandmother have thought, her face impassive, as she received Ellsbeth's body, took her in her arms? And as she bent over her labors, her mind working with such thoughts as I can only imagine, the shape of Jack himself would have appeared in the door.

At least this is what I have imagined, the shape of Jack Benoit, looming in the door. This is what the facts, such as they are, lead me to imagine.

Remember, Jack was free then at that moment; they were both free.

But not there, Jack, not in that chapel-like room, not while my grandmother was at work.

But what he did then, what he sought to do in his terrible and misguided way—well, I have lived with the tragic result of it.

Jack stepped forward then toward his wife's body.

And can you not see it? Can you imagine any other scenario? I have thought and thought, and every time, I see the same terrible moment again and again, like a nightmare that refuses to release the tormented dreamer. I must believe that Jack was aiming for a symbolic release, aiming to twist Ellsbeth's wedding ring from her, his strong fingers wrenching the little hand, wrenching to remove the ring, which he had thought would yield easily enough. Did he think he would turn with it glinting in his palm and offer it to my grandmother? That she might be pleased by that? Or did he think he would turn and heave it like a star out over the cliff into the dark sea, its vanishing course like the tail of a dying comet? Did he believe, once that ring was gone, that he could take my grandmother in his arms at last, that she would receive him there?

What made him waste it all, all those years?

The ring would not come loose, it would *not;* he failed and, sweeping the room, seized, from the pile of lumber hewed for coffins, the ax, all those years of stifled ardor exploding. My grandmother would have been too late. It was all too late then. Jack tore out the door, his wife's hand in his own, to be dropped somewhere in the scrub pine as he fled.

Those pleasant rooms. I hate the thought of my grandmother down there after that, after what she had to contrive in Ellsbeth's coffin to hide Jack's terrible error. For he had spoiled it, of course, spoiled everything: the cleanliness, the dense quiet, the godly work she performed, her grace.

After her death, her fall from the roof—I must believe it was an accidental fall, a slip of the foot; it is too terrible to imagine otherwise—my father and his brothers returned to the house to close it up and make arrangements with a caretaker to have it looked after.

At the dinner table the night of my father's return from Belle Isle, he sat, his hand over his eyes, his food untasted, his plate pushed aside. "We didn't touch the basement," he told my mother, speaking over our heads as though we weren't there. "Matthias just closed the door, said to let it be. Good God, I hate even to think about it."

I looked up at my father then, my father the cellist. I looked at his long, womanly fingers, which he protected so jealously from injury or harm that he wore gloves while shaving and forbore cutting his own meat, passing his plate instead to my mother for her meek and efficient work. I looked at the cold indifference in his face, which I suddenly understood as fury, and I felt I could, just once in my life, become something sharp and fatal and yet infinitely just.

"It was nice down there!" I shouted, bringing my knife down on my plate, tears cresting unaccountably in my eyes. "It was good! You never even saw it."

My father stared at me, his expression wooden as he beheld my stricken face.

"I'm sorry," I said, and bowed my head.

Not long after, I had to make the terrible announcement to my parents that my musical career was finished. I had already found a partner to help finance starting the music store; I was able, thankfully, to set forth those plans in the same breath in which I announced I would no longer play the piano. It was a disappointment to us all, of course. And when I came back here, my whole life contracting behind me like a closing telescope as I again opened the doors to this house, paced its rooms, stood before the view, I remembered for a moment that awkward conversation with my parents, my departure from the room after their silence.

And then the memory was gone, and the Atlantic with its hypnotic roll drew me near to the cliff's edge. All I could hear was the sea.

OF COURSE, I FOUND the hand, Ellsbeth's hand with its tiny ring, among my grandmother's possessions. I can imagine her hunting along the cliff edge with a torch that night, looking for what could never be put back together but must be saved nonetheless, preserved against the forces of time, which can so easily, so lightly, sweep us all away, one generation no wiser than the next, repeating the same errors of love and pride again and again.

For a long time I didn't know what to do with it. It couldn't be displayed, of course, like my grandmother's other odd possessions, though the dusty bell jar that houses it in a cupboard in the basement doesn't seem permanent either. Once I thought of Joshua Benoit, Jack's great-great-grandson and Ann's friend, a guidance counselor at the high school here who sometimes takes Ann out to a movie when she visits—a twist of fate that fills me with trembling. But I hardly know the young man, really, and I can't imagine what I would say to him. In a certain light, it doesn't even make sense. He'd probably think I'd lost my mind.

Still, I am fairly sure of all of this, as sure as one can be of such things. When I am gone, there will be no one who

can tell this story, who can explain the presence of this—
artifact. However little I have earned the attention of history, at least it can be said that I have been a faithful guard
at the door, that I have sensed, always sensed, the obliterat-
ing force of time, the savage way our lives and all their
meanings are erased.

Someone else must know what happened here in this
house on Belle Isle. That should be perfectly obvious by
now.

And so when Ann wakes, as she soon will, I will tell her
this story. I will draw back the curtains in this room, admit
the forgiving light of early afternoon as it falls upon this
house, this hurricane lamp glowing at the edge of the ocean.
I will draw her near the edge of the sea, direct her gaze,
show her what I see. I am old, you understand, but not so
old that I cannot find the strength to do this last thing, to
step aside and make a gift of my place in the world, the
small place I have cleared in the thicket of history, the small
role I have played. To be sure, it is a wilderness out there,
and we are all equipped with different measures of the one
force that can guide us into the dark of virgin territory, give
us the strength to move on.

The same light that carries us forward also shows us the
way home. And so that is my gift to Ann, and to my grandmother. I have kept the fires burning here. This house,
situated like a station of light on the cliff, is Belle Isle's un-
acknowledged beacon, the port in the storm, a lighted sill at
the door of the night.

Ann will be persuaded, I hope. And then no one will be
forgotten. No one will be left out in the dark.